# A State of Jane

**Books by Meredith Schorr**

JUST FRIENDS WITH BENEFITS
A STATE OF JANE
HOW DO YOU KNOW?


**The Blogger Girl Series**

BLOGGER GIRL (#1)
NOVELISTA GIRL (#2)

## BLOGGER GIRL (Blogger Girl Series #1)

"What a fun book. The characters were incredibly well-written. I felt like I understood everyone's personalities and quirks, almost as if I knew them personally myself. Meredith Schorr is a talented author and I'm glad she has other books out for me to read!"
— Becky Monson, Bestselling Author of the Spinster Series

"Sassy, sexy, endlessly entertaining, and full of laughs (as well as some heart-wrenching moments), *Blogger Girl* is one of those books that keeps you up at night because you can't wait to see what happens next."
— Tracie Banister, Author of *Mixing It Up*

"America finally has its own version of Britain's Bridget Jones!"
— *Books in the Burbs*

## NOVELISTA GIRL (Blogger Girl Series #2)

"A strong and confident heroine, a sexy boyfriend you can crush on, supportive friends, and plenty of conflict leading to comical results, culminating in a very satisfying ending...Once you start this book, you won't be able to put it down."
— Erin Brady, Bestselling Author of *The Shopping Swap*

"A perfect mix of romance, conflict, and humor, *Novelista Girl* solidifies Schorr's place among best-sellers Sophie Kinsella and Emily Giffin."
— Carolyn Ridder Aspenson, Bestselling Author of *Unbinding Love*

"Absolutely brilliant chick lit, I couldn't put it down, and I highly, highly recommend."
— *Chick Lit Plus*

## JUST FRIENDS WITH BENEFITS

"Meredith writes with wit, candor, humor and vulnerability that illuminates the struggles of dating and relationships."
— Nancy Slotnick, Author of *Turn Your Cablight On*

"The perfect vacation read. The dialogue flows like beer at a beach party."
– K.C. Wilder, Author of *Fifty Ways to Leave Your Husband*

## A STATE OF JANE

"I laughed my way through this novel. A must-read."
– *Chick Lit Plus*

"A witty true-to-life story that will not disappoint you, it is chick lit at it's very best!"
– *Jersey Girl Book Reviews*

"I am a huge fan of chick lit, but this book was so much more. It has become one of my favorite reads!"
– *The Little Black Book Blog*

## HOW DO YOU KNOW?

"Meredith Schorr is an author to watch."
– Tracy Kaler, Founder and Editor of *Tracy's New York Life*

"You won't forget this delightful cast of characters or Schorr's sharp, candid insights about the plight of the modern woman."
– Diana Spechler, Author of *Who by Fire* and *Skinny*

"I think every woman will relate to Maggie and her friends, no matter her age or relationship status."
– *Chick Lit Club*

# A State of Jane

## Meredith Schorr

HENERY PRESS

A STATE OF JANE
Part of the Henery Press Chick Lit Collection

Second Edition | February 2017

Henery Press, LLC
www.henerypress.com

Trade Paperback ISBN-13: 978-1-63511-153-8
Digital epub ISBN-13: 978-1-63511-154-5
Kindle ISBN-13: 978-1-63511-155-2
Hardcover Paperback ISBN-13: 978-1-63511-156-9

Printed in the United States of America

*To all of my single sisters
navigating the New York City dating jungle.*

## ACKNOWLEDGMENTS

I knew I wanted to make changes to the original edition of *A State of Jane*, but wasn't sure where to start. That is where my brilliant editor, Erin George, came in. She knew exactly what areas needed the most work. Thanks to Erin's guidance and direction, I'm so thrilled with the finished project. Thank you to Erin and everyone else at Henery Press for believing in me and making the republication of this book possible.

I'd like to express gratitude to Diana Spechler and Gabriella Roman for their help with the first edition of the book. I also owe thanks to my late great best friend, Alan Blum, for helping me find the perfect ending for Jane's story. Special thanks to Samantha Stroh Bailey for always motivating me to keep going.

Thank you to my friends and family for supporting me through this journey and for seeing no resemblance between the character of Jane and myself despite sharing some similar bad luck in the dating arena.

Finally, this book would not be possible without all of you flakes out there.

# Chapter 1

Holding the phone against my ear with my shoulder as I painted my toenails in OPI's *That's Hot Pink*, I said to my sister, "Wish me a happy anniversary."

"Happy Anniversary, little sister." Claire was only seventeen months older than me, practically my Irish twin, but she always insisted on referring to me as her "little sister." "May I ask what anniversary you're celebrating?"

"My first one. And hopefully my last."

Claire replied, "Clarify."

"My first anniversary as a single person. It's been exactly a year since Bob and I broke up, and I'm officially ready to fall in love again." I looked toward my computer screen where my eHarmony profile was 28 percent completed.

Claire snorted. "Says who?"

"I've done extensive research online, and my scores on several questionnaires clearly indicate that I'm emotionally available for a new relationship."

A hint of doubt in her voice, Claire questioned, "'Cause it's been exactly a year?"

"Precisely. Three hundred and sixty-five days." I wasn't going to let Claire's teasing get to me. I knew waiting a year meant I'd be less likely to waste my time in a rebound relationship.

"Only you would actually believe a few days could make a difference," Claire said in obvious amusement.

"Ha ha, Claire. Keep laughing all the way down the aisle on my wedding day when you're my matron of honor."

"Who do you intend to start this new relationship with?"

"Someone amazing. I just have to find him. Could be anywhere—eHarmony, the subway, a bar, at work. In fact, a new set of first year associates is starting this week." I bit my lip. "Although, if they started law school right after college, they might only be twenty-five." Not everyone worked as a paralegal first like I did.

"And that's a problem because?"

"I'm twenty-six! I'd rather date someone older. Or my age." Thirty would be ideal since men matured less quickly than women. A four-year age difference might mean we'd be ready to settle down at the same time.

"It's a one-year difference, Jane. Keep your options open."

"They are open."

"Whatever you say."

I blew on my toes, willing the polish to dry faster. "I hate when you do that, you know."

"Do what?" Claire asked innocently.

"Dismiss me."

Claire sighed dramatically. "You're not in high school anymore, Jane, and guys in New York are not gonna fall at your feet." Laughing, she added, "Except the really short, nerdy ones with balance problems. Just don't expect to meet Dr. Right who looks like Eric Bana. It ain't easy, and you've got lots of competition."

I met Bob the summer between our sophomore and junior years in high school, when we were co-counselors for the same group of seven-year-old boys. We became good friends, but when I told Claire I had a crush on him, she said I'd never have the guts to make a move and should just use his friendship as practice for talking to guys. "As always, thanks for the uplifting pep talk. And it's not as if guys fell at my feet in high school either. Bob was my first boyfriend, remember?"

Softening her voice, Claire said, "Sorry if I sounded mean. You're a definite catch, sis. But you're naive, and I don't want you to be unprepared. Just go in with no expectations, okay?"

"Okay," I said quietly. I had hoped Claire would share my excitement, not give me unsolicited advice.

Her voice brightened. "You do realize you'll need to actually go on dates first, right? Which means no more back-to-back episodes of the *Barefoot Contessa* and *Iron Chef* on the Food Network on Saturday nights."

"It's not like I'm a hermit, Claire. I wanted to make sure I gave myself enough time to move on after a nine-year relationship." The fact that I broke up with Bob and not the other way around didn't make the split any less traumatic. Or at least not *that* much less traumatic. On a positive note, I'd learned a lot of new recipes over the past year. "Anyway, I'm ready now."

"I'm sure you are. Just please don't expect things to be as easy as they were when you met Bob. The dating world post-millennium is an entirely different animal, and you're dealing with experienced men, not innocent boys. It might not be as easy to meet another Bob. If you don't believe me, ask Pin Cushion."

Pin Cushion was my sister's secret nickname for my far from virginal roommate, Lainie, and she was the last person I'd ask for relationship advice. Birth control advice, maybe. We'd met through Craigslist and although she was often negligent in the way of household duties, I was happy she wasn't a psychopath.

"I'll be myself and things will happen. Like they eventually did for you."

Claire groaned. "Eventually is the operative word. And now we can't make a baby to save our lives."

I remembered how Claire had dyed her dirty blond hair jet black when she dated a drummer in college, and how she gave up meat when she dated a vegetarian. She wound up married to Kevin, another high school teacher from the suburbs who, ten times out of ten, also chose cheeseburgers over tofu and soy milk. They were a perfect match, but baby making had proved to be a challenge. "It will happen when it's supposed to, Claire. I truly believe that." Secretly, I wished it would happen sooner rather than later so I could start buying cute baby clothes for my little niece or nephew.

"My advice to you—take your own advice. It will happen when it's supposed to happen. Don't look at every guy as the potential 'one.'"

"Not every guy, Claire. Just the single, handsome, ambitious, generous, funny ones." A message popped up on my computer saying my session on eHarmony was going to timeout if I remained idle for another sixty seconds, so after I told Claire I loved her and would cross my fingers she didn't get her period that month, we hung up and I finished my online profile. I couldn't wait to be matched with someone with whom I was compatible on twenty-nine dimensions.

# Chapter 2

The next night, I had drinks at the Brass Monkey with my best friend, Marissa, and her older sister, Katherine. We sat on the rooftop sipping pear cider and enjoying a view of the West Side Highway and the Hudson River. It was an Indian summer, but there was still a chill in the air. I reached behind my chair for my pink and green Lilly Pulitzer cardigan, wrapping it around my shoulders. Gesturing toward Marissa, I asked, "How are things going with that guy Eric?" She had met him on PlentyOfFish. When I asked why she didn't try eHarmony, she said she lacked the patience to complete the extensive questionnaire. I, on the other hand, was certain the extra labor would pay out in finding me my consummate other half.

Marissa took a sip of her drink. "I don't know. He's really nice, but totally clueless."

"In what way?" I asked.

Snorting, Katherine said, "Do you have all night?"

I ignored Katherine. She'd been a know-it-all ever since she got married the year before, and I never forgave her for making Marissa wear a beige maid of honor dress. With Marissa's pale complexion, she looked naked. And besides, beige was only flattering on girls who wore a size four or less. Marissa was not one of those girls. Neither was I.

I nodded toward Marissa. "Details, please."

Marissa gave an embarrassed smile. "I guess his first offense was taking me to Smiler's Deli on our first date. It was approaching closing time, but we managed to snag some grilled vegetables and stale California rolls before they cleared out the salad bar. Second, and more ridiculous, was telling me on our second date that he was in therapy because his ex-wife left him. Too much information *way too soon.*" Marissa shook her head of long plum brown hair as if bewildered by it all.

"Are you talking to anyone else?" The whole internet dating phenomenon fascinated me since I hadn't been on a date with anyone except Bob since the summer of 1999.

"Yeah, but still at the email stage. Eric already asked me out for a third date."

"Did you let him down easy?" I asked.

"She said yes," Katherine said matter-of-factly. "He's nice, not ugly, and he asked. She has to give it another chance. Pickings are slim."

How would Katherine know this, being that she was the opposite of single? Oh, yeah, because Katherine knew *everything.* Tuning her out, I asked Marisa, "But do you like him? You shouldn't force yourself to go out with him if you don't."

"He's really nice, but I'm not sure if I could ever be attracted to him. I'm trying though."

It pained me to watch Marissa practice this ritual time and time again, believing she could create chemistry if she tried harder. She'd been my best friend since she lived across the hall from me our freshmen year in college, and I wanted her to meet her soul mate almost as much as I wanted to meet my own. "Why are you even trying? You shouldn't have to try to be attracted to someone. You either are or you're not."

"Or you close your eyes and pretend he's Bradley Cooper," Katherine said, laughing.

I took a sip of my drink, thankful it was diluted with ice. I wanted to squeeze in an hour of studying for the LSAT before bed. "You can't settle. New York City is full of eligible bachelors. Onward and upward, I say."

Looking at me like I was a clueless intern on my first day of work, Katherine raised her chin toward the air. "Yes. Manhattan is full of eligible bachelors. Eligible bachelors who are unemployed, uninterested, gay, or looking to get laid."

Marissa nodded her head in agreement. "Jane will see soon enough. She's ready to start dating again."

"Really? One piece of advice. Try to refrain from telling every guy who hits on you all about how you and Bob 'lost the spark' and how important it is to find 'the spark.' Ranting about your ex-boyfriend is not the best way to get a new one."

While Katherine's face distorted into an obnoxious laugh, I glared at Marissa. She mouthed, "Sorry" and quickly looked away.

"I did that once, and I wasn't even interested in the guy," I muttered. And how kind of my big-mouthed best friend to share it with her bigger-mouthed older sister. "Besides, the spark *is* important."

Katherine downed the rest of her cider and placed her empty glass on the table. "Well, best of luck finding the spark, Jane. I can't wait to hear about your dating disasters. Marissa's are getting old."

Katherine was so cynical, I wondered how she ever managed to get married. Then I remembered what her husband looked like and smiled to myself. Placing my hand over Marissa's, I said, "You'll meet the right guy someday. Don't waste time on the wrong ones. Remember when I told you Christopher would say yes if you asked him to the formal senior year?"

Marissa nodded somberly. "Yeah."

"I was right then, and I'm right now."

"What about you?" Marissa asked. "Have you spoken to anyone yet?"

"Not yet, but ask me again tomorrow and I might have a different answer." I handed my credit card to the waitress. "These drinks are on me, ladies. I'm feeling generous tonight."

"Thanks, Jane. What's the occasion?" Katherine asked.

Tucking a strand of dirty blond hair behind my ears, I said, "Love is in the air. I feel it. I'm checking my eHarmony matches as soon as I get home. Maybe the love of my life is waiting in my inbox."

Katherine looked at me doubtfully. "Your optimism is inspiring."

Half laughing, Marissa said, "With Jane's luck, the 'one' will be the first guy she goes out with. She'll be married before I get past the fifth date with someone."

"I hope so." I paused and looked at Marissa. "Not the part about you and the fifth date, of course. But just in case eHarmony doesn't pan out, I've also joined a group on Meetup for singles in their twenties through thirties, and I'm smiling at every cute boy I pass on the street. I want to be settled in a committed relationship by the time I start law school next year, when I'll be too busy studying to meet anyone."

Katherine stood up and flung her bag across her shoulder. "I hate to drink and run, but I told Martin I'd be home twenty minutes ago." To me, she said, "Thanks again for the drink and best of luck in the dating jungle. Don't get eaten alive."

We waved goodbye before I said to Marissa, "Alone at last."

Marissa frowned.

"Why are you looking at me like that? I didn't mean it as an insult to Katherine. I just haven't spoken to you in a while." Marissa and Katherine were also less than two years apart in age, but you'd think they were twins from the way Marissa told Katherine everything.

Marissa furrowed her dark brows. "This has nothing to do with Katherine. I'm just afraid your expectations with this dating thing are too high. It's not easy."

"You sound like Claire."

"Maybe Claire knows what she's talking about."

I waved my hand in protest. "I appreciate your concern, but I know what I'm doing." Marissa's cautious attitude toward dating wasn't exactly confidence inspiring. Anxious to change the subject, I said, "How's work? Any samples you can spare?" Marissa worked in the corporate department of a cosmetics company. Along with a 25 percent discount off of the wholesale price of products, they were always passing along free samples.

Marissa's face brightened as she reached into her bag. "Yes. I completely forgot. Here," she said, handing me an assortment of sample-sized perfumes. "I'm not sure if any of them are good, but you can have them all."

I happily threw them into my purse. "Thank you. I'm almost out of my Michael Kors."

Smiling, Marissa said, "What are friends for?"

"We're meeting tomorrow morning at the Greenmarket, right?" I bought all of my produce at the farmer's market in Union Square, but it was only open on Mondays, Wednesdays, Fridays, and Saturdays. "I'll be there by eight thirty to beat the crowds."

Marissa smirked. "I'll aim for ten thirty. No fruit is worth getting up early on a Saturday morning."

I stood up. "We'll agree to disagree on that." With a hug goodbye, I said, "Sleep well."

Later that night, I sat at my computer desk and logged onto eHarmony. I wondered if my future husband was among my twenty-three new matches. The first eligible bachelor was Peter. He was five foot five. Since I was five foot six, I clicked "not interested."

The second match was Nate. He was cute with short brown hair, dark skin, and broad shoulders. And at five foot eleven, he was a nice height for me. He was a financial consultant, so he could probably meet my intellectual standards, and since he loved home-cooked meals and I was a master in the kitchen, we were probably a perfect match.

I confirmed my interest and moved on to the next—Brett. Brett posed shirtless with a harem of women in every picture. I clicked "not interested," figuring he didn't need another girlfriend.

I finished reviewing the remaining twenty matches, confirming interest in four of them, and climbed into bed.

I closed my eyes and imagined where Nate would take me on our first date. Hopefully not Smiler's Deli. Later, I dreamed about swim-up bars and sex on the beach with Nate on our honeymoon. The dreams were interrupted only once when I woke up in a panic, remembering I had forgotten to study for the LSAT. I made a mental vow to spend an extra hour the following night and fell back against the pillow, anxious to return to the Caribbean and beach-side massages with my future husband.

I brought a ripe nectarine to my nose, breathed in the sweet fragrance, and placed three in my basket. I wanted to take full advantage while the fruit was still in season. I could use it in a fresh fruit salad or maybe make a relish. I paid for my fruit and glanced at my watch. I was meeting Marissa at the Deep Mountain Maple vendor in five minutes, we'd walk around for a few more minutes, and then head to Max Brennar for coffee and breakfast. It was Marissa's favorite spot for hot chocolate and how I bribed her to meet me on Saturday mornings when she'd rather curl on the couch and catch up on her DVR.

I spotted her fawning over a jar of syrup and poked her lightly in the back. "Hey, you."

Without turning around, Marissa said, "If I buy the syrup, will you make the French toast?"

"It's a deal. I even saved an article from BuzzFeed with recipes using maple syrup. There was one with sausage I'm dying to try." My mouth watered just thinking about how a hint of sweet could enhance a savory dish like sausage.

"God bless you for being you and loving me," Marissa said.

Thirty minutes later, with my grocery bags tucked safely underneath my chair, Marissa and I sat comfortably in a booth at Max Brennar. "How was the rest of your night?" I asked.

"I fell asleep watching *Breaking Bad* and have to watch the episode again. I hate when that happens." She pouted. "How about you?"

I told her about Nate. "I can't wait for you to meet him."

Marissa laughed. "Shouldn't *you* meet him first?"

My cheeks warmed. "Of course. But once we settle into a routine, I'll introduce you guys. Maybe he has a friend and we can double date."

Marissa took a sip of her hot chocolate. "I think you've been watching too many Hallmark Channel movies, my friend."

I pointed at her. "And you, my friend, need to step away from the *Breaking Bad.*"

# Chapter 3

"My routine follow-up regarding the status of your hair," I said into the phone a few days later. When Bob and I broke up, we promised to keep in touch. He told me he'd forget to get his hair cut without me to remind him, and so I vowed to call him periodically. Not too often, since I actually preferred when his thick locks got a little unruly and cartoonish, but often enough so he wouldn't look like a bum.

Chuckling, Bob said, "I got a haircut a couple weeks ago. I'm running my hand through my mop now and it's not getting stuck."

"Wonderful. What else is new?" I got ready to feign interest in the newest addition to his video game collection.

"Actually, there's something I wanted to tell you."

"Okay."

"This is weird."

"What could be too weird to tell me? You told me once you fantasized about a three-way with me and Judy Jetson. Talk about strange."

"She's hot, Jane. No apologies for that one. But this is something else."

I felt my insides tighten. "What? Just tell me." For a moment, all I could hear was the sound of my own breathing, but then he said it.

"I'm seeing someone, Jane."

I sat down on the edge of my bed and took a deep breath. Bob was dating someone? I'd estimated his recovery time at least six months longer than mine, since he was on the receiving end of the breakup. "That's great, Bob. I've started dating again too." Technically. And I was sure whatever he had going on was casual.

Clearing his throat, Bob said, "Actually, it got serious kind of fast."

I lay back on the bed, held the phone away from my ear for a moment, and swallowed hard. I brought the phone back to my ear. "Oh? Has she met Arlene yet?" Bob was the ultimate mama's boy. Arlene had to be on board with any girl before he got serious.

"Yeah. Mom loves her."

"Really? I mean cool. Congratulations, Bob."

"There's more."

"Okay?" Did she and Mr. Krauss bond on a fishing trip or something?

"We're moving in together. She has a one-bedroom in the West Village, so I'm giving up my studio when the lease expires in a couple of months."

Words continued to escape Bob's lips, but I stopped listening. I couldn't believe he was moving on faster than me. If I'd waited only six months instead of a year, this wouldn't have happened. "Great, Bob. I'm happy for you. Can't wait to meet her."

"We're having a party after I move in. You'll meet Trish then. You'll like her."

Trish? I went to high school with a girl named Trish. Hated her.

No need to panic, Jane. The party was at least a month away. I'd totally have a boyfriend by then. Maybe even Nate. Everything would be fine. So I hadn't given much thought to Bob moving on, but it had to happen someday, right? The timing could have been better, like after I was already settled, but it wasn't the worst thing in the world. It wasn't like I wanted to be with Bob, and I certainly didn't want him to be alone for the rest of his life. It just proved what I'd said to Claire earlier, that I was ready. It was time. Time for Bob to move on and time for me to move on.

After I hung up the phone, I immediately logged onto eHarmony. Nate and I had completed all of the steps and were now given access to "open communication," which I learned meant we could email each other directly. I had discovered during the various stages of, I'd guess you'd call it "closed communication," that among Nate's must-haves were compassion, fidelity, and honesty. Among his must-NOT-haves were laziness, intolerance, and insensitivity. He seemed perfect, and I was certain there would be an email from him waiting for me.

I scrolled the list of active matches, past Andrew, Todd, and Christian, to the thumbnail picture of Nate leaning against the side of a sail boat. But his picture wasn't there. I figured in my haste I had scrolled too fast, so I went back to the top of the page and gave it another scan. Nate's profile was still not there. Thinking there might be a separate section on the site for open-communication matches, I carefully scrutinized the page, but I didn't see any other sections aside from closed matches.

I got up and took my dirty coffee cup to the kitchen. Lainie was sitting at our kitchen table. She was speaking with her Southern accent, which I noticed only came out when she talked to her mom. She held the phone in one hand and played with her curly hair in the other, but she looked up, removed her hand from her hair, and waved. I mouthed "hello," put my coffee mug in the dishwasher, and left the kitchen.

Back in my room, I searched one more time for Nate under active matches and he still wasn't there. I muttered, "Freakin' weird," double-clicked closed matches, and there he was, smiling at me from what I had hoped was his parents' boat. (I'd always wished my parents would buy a boat, but my dad said, "The two best days in a boat owner's life are the day he buys a boat and the day he sells it.")

I didn't understand why Nate's profile was now in my closed matches. There had to be an explanation. We had breezed through the entire process. I knew he was as anxious to meet me as I was to meet him. Firmly gripping my mouse, I held my breath and scanned the page until I saw it. Nate had closed me out earlier that day, citing "different values" as his reason.

Pacing my room, I nervously picked up clothes I had strewn across the floor that morning when I'd noticed the black pants I intended to wear weren't as flattering as the last time I'd worn them. I had to try on three other pairs before finding ones that didn't emphasize my saddlebags. I vowed to add squats to my workout routine even though I hated them.

Different values? We shared almost all of the same must-haves and must-not-haves! I reviewed his profile one more time. I wondered if I could write eHarmony and request a further explanation. I logged off my computer and fell back on my bed. How was I supposed to focus on studying after this disturbing turn of events?

My eyes closed, I took deep breaths in and out and visualized myself eating pastries and people watching with my fiancé in Paris. I had trouble picturing what he looked like, but it wasn't Nate. Maybe it was Andrew, Todd, or Christian, but not Nate. And it was probably just as well. The right guy for me would never be so hasty as to assume our values were different based on a silly profile. God was doing me a favor by showing me Nate's true colors before we even met, so I wouldn't waste my time. It was all for the best.

# Chapter 4

"You went to bed early last night, Jane. You didn't come out to watch *Suits*. It was a new one."

I grabbed my Greek yogurt from the fridge and threw it in the pink Gucci bag Claire had bought me on her honeymoon in Italy. "I know. I wasn't in the mood. I'll watch it online later." After I study for the LSAT. "Some guy on eHarmony closed me out right after we got to open communication. Odd, right?"

"Not really," Lainie said. "Happens all the time. That's why I never get excited about a guy until we've met face to face. Or mouth to mouth." She winked.

Nodding, I said, "You're right. I dodged a bullet. If he wasn't able to follow through with an email, he's probably a commitment-phobe."

Lainie leaned against the refrigerator. "Look at Jane, always putting on a positive spin."

"Everything happens for a reason," I said matter-of-factly. I couldn't even remember the name of the guy I had crushed on before meeting Bob, but I remembered feeling rejected when he didn't pay any attention to me. Later, I knew it was because Bob, not him, was supposed to be my first boyfriend.

"I'd love to know the reason God put all the asshole single guys on the island of Manhattan. They are only good for one thing, some of them better than others."

"You're so jaded, Lainie. They aren't all bad. You just haven't met the right guy yet."

"I'm all about trial and error. Who knows, maybe my next

guinea pig will be on the 6 train this morning. I have a pitch meeting at nine thirty." Lainie worked as a production assistant for the WE Network. They had weekly meetings to brainstorm original content. She wanted to work for the male-targeted Spike Network, but they only had offices in California. She removed her sunglasses from the neckline of her low-cut sweater, placed them on her head, and began walking out of the kitchen. "You coming?"

"Sure."

I followed her down two flights of stairs and onto 82nd Street. I breathed in the fresh air and looked upwards at the cloudless sky. Since it was usually rainy and cold, hot and humid, or some other "extreme" weather condition, the weather we were having on that day was a rarity. "You know what? I'm gonna walk. It's only thirty blocks and it's still early." I had to stop at the bank anyway, and there was an HSBC on 68th and Third.

Enjoying the crisp breeze, I picked up the pace and smiled as I walked to work. When the distinguished-looking older business man thought the smile was directed at him and winked at me, I considered it an added benefit. I would include his wink on my daily "grateful" list. He was too old for me, but it reinforced my confidence that someone besides Bob would find me attractive. According to a poll in *Cosmopolitan,* confidence was the biggest turn-on for men.

Men. My noteworthy experiences with the gender were limited to my nine-year relationship with Bob. I had defined myself as his girlfriend for my entire adult life up until a year ago, and some people thought I was a fool to have broken up with him. I hadn't ended things because Bob did something wrong, like cheat on me or treat me badly, and I didn't think I was better than him. I just knew in my gut he wasn't "The One."

When I first met him at camp at the age of sixteen, having done nothing more than kiss a few boys at high school dances and in closets during Seven Minutes in Heaven, I woke up each morning infused with nervous excitement to see him. I wondered if he'd show any signs his interest went beyond co-counselor camaraderie, and it gave me something to look forward to each day besides bug juice and chasing sweaty little boys across the soccer field. He'd hug me after I got a base hit in softball or walk away from other girls at parties to talk to me, and it made me feel special. We made out for the first time in the hot tub at Glenn Kellerman's house party. I was afraid he would blow it off as a result of too much cheap keg beer, but the next morning at camp, he pulled me to a corner of our musty bunk, told me he liked me, and asked me to the movies that night.

After that, we officially became girlfriend and boyfriend and the nervous excitement and uncertainty were replaced by passion and exploding hormones. In nine years, we'd experienced the thrills of first love, the scariness of letting someone else in, and the adventures of learning what made each other tick. It wasn't always the stuff of romcoms and we rode the emotional roller coaster of fighting and making up quite a few times, but in the last couple of years, the thrills were not many, we ran out of things to learn, and the emotional rollercoaster turned into a boring Ferris wheel. We felt like an old married couple, which would have been fine if we weren't in our twenties. Or were married. But we were neither of the two, and I knew we never should be. We were meant to be each other's first loves, but not our forever-and-always loves.

Even though I knew breaking up with Bob was the right thing to do, I missed having a boyfriend. Sometimes it was the little things, like standing alone in line every week at H & H for Sunday morning bagels and coffee surrounded by couples with morning sex hair. Sometimes it was the bigger things like being the fifth wheel at holiday dinners with my family. And then there was the sex. I hadn't had any in over a year. I hadn't even kissed anyone. Except for the drunken kiss last Halloween with a guy dressed up like a doctor. I was a nurse.

At first I missed sex terribly, but I'd practically forgotten what it felt like at this point. I absently let my hand wander to the front of my sweater and shook my head in disgust that no one had touched my breasts in over a year. Was I considered a born-again virgin by now? What if I forgot how to do it? Or what if it hurt again?

As my stomach turned in agony at my impending re-entrance into the sexual world, I noticed that the guy in front of me at the ATM had a really cute butt. It fit nicely into his dark brown cords.

I was enjoying the view when it suddenly changed, and instead of looking upon his rear end, I was caught staring right at his crotch.

"All yours," he said, motioning to the ATM.

Feeling my face get hot, I looked up, muttered "thanks" and caught a glimpse of his wiseass grin before I scurried to the machine. As I entered the first two numbers of my pin, I felt the card slip between my fingers and drop to the ground. I would not be adding this incident to my grateful list, I thought as I completed my transaction.

Finished, I carefully placed the cash in my wallet, spun around to see where my card had landed and found myself looking once again at a pair of brown corduroy pants and Crotch Man with his hand extended to me, firmly gripping my debit card.

"I think you dropped this," he said. I noticed his eyes matched his pants perfectly.

Maybe I would add this incident to my grateful list. Gently removing the card from his hand, I joked "Stealing my card, huh?"

Crinkling his forehead, he said, "I thought I just handed it to you."

Okay, so my flirting skills needed work. "Joking. Thanks so much. It was nice of you to wait."

"I had an ulterior motive," he said.

"Really, and what would that be?"

"Have a drink with me."

"I don't even know your name."

"Randall. Now will you have a drink with me?"

"You don't even know *my* name," I said laughing.

"Jane Alexis Frank."

My heart raced as I wondered how he knew my name and

what else he knew about me. I zipped up my purse, prepared to run.

"Jane," he said. Then he reached over, touched my shoulder gently, and repeated, "Jane. Your name is on your debit card."

No longer fearing for my life, I marveled at how lucky I was. He was handsome *and* smart. Batting my eyelashes, I said, "Well then...a drink would be nice."

My friends didn't know what they were talking about. New York was full of cute eligible men, and I had just snagged one.

# Chapter 5

"Yes, Dad, I've been studying for the LSAT," I lied. I'd start this weekend. I was having drinks with Randall on Thursday night so I decided not to bother with the Meetup singles' bowling event on Saturday.

"If you want to get into NYU, you should aim for a score of 170. But, if not, Fordham or Brooklyn Law would be fine, and they're not as particular. You graduated college with a 3.5, right?"

"A 3.75 in my major. I was thinking Columbia."

"That's my girl! Aiming high."

I smiled as I pictured sitting next to my dad at a conference table negotiating million-dollar deals with one of our Fortune 500 clients. I wasn't clear on what exactly I'd be doing, but I'd find out in law school. My dad was a partner at a small but prestigious boutique corporate law firm. He wanted me to work for a large global firm first to gain experience, but he'd talked about us working together since I was ten. I just hoped he wouldn't retire before I was ready. He loved being a lawyer. But he also loved golf. I had made Bob teach me how to play, but I kind of sucked. Claire was a natural. I took after my mother and had no athletic ability whatsoever. "Is Mom home?" I asked.

"She's playing Bunko with the ladies."

"Oh." I wanted to tell her about Randall. She hadn't been thrilled when I broke up with Bob. "He comes from a nice family, he treats you well, blah, blah, blah." If there was a new guy on the horizon, maybe she'd get over it. "Can you tell her to call me when she has a minute?"

"Of course. Talk to you later, Pumpkin."

"Love you, Dad."

"Love you too."

After I hung up the phone, I opened my Kaplan practice LSAT book.

Chewing my pen, I pondered the first question for a few minutes, taking notes on the side of the page. Easy. I read the passage twice to make sure, checked the answer, and confirmed I'd nailed it. Columbia, here I come. I put the pen down and thought about what I'd make for dinner. I was in the mood for spaghetti and my homemade garlic meatballs, but eating garlic the night before a date could be dangerous. Sometimes it took days to get rid of the smell no matter how many times I brushed my teeth or gargled with mouthwash. I'd make chicken teriyaki instead—enough to share with Lainie. I glanced at my half-opened closet and realized I had no idea what to wear out with Randall. I wished my mom had been home, but she'd probably have told me to wear whatever I wanted. *With slimming black pants.*

The following evening, with nervous knots in my belly, I logged off computer, freshened up my makeup in the bathroom, and left for my date with Randall. I was meeting him at Vero at seven, so it made sense to go straight from work since both my office and the bar were in the 50s. I had picked up a form-fitting zebra-print V-neck cashmere sweater the night before at Lord and Taylor to wear with my favorite black pants. Sexy yet sophisticated. It was my first "first" date in a decade, and I was so nervous, my legs felt like Jell-O as I entered the bar and spotted Randall talking to the young female bartender.

His back was to me, but his butt looked familiar. I approached where he was standing and smiled at the bartender, who gave me a once-over. Patting Randall on the back, I said, "Hi. Sorry I'm late."

Turning toward me, Randall grinned. "You're right on time, Jane Alexis." Then he handed me the expansive menu of wine choices. "Let's get you a drink."

Noting his full glass of white wine, I asked, "What are you drinking?"

"Cassandra," he called to the bartender, who had walked to the other side of the bar. When she looked over, he asked, "What is this fine wine you chose for me?"

Cassandra ran a hand through her smooth long blond hair and shook her head casually. "It's an Australian sauvignon blanc. Fruity, just like you."

Randall said, "Hey, don't give my date here the wrong idea." He turned back to me. "I assure you. I'm very manly."

Giggling, I said, "I can tell." I glanced around the relatively uncrowded seating area. "Want to get a table or something?" I felt Cassandra's blue eyes on us and didn't need her eavesdropping on our date.

"Anything you want, Jane. Let's grab a menu so you can take your time choosing your wine. We can order appetizers too if you want." He led me to an open table and when the palm of his hand touched the small of my back, I felt a jolt of electricity through my entire body. My legs still felt wobbly, and I hoped I wouldn't break out in a sweat. I was unaccustomed to feeling so wonderfully ill at ease in a guy's company.

About an hour and one and a half glasses of Gewürztraminer later, peppered with a few cubes of cheese, Randall and I were making moon eyes at each other and holding hands across the table. He told me the most charming story about how he got lost at the zoo when he was seven and his grandmother only found him because he told the security guard his name was GI Joe, his favorite toy at the time.

"What about you, Jane? Any childhood stories you want to confide?"

I consciously avoided biting my lip as I thought of a memory I wasn't too embarrassed to share. "Well, there was the time I played the wrong song at my piano recital and—"

Interrupting me, Randall said, "You play the piano? Sexy *and* talented."

Blushing, I said, "I actually was pretty good for a while. Anyway, I was supposed to play Mozart's *Papagano*, but my teacher had also taught me 'Hero' by Mariah Carey. I played that instead because I thought it was hipper. But it was a classical recital, and I wasn't allowed to watch television for a week as a punishment. And I missed the season finale of *Boy Meets World*— my favorite show at the time."

I instantly regretted telling him a true story and wished I'd come up with a lie that would make me appear charming rather than completely dorky, but Randall didn't seem to notice. He reached over, moving a wavy strand of hair away from my face. "Jane, the rebel. I like it."

Bravely, I responded, "I have my moments."

"I like that in a girl," he said with a soft smile.

I wanted to ask what else he found attractive in women, but before I had the chance, Cassandra appeared at our table. "Can I get you guys anything else?" As she leaned down to remove our empty plates, a hint of red from her bra strap peeked out from her tight and low-cut black t-shirt. I glanced at Randall to see if she'd distracted him with her cleavage and was thrilled to see his eyes were firmly on me.

"Did you want anything else, Jane?" he asked.

I shook my head. "I'm good."

"We'll take the check, Cass. Thanks." He winked at her.

"Your drink at the bar earlier is on me," she said before ruffling his hair and placing the bill on the table. With a sense of unease, my eyes followed her as she sashayed back to the bar until Randall snapped me out of it. "It's a nice night. Can I walk you home?" he asked.

My face brightened. "I'd like that."

"I promise I won't ask for an invite inside. Although I might try to kiss you."

My lips had barely touched anything besides food and my toothbrush in the past year. I thought I might die if they weren't kissed soon. "And I might let you."

Throwing a wad of cash on the table, Randall stood up. "Then let's get out of here before you change your mind."

As I grabbed his hand and began walking towards the exit, I said, "I won't change my mind."

With his free hand, Randall waved goodbye to Cassandra and followed me outside.


"It was so good," I told Marissa over bagels and coffee on Saturday.

"Yay! I can live vicariously through your amazing date, since I haven't had a great one in over a year." Marissa frowned. "It's always the ones I don't like who won't leave me alone and the ones I like who never call. Not that I've even liked anyone in the last few months."

I reached over and squeezed Marissa's hand. "I'm sorry you're in such a long dry spell. Maybe you should switch dating sites. Guys on eHarmony are probably less likely to flake after spending two hours completing the profile. And there are some cute ones." The only reason I could think to explain why Marissa was meeting such unappealing guys was that she was on the free sites. You got what you paid for. She was pretty, but Bob said she was a "sleeper." At first glance, you might not notice her, but if you looked twice, you'd realize how attractive she was with her large hazel eyes, full lips, and thick dark hair. He also said she had a nice rack. So unless she spent the entire date babbling other people's secrets, which actually wouldn't shock me, it had to be the guys.

"No, eHarmony is no better. When I told Katherine what happened with your match Nate, she agreed. All the sites are the same."

I took another sip of coffee and shook my head at her. "You told Katherine about Nate?"

Marissa's face turned red. "I'm sorry, Jane. I know, but Katherine met Martin online. She's been there."

"Whatever." I didn't want to talk about Katherine. "Back to my date."

Nodding eagerly, and likely relieved at the change of topic, Marissa said, "Yes, do tell."

"I forgot how much I loved to kiss. He was such a good kisser."

Raising her eyebrows, Marissa said, "Better than Bob? You always said Bob's kisses still blew you away even after nine years."

I had said that. Whenever Bob and I argued over what movie to see or where to go for dessert and I was this close to winning, Bob would dip me into a Hollywood kiss and I'd let him have his way. "Not better. Just different. Which made it even more exciting."

"How'd you end things?"

"After kissing on my front steps for about twenty minutes, he said he was reluctantly going to head home but would call me soon. He sent me a text this morning asking if I would be around tomorrow night to chat. He said he was working all weekend."

With mock annoyance, she said, "Jane, if you end up marrying this guy, I might have to kill you. I've been on at least forty dates in the past two years and haven't made it past a third date with anyone."

"We've only had one date. Nothing to get excited about yet," I said. Secretly, I was way excited, but I didn't want Marissa to feel bad that I had better luck with men. Maybe my good fortune would rub off on her. "Hey, are you doing okay?"

"Yeah. Why do you ask?"

"Just wondering if you ever think about Dovid." Dovid had been Marissa's only boyfriend. They'd met when Marissa went on a European tour the summer after we graduated college, and they were on and off for a few years. They ended things permanently two years ago.

"I don't think about him much anymore." Turning red, she said, "But he's in my dreams every few months." She waggled her eyebrows. "*Those* kinds of dreams if you know what I mean."

I shivered. "Gross." I was not a fan of Dovid. He was extremely controlling and possessive. The only positive influence he'd had on Marissa was getting her to quit smoking. He'd threatened to break up with her if she didn't.

Marissa shook her head at me. "I know you hated him. Trust me, I would never go back." Looking sad, she said, "Although I miss regular sex. With my dating luck, I worry I'll never have any again."

Laughing, I said, "You're afraid of never having sex again, and I'm terrified of the opposite since I've only been with one person my entire life."

Marissa put her arm around me. "It's like riding a bike, my friend. No worries."

# Chapter 6

"You're so sexy, Jane," Randall whispered, blowing his warm breath in my ear. "I love your curves."

Tingles shot through me. "You're not so bad yourself." I traced the outline of his face with my fingers before drawing him into another kiss. "I haven't felt this way in a long, long time, Randall," I confessed.

"Hold that thought." Waving at the waitress, he said, "Can we get another round, darlin'?"

We were on the roof at the Gramercy Hotel, sitting side by side on a couch, and I scanned the room wondering if anyone was watching us make out. There were some girls sitting a few tables away. They kept glancing our way, and I possessively placed my hand on top of Randall's.

Handing me a full glass of wine, he said, "Where were we? Oh, you were saying you hadn't felt this way in a long time. What way would that be?"

"I guess 'content' is the right word for how I'm feeling."

"I hope I have something to do with your contentment."

"You do," I assured him.

"Then I must kiss you again," he said.

Sliding even closer to him with my head a mere inch from his, I said, "Go for it."

After another amazing kiss, he pulled away from me. "I can taste your wine." He licked his lips. "Good stuff."

"Good stuff indeed," I repeated before kissing him again.

I continued to revel in the fullness of his lips against mine and the contrast of his cold hands rubbing the warm skin on my back. I unsuccessfully wracked my brain for something interesting to say, but kissing instead of talking was fine with me. Randall didn't seem to mind either. Stopping momentarily to catch my breath, I gazed at him dreamily.

"Great eyes, Jane. Not quite brown, but not green. Almost gold."

"I call them amber."

Lacing his fingers with mine, he nodded. "Amber is about right. So Amber, want to get out of here?"

Startled, I said, "Why? Are you bored with me already?" I was happy to stay on that couch forever.

"Never. I thought we'd take this party somewhere else. My place. Or yours. Whatever you're most comfortable with."

I swallowed hard. "I'm kind of happy here. Not quite ready to, well…" I didn't know how to complete the sentence.

"No worries, Jane," he said. He kissed the top of my head. "No worries at all. We can stay here as long as you want."

Relieved, I placed my head on his shoulder and closed my eyes. "It's just…I recently ended a long relationship and think I should take things slow." I opened my eyes, sat up, and faced Randall. "You understand, right?"

Randall nodded and kissed my forehead again. "Of course. We have all the time in the world."

Content once again, I took another sip of wine and returned my head to Randall's shoulder.

We left after we finished that round of drinks, since Randall had to drop his roommate at the airport early the next morning. He hailed me a taxi back to the Upper East Side and, as he opened the door for me, said, "Get home safely, sweetheart."

"I will. Thanks for another great night."

"My pleasure."

Reluctant to leave, I asked, "One more kiss?"

"I could kiss you all night, Jane." Motioning in the direction of the driver, he said, "But the meter's running, and the big guy here probably wants to get going. We'll have to save the kissing for next time. Something to look forward to."

I slid into the cab. "Yes, something to look forward to." Randall closed the door and waved goodbye.

I waved and watched him walk back into the hotel. "Eighty-second and Lexington, thanks," I said before resting my head against the seat and closing my eyes for the ride.

# Chapter 7

From her seat on the opposite side of the kitchen table, my mom said, "I ran into the Krausses at Stu Leonard's last week. Did you know Bob was moving in with his new girlfriend in a few months?"

"Of course I know, Mom. Bob and I are still friends." I refused to give her the satisfaction of thinking she knew something about my ex-boyfriend that I didn't.

"Oh? Arlene mentioned that Bob only told you about Trish a couple of weeks ago. They've been dating several months now."

I got up to bring over the coffee cake I had made, and with my back to my family said, "I know about Trish, Mom. I'm happy for them. Besides, I'm dating someone too."

Piping in, Claire said, "Don't get ahead of yourself, Jane. It's only been two dates."

I turned around and glared at my sister. "Two great dates, Claire."

"Yes, Jane. What does this Randall do?" my mom asked.

"He works in business. Doing something. Not sure," I said, placing a piece of cake on everyone's plate before sitting down.

"Business doing something," my dad repeated. "Way to ask the hard questions, Pumpkin." He leaned over the table and cut another slice of cake even though he wasn't finished with his first once.

Ignoring my dad, I said, "He makes good money, whatever he does. Very generous too. He wouldn't let me pay for anything on either of our dates."

"Good," my mom said, taking a dainty bite of cake. "Good cake, Jane."

I took a forkful into my mouth and felt a wave of disappointment. "Not my best effort. Could have been flakier. I mixed with a spoon instead of using my hands."

Not bothering to use her fork, Claire shoved a big piece in her mouth. After swallowing, she said, "You're insane, little sister. This cake is awesome. When are you going out with him again?"

Fidgeting with my cell phone under the table, I said, "Probably this week." I was anxious to hear from him, but knew it was a busy season at work.

"Sounds promising," my mom said. She turned in Claire's direction. "On to you. Any news?"

Shaking her head, Claire said, "Still not pregnant. We're having fun trying, though."

I was glad her husband, Kevin, wasn't around. He hated when she mentioned sex in front of my parents. So did my father.

Turning back to me, my dad asked, "How's the studying going?"

The LSAT. In favor of studying, I had been daydreaming about my future with Randall. "Fine. It's going fine."

My mom got up from the table, stood behind my dad's chair, and squeezed his shoulder before walking out of the room. From down the hall, she called out, "Girls, let's get going," which I assumed was my cue to chug the rest of my coffee and freshen up.

After brunch, my mom, Claire, and I headed to the Tanger outlets. I bought three sweaters at Ann Taylor Loft for nineteen dollars and tried on a few pairs of jeans at J Crew.

Modeling a pair of black ones for them in the dressing room, I checked myself out in the 360-degree mirror. "What do you guys think?"

After eyeing me up and down for what felt like a really long time, my mom finally nodded her approval. "I like them. Dark black is good for you. Save the colors for your upper body."

"I know, Mom. Thanks for insinuating I have a huge ass." Standing next to my size two mother, I was well aware I had junk in the trunk.

Giving me a kiss on the cheek, my mom said, "You have a lovely figure, Jane. I just want you to play up your best features for Randall."

Turning to Claire, who was examining a silk scarf for pulls, I asked, "What about you, Claire? Like them?"

She looked up, smiling brightly. "Love them. Your ass looks really good."

I turned to my mother to shoot her a look, but she was holding a cardigan against her chest and examining her reflection in the mirror.

Winking, Claire said, "Third date material, if you know what I mean."

I had no clue what she meant, which I assumed she realized by my blank expression. While our mother generously got in line to pay for our items, she whispered, "Third date rule."

Still clueless, I said, "What does that mean?"

Shaking her head, she said, "I can't believe your girlfriends didn't share this with you."

"Share what?"

Grabbing my elbow and directing me to an unoccupied corner of the store, she said, "Well, I haven't been single in a while, but from everything I hear, the third date equals sex these days."

More than a little aware my next date with Randall would be our third, I said, "Isn't it too soon? I was dating Bob for almost a year before we did it."

"You were sixteen."

"Seventeen." Much less slutty.

"Anyway, I understand you might not be ready, and it's not a set rule, but seriously, Jane, it's been a while. Don't you want to?"

Half-truthfully, I replied, "Of course."

There was a part of me that wanted it so badly, I was ready to climb on top of Randall on the *first* date. But there was also a part of me that was so terrified, I wanted to go home, put on my feety pajamas, and hibernate for the winter.

# Chapter 8

In nervous anticipation of my third date with Randall, I went through my underwear drawer and sorted out which of my panties were sex worthy. Most of them weren't. Hanes briefs were out of the question. I had a bunch of G-strings that served their purpose by avoiding panty lines, but my tummy spilled over and the lines cut me in weird places and made me look flabbier than I actually was. After looking up the best fit for my body type online, I went to Bloomingdale's and bought four pairs of Hanky Panky low-rise thongs for twenty dollars each. Lainie and I were both craving a spicy tuna roll, so I met her at Iron Sushi on the way home.

Eyeing my Small Brown Bag, she asked, "What did you buy?"

Trying to be as discreet as possible, I slipped the bag to Lainie under the table and whispered, "Sexy underwear."

Lainie removed a red lace thong from the bag and waved it around. "What's the occasion?"

Not really wanting to discuss sex with Lainie, I jerked the thong from her hand, said, "Just time to buy new stuff," and popped an edamame in my mouth.

"You and Randall do it yet?"

Feeling my face turn red, I sucked the salt from the edamame, placed the shell on the empty plate and muttered, "No. But probably soon."

Grinning in response to my reaction to the topic of conversation, Lainie asked, "When are you seeing him again?"

I shrugged in response.

"No dates planned?"

"Not yet, but it's only been a few days since our last date."

"Have you spoken to him?"

"Not in a while, but I'm sure he'll call soon." I didn't want to admit it to Lainie, but I was getting antsy. Maybe he wanted to plan something special for the big third date and it took time.

Lainie crinkled her nose. "Have you heard from him since your date?"

I shook my head. "No, but he's like a workaholic. Quite typical for guys in their late twenties. Ambition is a turn on."

"How did you leave things?"

"He kissed me goodbye and put me in a cab." I narrowed my eyes at her. "What's with the interrogation, Lainie?"

Ignoring my question, she asked another one of her own. "What did he say?"

"I don't know. It was kind of fuzzy. Too much wine. He had to get up early the next day."

Lainie snorted. "What? To drive his sister to the airport or something?"

"His roommate actually. What's so funny?"

Lainie stared at me. Waiting for an answer, I stared back. Finally, she said, "He really said he had to take his roommate to the airport?"

I nodded.

"And you believed him?"

"Yes. Why not? You think he was lying?" *Please say no.*

"I don't know. What happened on your date?"

"What do you mean? We had dinner, drank some wine, smooched. Randall wanted me to go home with him but totally understood when I said I wanted to take things slow."

Lainie pushed away her plate of sushi, reached across the table, and put her hand over mine. She shook her head. "Sweetie, I don't think Randall will have the pleasure of seeing you in your sexy new underwear."

I felt my muscles tighten and swallowed hard. "Why not?"

Looking at me in disbelief, Lainie raised her voice. "Girl,

you've been blown off. Randall the Great is really Randall the Rat!" Lowering her voice, she said, "Don't feel bad though. You didn't do anything wrong aside from refusing to do *him*. I applaud you. He's a slug."

I pictured us sitting side by side on the couch at the Gramercy Hotel and how my head fit so neatly in the curve of his arm. Lainie was out of her mind. "No. He was so great about it. He kissed me even after I said I wasn't ready to have sex. He called me 'sweetheart.' He hailed the taxi for me and opened the door too. And he waited for the cab to leave before going back in the..." I looked down at the blond hairs standing up on my arms. "Oh God."

Lainie opened her eyes wide. "What?"

"Why did he go back in the bar if he needed to go to sleep early?"

Bursting into laughter, Lainie said, "He seriously went back inside the bar after putting you in the cab?"

I absently nodded my head at Lainie, who continued to call Randall various derogatory names. But I was no longer listening. And I had lost my appetite for spicy tuna.

# Chapter 9

The next day, I stayed at work late to study for the LSAT. My cases were slow but I didn't want to go home. Lainie was having a male guest over and called dibs on the living room. I didn't understand why, since the date would inevitably end in her bedroom. I hoped she didn't plan on having sex on the couch. It was technically mine.

I was baffled. It didn't make sense. None of it made sense. Why would Randall blow me off just because I wouldn't have sex with him on our second date? Especially since we hadn't gotten to the third date yet and, according to Claire, it was the third date rule—not the second. And when I told Randall I wasn't ready, he said we had all the time in the world.

By my reasoning, Lainie was totally wrong about Randall being a slug.

But that didn't explain why he hadn't called since our date or why he went back inside the Gramercy Hotel after putting me in the cab when he said he needed to get to bed early.

I had always told Marissa to wait for the guy to call her, but I needed to talk to Randall and get his side of the story. He deserved the benefit of the doubt. I knew he liked me. There had to be a reasonable explanation for why he hadn't called. So I ignored my own advice and called him.

After the first ring, I stopped chewing my pen. A nasty habit my mom said would give me an overbite. He wasn't picking up. Voicemail. "Hi Randall. It's me. Jane. Amber. Ha! Just calling to say hi. Haven't heard from you and wanted to make sure you were all right. Give me a call, okay? Bye."

Deep breath. I wondered when he'd call me back. I also wondered if he was screening my call and would never, ever return it. I turned to my officemate. "Andrew?"

Andrew looked up from his desk. "Yeah?"

"How can I tell if a guy is screening my calls?" Andrew's sweet smile and playfulness around the office made him very popular with the female paralegals and probably girls in general. I figured he'd screened many calls in his time.

Grinning, Andrew said, "Wanna catch your man in the act, huh?"

I nodded. "I guess."

"Have you been calling him from your cell?"

Waving my phone at him, I said, "Uh-huh."

"Does he know where you work or your number here?"

We hadn't talked much about work. "No."

"Call him from your work phone and see if he picks up."

My hands shaking, I started dialing his number when Andrew stopped me.

"Wait," he said. "I have a better idea. Let's call from my phone just in case. I'll put it on speaker."

I gave Andrew the number and held my breath as he dialed and we waited for the ring.

After one ring, he picked up. "Randall here."

Andrew looked at me waiting for my response. I didn't say anything. He gave me bug eyes and mouthed, "Well?"

I whispered, "Hang up. Hang up!"

Andrew hung up. "There's your answer, I guess."

Feeling sick to my stomach, I logged out, grabbed my bag, and waved goodbye to Andrew. I was going home, and Lainie and her date would just have to deal with it. "Thanks for your help. See you tomorrow."

As I exited our office and turned left toward the elevator bank, I heard Andrew call out, "He's a fool, Jane. Chin up."

\*   \*   \*

Marissa didn't have cable, so she came over every Sunday and watched *The Walking Dead* with Lainie. I wasn't into it, but I had made enough lasagna to feed all three of us and our future grandchildren, so I sat with them anyway.

Lainie insisted on talking about Randall the Rat.

"I'm so sorry, Jane," Marissa said. "He sounded so charming."

"The biggest scumbags always put on the best show. That's how they operate," Lainie said. "Mind if I take more lasagna?"

I shook my head and returned the recliner to the upright position. "It's no biggie, guys. I suppose I was due a bad egg after dating the same great guy for nine years."

"I still don't get how you possibly thought you'd do better than Bob. Not that I've met him, but he seemed like state of the art boyfriend material. Being in a committed relationship seems to be your goal in life, and you were in one. Kind of blew it if you ask me," Lainie said, before walking into the kitchen.

"It wasn't about wanting someone better than Bob. We just fell out of love, that's all. It was too convenient. Too easy, you know?" I looked at Marissa, hoping for her support.

Laughing, she said, "Dating in New York is neither convenient nor easy, so maybe you'll like it."

Lainie sat back down with the plate of lasagna on her lap. "Yes, it's most inconvenient and difficult to say the least," she said before taking a bite.

Bored with the conversation, I got up and headed to the bathroom to get ready for bed. I had a wine tasting event through Meetup the next night and hadn't picked out an outfit.

"Randall wasn't the one, girls. Over and out. The search continues. I'll call you soon, Ris. Night, Lainie. See you tomorrow."

As I changed into my pajamas, I heard them whispering about how great my attitude was until they finally shut up and watched the show.

In bed, I played back my time with Randall. Maybe I'd freaked him out when I said I had just gotten out of a relationship and wanted to take things slow. He probably liked me but assumed I was looking for something serious. I was, so it was a blessing I found out he wasn't on the same page before I slept with him. Just the same, I shouldn't have made it so obvious. But it was his loss. The next guy would reap the benefits of my education. Claire was right—dating post-millennium was a whole different animal, and I'd just had my first blunder. I should never have mentioned my past relationship and desire to take things slow. It wouldn't happen again.

# Chapter 10

I second-guessed my decision to go stag to the singles event when I walked into the room full of complete strangers laughing together. I had purposely arrived fashionably late, but it seemed like everyone already knew each other. I glanced around the room contemplating my first move, grabbed an empty wine glass, and headed to a table where a man was explaining the difference between a Shiraz and a Syrah. I pretended to listen until he noticed me standing there and asked if I wanted to try the wine. The group of people surrounding the table took notice of me and, feeling awkward, my cheeks heated up.

I extended my glass. "Yes. Thanks." I took a small sip and nodded my approval even though I wasn't sure I really liked it.

After a few more tastings at that table, it was time to move on, so I scoped out the room for cute guys. Marissa had warned me singles events were usually attended by more girls than boys, and the girls were typically better looking. I reluctantly agreed with her and chugged the rest of my wine. I noticed the cheese buffet and got in line. I popped a cube of cheddar in my mouth, filled my plate with an assortment of other cheeses, crackers, and dried fruit, and sat down on one of the couches.

On the couches next to me sat five giggling girls. I wondered what was so funny and knew I would have enjoyed myself more if I had gone with friends. My mother had advised me to go to these things alone though, because men were more likely to approach a girl on her own.

Determined to meet someone before the night was over, I put

my cheese plate on the floor and scanned the room again. I smiled at the group of guys standing to my left. They smiled back but continued their conversation. I picked the cheese plate off the floor and returned it to my lap. I took a second look at the guys, concluded they weren't cute anyway, and laughed. I quickly put my hand over my mouth as I realized I might look slightly psycho.

"Want to let me in on the joke?"

Startled, I looked up at the guy standing before me and took a sip of my wine. "I didn't realize I had laughed out loud. Embarrassing!"

"Care to share?"

I cocked my head to the side. "This whole event is kind of humorous in general."

"Tell me about it," he said, nodding. "You mind if I join you?"

Sliding over to give him more room, I said, "Not at all." With his jet black hair, tall frame, and dimples, he was way cuter than any of those other guys who were now looking in our direction.

"Have you been to one of these before?"

"No. This is my first one. You?"

Shaking his head, he said, "First timer too. I just moved here from Detroit. I don't really know anyone aside from the people I work with. My boss actually told me about this group and suggested I give it a shot."

"Are you going to yell at him tomorrow?"

"Yell at *her*. She's a woman, and no, I might have to thank her," he said before smiling shyly.

I realized he was flirting with me and butterflies danced in my stomach. "I'm Jane."

He turned back to face me. "Jim. Good to meet you."

"Same here. Have you tried all the wines yet?" I asked.

"Just about. All except table A. What about you?"

"I've only been to table C—reds from France. I don't think I can handle trying all of them, but I'll join you at table A if you want."

Standing up, he said, "Let's go for it."

After I traded in my dirty glass for a new one, Jim and I joined the small group surrounding table A. I half listened to the curly-haired woman discuss the floral flavors of the New Zealand Pinot Grigio while secretly hoping Jim would ask for my number.

After we'd tried all six of the wines on the list, Jim asked, "Which was your favorite?"

"The Chilean Sauvignon Blanc. I liked the grapefruit aftertaste. I bet it would taste good with Thai food, or even sushi. Which did you like the best?"

"To be honest, I'd prefer a Guinness over a glass of wine any day."

"A beer guy, huh? I never acquired much of a taste for beer, except maybe Hoegaarden. It's lighter than most beers."

"I'm not much into fruity beers."

I thought about Randall's fruity wine and decided Jim's preference for beer was a good sign. Poking him playfully in the arm, I said, "Not manly enough for you, huh?"

His eyes piercing mine, he asked, "Is that bad?"

"Not at all. I prefer my men 'manly,'" I flirted.

"Not into metrosexuals?"

Noticing his Detroit Lions jersey, I said, "Not at all. I like guys who enjoy sports and beer. They can leave the shopping to me."

"My kind of girl, Jane. Into football?"

"Admittedly, I don't understand the game." Lying, I said, "But I've always wanted to learn."

"Really? Well, I'd be willing to teach you, if you want. I'm a diehard Lions fan. I never miss a game. If you watch one with me, I'd be happy to give you a play-by-play lesson."

"That would be awesome." I'd gladly suffer through a football lesson for those dimples.

"How about Sunday? There's a game at four against the Titans. Want to watch it with me?"

"Would love to," I said.

With a toothy smile, Jim removed his phone from his pocket. "What's your number?"

I gave Jim my number, trying to contain my excitement. If things had worked out with Randall, I'd never have met Jim, who I could already tell was a much better match. My dad would totally approve of a fellow football fan. Although, being a Giants fan himself, he might question Jim's allegiance.

I practically skipped to the subway station and was barely shaken when the E train didn't stop at 53rd and I had to take a cab to get back to the east side. I'd put in a lot of overtime that month and had certainly earned the right to splurge on a single taxi ride. Besides, my mom didn't like me to take the subway after ten p.m. She said she didn't like the "element." She and my dad had lived in Manhattan well before Rudy Giuliani had cleaned it up.

Lainie was sprawled across the couch watching the *Real Housewives of Atlanta*, but she muted it when I walked into the apartment. "How was the wine event?"

I threw my bag on the coffee table and plopped myself on the couch next to her. "It was a lot of fun."

Lainie sat up. "Seriously?"

"Yes. Seriously! I met the greatest guy."

"You said that about Randall, if I recall."

"Yes, but Randall was Mr. Smooth. I should have spotted him a mile away. Nothing like Jim."

"Jim, huh? What's he like?"

"He's a chemist. Works for Becton Dickenson and was just transferred from their Detroit office."

Patting me on the shoulder patronizingly, Lainie said, "Sounds like a nerd, Jane."

"Not at all. He's dorky-cute," I said.

"Did he take your number?"

"Yep. He already asked me to watch football with him on Sunday."

Lainie laughed. "Football? You? You don't even know who won the Super Bowl last year."

"The Giants." Thankfully, Jim had mentioned it in conversation.

"I had no idea you were such a football fan."

"I wasn't until today," I said before walking into my bedroom and shutting the door.

A few minutes later, I was sitting in front of my computer reading about the history of the Detroit Lions on the NFL website when Lainie tapped on my door. I turned around. "What's up?"

Lainie sat on my bed. "I'm glad you met another guy tonight. I hope he's more worthy than Randall."

The unexpected kind words left me momentarily speechless, but I recovered quickly. "Thanks, Lainie." I pointed to my computer screen. "To be honest, I'm clueless about football. I'm studying up now so I'll have something to contribute on our date."

Lainie gave me a soft smile and stood up. "You're sweet, Jane. You deserve a good guy."

I felt a lump in my throat at the sincerity in her words. "You do too, Lainie."

"Thanks. Unfortunately, I always find the bad ones so much more attractive. Well, goodnight."

"Goodnight."

After she closed the door, I continued reading about the Lions. I gave up after five minutes and prayed the game itself would be more interesting.

Tingling in anticipation, I turned off my computer and crawled into bed hoping Sunday would come fast.

# Chapter 11

"So they have ten chances to go four downs?"

Laughing, Jim said, "Close. They have four downs to go ten yards."

We were watching the game at East End Tavern, not far from my apartment. "What are downs again?"

"You're adorable. You know that?"

Blushing, due more to being giddy from the compliment than embarrassed over my ignorance, I responded, "Thanks" and took a sip of my apple martini. It didn't exactly go with the football theme, but there was a five-dollar special, so I wasn't the only girl not drinking beer.

"This place is great."

"I've never been here before, but the website said each booth had its own television screen and I figured you'd like it."

"You did research?"

I said, "Yep" and took a sip of my drink before turning toward the television monitor where a bunch of players in dark blue jerseys had just jumped on top of one guy in a lighter blue jersey. When I looked back at Jim, he was staring at me. I glanced down and hoped I hadn't dribbled my martini onto my white long-sleeved t-shirt. I wore it with dark blue jeans to go with the colors of the Lions. "Do I have wings in my teeth?" Chicken fingers would have been a safer choice, but they'd probably be too salty whereas the place was known for its crispy wings.

Jim chuckled. "No, nothing nearly as dire as that. It was very sweet of you to put so much thought into where we watched the game."

Blushing again, I said, "It was nothing. I like researching places before I go to them."

"It was still nice. You did good."

Jim got up from the table. I thought he was going to excuse himself to the bathroom, but instead he walked to my side of the table, sat down, and surprised me with a soft kiss on the lips.

Grabbing my hand, he said, "I'm having a great time, Jane."

Startled, but in a good way, I said, "Me too" before Jim reached over and kissed me again. Since I wasn't caught off guard like the last time, I kissed him back.

After that, there was no point faking any interest in football, so I gazed longingly at Jim while he stared intently at the television and kissed me during timeouts. We held hands except when Jim clapped excitedly or slammed his palm against the table in frustration.

After the game, Jim walked me home and we sat on my front steps. "I'm very happy the Lions won for more reasons than one," he said.

I squeezed his hand. "I'm happy the Lions won too. Happy for you, that is. I won't pretend to suddenly be a football fanatic."

"Well, besides the obvious reason that I always prefer when my team wins, I can be quite a sore loser, and I'd hate to make a bad impression on our first date."

"Since you only kissed me when the Lions did something good and sulked whenever the Titans scored, I kind of figured you might be a sore loser. It doesn't bother me. My ex-boyfriend was a sore loser too, so I'm used to it."

Releasing my hand, Jim asked, "How 'ex' is the ex-boyfriend?"

Crap. I wasn't supposed to mention the ex. I chewed on my lip. "Very 'ex.' We broke up over a year ago." I hoped I sounded casual and completely available for a new relationship.

Jim took my hand back and kissed it. "Good. So, do I get a second date? I promise it will be more upscale than a sports bar."

Happy he didn't ask for more details about Bob, I said, "I look forward to it."

Jim stood and extended his hand to help me up with him. "I'd better run to catch the bus to Weehawken. But I'll call you to set up date number two. I promise you'll have my undivided attention." He hugged me goodbye.

I walked in the apartment, shut the door behind me, and, through the peep hole, watched Jim walk back down the stairs.

I totally lucked out meeting Jim right after the Randall disaster. I thanked God I hadn't slept with Randall. If he couldn't wait for the third date, that was his problem, which is what I told Claire at the Tasti D-Lite on First and 73rd, right between my apartment and hers on 62nd and Second. She asked why I was so excited about some guy named Jim and didn't I mean Randall?

"Randall was a slug. Just like Lainie said. He was only out to get laid. He did me a favor by not calling again."

Claire took a spoonful of her toasted almond fudge ice cream, if you could even call it ice cream. It tasted more like flavored air. "You're certainly taking this well for someone who was so into Randall a week ago," she said, raising her eyebrow.

I pouted. "I've been out of the game a while—"

Before I could finish, Claire interrupted. "You were never in the game."

"Whatever. I fell for Randall's fake charm, but I'm not going to beat myself up over it. It's done. And now I have Jim, who's so much better."

# Chapter 12

On our second date, after Jim paid the bill for the slice of seven-layer cake we shared at the cafe across the street from the movie theater, he excused himself to go to the bathroom. And I wracked my brain for a way to subtly let him know I was game for third-date sex without coming out and saying it. I wasn't ready to bring him home yet, but I needed to send the message I was almost ready to progress to the next level.

Returning from the bathroom, Jim sat down. "I still can't believe you liked the movie. What exactly did you like about it?"

"Do I think it was Oscar-worthy? No. But I don't get why you hated it so much."

"So you think it was Golden Globe-worthy but not Oscar, huh?"

When he teased me, Jim got slight laugh lines on the corners of his eyes, making his otherwise flawless skin less pristine, but I liked it. I reached across the table, locking his fingers with mine. "I had fun watching the movie with you, and I totally forgive you for making fun of my taste in theater."

Jim let out a snort. "Theater? What we just experienced doesn't qualify as 'film' or even 'cinema.' Certainly not theater. It was a movie. Plain and simple." Smiling, he said, "But I'd watch it again with you and only you."

Holding my breath, I asked, "Does that mean you want to see me again?"

Squeezing my hand, he said, "It sure does."

"How about I cook for you?"

"Do you cook?"

"Actually, I do. My skills are not limited to spaghetti either."

The laugh lines appeared again. "Oh, you cook penne too? And rigatoni?"

"Just for that, there will be no pasta on the menu at all. How do you feel about rack of lamb?"

"Sounds delicious. I'll bring the wine. And dessert. Unless you're a pastry chef as well."

Locking eyes with Jim, I said, "I had my own ideas for dessert. But you're welcome to bring some too."


I paid Lainie fifty dollars to occupy herself elsewhere so Jim and I could have the apartment to ourselves. I probably didn't need to compensate her considering how many times our roles had been reversed, but I wanted to give her an added incentive to stay away. The lamb was browning in the skillet and, after Jim arrived, I'd add the potatoes and shallots. We'd have salad and melon, Jamón and mini mozzarella skewers to start. And I made Nutella mousse for dessert. Although I hoped we'd eat it in bed later.

I had on a black lace thong and matching bra under my belted midnight blue sweater dress, textured tights and high suede black boots and hoped the wine would sooth my apprehension over being naked with someone for the first time in over a year. I also hoped it would alter Jim's perception such that he would think I was a size two instead of a size ten, and on skinny days, a size eight.

As I drizzled the homemade dressing over the salad, the buzzer sounded Jim's arrival.

Dashing to the phone, I picked it up. "Hello?"

"It's Jim. Hope I'm not too early."

"You're right on time. Come on up. I'm on the third floor."

Figuring it would take Jim about thirty seconds to make his way up two flights of stairs, I took one last glance in my bedroom to make sure I hadn't left any embarrassing items lying on the floor or on my bed. All clear, I made my way to the front door just as Jim rang the bell.

I opened the door to find him standing in front of me in blue jeans and a red sweater and holding a bouquet of mixed flowers in a variety of colors. Leaning down to kiss me, he said, "These are for you."

I kissed him back. "Thank you so much. They're beautiful."

"Just like the girl I bought them for."

I relocated Jim to the living room while I sliced the rack into chops and added the roasted potatoes and tomatoes to the platter. I had Jim uncork the bottle of Merlot he had brought with him to let it breathe, but while setting the table, I drank a glass, or maybe it was two, of a half-opened bottle of white Lainie had left in the refrigerator. The first course ready, I lit two candles, dimmed the lights, took one more sip of wine, and called Jim back to the kitchen table to eat.

After cleaning his plate of potatoes, Jim rubbed his stomach. "Wow, Jane. You weren't kidding about being able to cook. This meal was outstanding."

I was glad he had enjoyed it. My stomach was too crowded with nervous knots to eat. Instead, I moved the food around my plate and took small bites when Jim was watching me. "Glad you liked it. Dessert?"

Stretching his arms above his head, Jim said, "I don't think I can do dessert right now. I'm stuffed."

It was now or never. I gulped the rest of the wine in my glass, stood up and walked over to Jim's chair on the other side of the kitchen table. I sat on his lap and kissed his neck. "Dessert need not be limited to food, you know."

Jim moved aside my hair and gave me a kiss, gently biting my lip. "Oh? What did you have in mind?"

"Kissing is a good start." Hoping I sounded seductive, I said, "And you never know what can happen from there."

As I said this, I fumbled with the bottom of Jim's sweater in an attempt to lift it over his head. A button-down shirt would have been easier.

With his sweater still on, Jim stood up, lifting me up with him since I was on his lap. When we were standing face to face, he took both of my hands in his. "Wow. This is a side of you I haven't seen before."

I bravely responded, "There are many sides to Jane." I paused. "Including the sexy side."

Jim released my hands and laughed. "I don't doubt that. I noticed the sexy side of Jane the first time we met. I was referring to the aggressive side."

Reaching for the buckle of his belt, I looked him dead in the eyes. "I just find you irresistibly attractive."

His face turning red, Jim took a step backwards. "I'm flattered. You're pretty easy on the eyes yourself."

"I'm glad you think so." Since I wasn't having any luck getting his clothes off, I grabbed his hand, led him to the living room, and gently pushed him on the couch. "Sit right there and don't move," I commanded before running back to the kitchen and taking a long swig of wine directly from the bottle.

Returning to the living room, I sat next to him on the couch and quickly removed my boots. Out of the corner of my eyes, I saw Jim looking at me waiting to see what I'd do next. I stood up in front of Jim, unbuckled the belt of my sweater, and tossed it on the couch next to him. Then I pulled the dress over my head in one motion. In only my underwear and tights, I asked, "Do you think I'm easy on the eyes now?"

Staring at me, Jim said, "Of course I do."

I shimmied my upper half. "I bet you want to see what's under this. Don't you?"

Jim's eyes flashed to my black lace bra and he lifted himself to a standing position.

Pushing him back down, I said, "Not yet." I turned my back on him and wiggled my butt while I unhooked my bra. I pinched both sides together, but the hooks wouldn't budge from the eyelets.

"Jane? Do you need—?"

Still entrapped in my bra, I raised a hand in the air. "It's all good." I felt my blood travel to my face as I exerted more effort into freeing my boobs. "Almost ready," I said in a high-pitched and hopefully sexy tone. At last, the hooks came loose and I let out a sigh. I removed the bra, tossed it over my shoulder, and turned around with a smoldering look. "What do you think of these apples?"

Jim swallowed hard and scratched his dark hair. "They're, uh, very ripe."

"I was thinking delicious, but ripe works too," I said before growling like a sexy tiger. "I need some help with the rest of my clothes. Wanna volunteer?"

Sitting up straight, Jim reached for my hand. "Sure."

When we got to my bedroom, I jumped on my bed and motioned for Jim to remove my tights. As I lay on my back, I noticed the room was spinning slightly, and I fought the urge to pass out. Jim's hands roamed my naked body until I felt his form hovering over mine. I absently pulled him toward me and kissed him. My mouth was dry and I wished I had a glass of water by my bed. Or root beer. I was vaguely aware that Jim had sat up to put on a condom. As I waited for him to finish, I imagined the sweet taste of root beer until he bent down toward me and our naked bodies pressed together. My body felt numb to Jim's touch, but I was anxious to get past the awkwardness of our first time together so we could be a real couple. As Jim finished with a loud groan, I smiled at the thought of us double dating with Claire and Kevin, or even Bob and Trish, and fell asleep.

An urgent need to go to the bathroom woke me up the next morning. When I sat up in bed, I instantly felt a throbbing in my temples which I was surprised hadn't jolted me out of my sleep earlier.

Momentarily forgetting where I was, I looked toward my opened door that led to the hallway, Lainie's room, and the bathroom. Confused as to why my door wasn't closed, I glanced around searching for clues and immediately took note of my tights and panties on the floor by my bed. Slowly, the details of the night came back to me. Jim had come over and I had made him dinner. I was oddly hungry for having made so much food. Carefully stepping onto the floor, I walked two steps toward the door, had a flashback of giving Jim a striptease, and returned to my bed. On my back with my feet dangling off the edge, I closed my eyes and vaguely recalled having sex with Jim. I had no idea if I had enjoyed it.

I peed, made my way into the kitchen and was greeted by a sink full of dirty dishes. I didn't even remember clearing the table, which was now covered with drippings of melted candle wax. I could almost hear my mother chastising me for not using a tablecloth and stuck a finger in each ear hoping to tune her out. Two empty bottles of wine were sitting next to the garbage can and, when I swallowed, I could still taste it at the back of my throat. It tasted better the first time around.

It suddenly made sense why I had no recollection whether the sex was good, and I laughed out loud. We had put away two bottles of wine and had drunk and most likely sloppy, sex. Lord knows Bob and I didn't have movie star sex every time either. Jim and I would just joke about it and make sure the second time was better.

I sat at my kitchen table, buried my head in my hands, and prayed there was aspirin in the apartment. Any plans for the day would be superseded by a long nap. I wondered how Jim was feeling and hoped, for his sake, he was in better shape than me. I didn't even remember him leaving but assumed he woke up early and didn't want to disturb me.

After my nap, I cleaned the dishes and, on my way downstairs to take out the trash, ran into Lainie.

She held the front door open for me while I tossed the bags into the dark green garbage bin and we walked back up together.

Climbing the stairs two at a time, she asked, "How'd it go?"

"Very well, I think." *From what I remember.* I looked Lainie up and down with interest. "I see you're wearing the same clothes you had on last night. Crazy night?"

"Nothing too crazy. I made out with a hottie, but I have my period, so I just crashed at my friend's place after a long night of karaoke." After taking a water bottle from the refrigerator, Lainie sat down at the table. "So...how was it?"

Indecisive as to whether I wanted to join her at the table, I remained standing. "It was fine."

"Just fine?"

I sat down. "Great. It was great."

"No details? Was he good in bed? Does he have a big you-know-what? C'mon, Jane. Help a sister out."

Realizing I had no idea how big Jim's penis was—not that it was any of Lainie's business—I stood up and backed slowly out of the room. "I don't kiss and tell. But I'm happy. Very happy."

"Nice. It would be nicer if you gave me some details, but it's still nice."

"Maybe some other time, Lainie." Like when I had details to give. Suddenly, I was exhausted again and ready for another nap, but my phone rang. Lainie picked it up from the table, answered, "Jane's phone" and handed it to me. Since I wanted to let it go to voicemail, I rolled my eyes at her as she mouthed, "It's Bob."

I muttered, "I'll take it in my room" to Lainie before saying, "Hi. What's up?"

"Hey. Just thought I'd check in with you."

My first thought was maybe he broke it off with Trish. My second thought was that God would punish me for wishing something bad on my first love. I didn't really wish anything bad on Bob; I was just bitter because he was in another committed relationship before me. I hoped God knew the difference. "That was nice of you. How are things?"

"Really hectic. I'm packing up my stuff for the move."

"So you're still going through with it. I mean, things are still good with Trish?"

"Yeah, of course."

"Great. I mean it." If God was listening, I hoped he knew I really meant it.

"The move is killing me. Which brings me to my call."

"I thought you called to check in."

Bob laughed. "Yeah, well that too."

"What do you need from me?"

"Just wondering if you ever returned my box set of all the *Beverly Hills 90210* seasons."

I walked with my phone to the living room and removed seasons one through three from the bottom drawer of the entertainment center. "You itching to watch the Walsh's bond over dinner or something?"

"Nah. You know Steve is the only character I liked. Maybe Valerie too. But when I told Trish I owned the entire collection, she acted like it was the equivalent of winning the lottery and now I can't find it."

"I wonder where you put it," I said.

"I thought I might have lent it to you."

Back in my room, I shoved the DVDs into the back of my closet. "Nope. Don't have them. But I'll double check later."

"Thanks. So what's new? My mom told me you were dating some guy named Randall. How's it going between you guys?"

Our mothers being friends had been great when we were dating, not so much anymore. "The relationship didn't work out. But I met someone else. Jim. He stayed over last night." Feeling dumb for announcing that last bit of unsolicited information, I said, "It got serious really fast." I paused. "Like you and Trish."

"Can't wait to meet him and tell him all your dirty secrets."

"I don't have any dirty secrets."

Bursting into laughter, Bob said, "You're right. Sad, Jane. Might want to work on that."

"Ha ha."

"Joking. Well, I gotta run. Let me know if you find the DVDs."

"I don't have them, but if they mysteriously appear, I'll let you know."

After we hung up, I removed my LSAT practice test book from my dresser and brought it to my bed.

Next thing I knew, I woke up fully clothed with the book resting on my chest. No sunlight peeking through my window, I checked the clock and saw it was past one in the morning. I reached over, set my alarm for seven and got under the covers. I was about to fall asleep when I realized I hadn't put more than two hours into studying for the LSAT in weeks. It would be hard to balance preparation with a new boyfriend, but I wouldn't let my father down. Tomorrow was another day.

## Chapter 13

Monday morning, I opened a new document on my computer and drafted my list of goals for the week: Spend at least two hours studying for the LSAT. Decide what to get parents for thirty-third wedding anniversary. Make appointment with gyno to get back on the pill...

"Is there a reason why you're whistling, Jane?"

I looked up at Andrew. His long arms were stretched above his head of light brown, almost red hair and his mouth was half opened, midway through a yawn. "Sorry," I said. "Am I bothering you?"

"Not really. Just curious why you're happy. It's only Monday."

"Exactly. It's the beginning of the week—plenty of time to accomplish goals by Friday."

Andrew rolled his blue eyes. "If you say so."

I returned to the screen and continued drafting: Go to gym at least twice after work. Make lunch plans with Claire...

"I guess you're over that guy, huh?"

Still focused on the computer screen, I said, "What guy?"

"The one who screened your calls?"

Swatting the air with my hands, I nodded. "Totally over him. Dating someone else now. So much better."

Andrew stood up, dragged his chair over to my desk and sat back down. "Tell me about him."

Not wanting Andrew to see my list, I minimized the screen and took a sip of coffee. "He's so nice."

"Does nice translate to ugly?"

"No. He's cute. Tall, in good shape, dark hair. Cute." Looking questioningly at Andrew, I said, "I thought you liked girls."

Andrew smirked. "I do like girls, Jane. I'm asking about your type."

"I'm very open-minded. As long as he doesn't screen my calls."

"So this dude takes your calls?"

Without hesitation, I said, "Yup." But then I remembered I had never actually called Jim. "On second thought, I don't know. I've never called him first."

"Good. If a guy really likes you, he'll do the calling."

"Exactly." I glanced at my phone sitting at the top of my opened purse. I removed it from the bag and checked whether I had any unread messages. I didn't. No missed calls either.

"What's wrong?"

I threw the phone back in my bag. "Nothing." I turned away from Andrew and pretended to focus on my desktop while circling my mouse over the various icons.

Andrew removed my hand from the mouse and forced me to face him. "Bullshit. You were whistling like one of Snow White's freakin' dwarves a few minutes ago. Now you've got a full bottom lip and sad puppy dog eyes."

"Jim hasn't called me in a couple of days," I reluctantly admitted.

Andrew raised one eyebrow. "Jim's the guy you're dating?"

I nodded.

"What's the deal?"

Shrugging, I said, "Don't know. We hung out on Saturday night, and I haven't heard from him since."

"Typical chick." Andrew chuckled. "Seriously, it's only Monday morning. No need to be alarmed, Jane."

But I was. "I suppose. But..."

"But what?"

I chewed on my lip. "We, uh, we..." My face heated up.

"You what?"

"We had sex for the first time on Saturday."

"Did he stay over?"

"Yes." *I think.*

With a devilish grin, Andrew asked, "How was the sex?"

"It was fine. From what I remember. But that's beside the point. He was gone when I woke up on Sunday, and I haven't heard from him since." I felt a quivering in my bottom lip and placed my hand over my mouth to hide it from Andrew.

"Aw, Jane. You really know how to pick 'em." Andrew sighed dramatically.

I looked hopefully at him. "You said yourself it's only Monday. No need to be alarmed. He might still call. Right?"

Andrew got up and returned his chair to his own desk. Before sitting down, he walked back over to me and placed his hand on my shoulder. "I don't know this dude. He might still call, but when I sleep with a girl I really like for the first time, I call the next day. If I don't, it's usually because I'm not interested."

"Oh."

"I'm sorry, Jane. Maybe I'm wrong."

I barely fought back the tears on the way home. How did I get it so right with the first guy I had sex with and screw up so badly with the second? As I walked up Lexington Avenue, drizzle hit my head in a slow and steady rhythm, but I didn't care. I needed to walk it off and vowed to be in better spirits by the time I got home. Jim was a total jerk who had charmed me into bed with his phony romantic act. I could do so much better. He wasn't even good in bed. Well, I didn't actually remember, but I was positive he sucked. Nope, he wasn't the one for me.

The rain picked up intensity, so I ran the remaining three blocks home. As promised, I felt better as I climbed the stairs to my apartment. Not fantastic, but better.

The following night, Marissa persuaded me to see the new Marvel movie. Even though comics weren't my thing, she promised Chris Evans would help get my mind off of Jim. She was right, although the film made me yearn to date an old-fashioned man from the '40s. Assuming he was enhanced to the peak of physicality like Captain America, of course.

On the way back to our apartments after the movie, I stopped walking and peered into the window of Roy's Fish Market. The different colors of the raw fish looked so pretty side by side—like a rainbow.

Marissa appeared by my side. "It took me a few seconds to realize you weren't with me anymore. I received a few weird looks from passing pedestrians for talking to myself."

"I'm sorry," I said with a chuckle. "Got pulled in by the colorful fish." I pointed to the market. It wasn't a restaurant, but they offered takeout and delivery and I'd read about it in a food blog.

Marissa made a sour face. "Sushi. Blech."

"You've made your feelings on raw fish clear over the years. Do you mind if we go in though?"

"How can you be hungry after all that popcorn?"

"I'm not, but I'm curious."

Marissa gave me a strange look, but followed me inside.

When I approached the counter, the guy at the counter smiled. "Can I help you with something?"

Marissa muttered, "It smells fishy in here," but I ignored her. "Can you make me a platter to feed two? Whatever you think is best." I wished I could say I asked for a big platter so I could share with Lainie, but it was really because I wanted a nice variety.

"How about a tray with a roll, sashimi, and nigiri?" He gestured to the counter. "I've got salmon, yellowtail, tuna, fluke, scallop, unagi, and a spicy salmon roll."

"I'll take it all. Can I watch you make it?"

"Sure." He gestured for me and Marissa to follow him to the back counter.

I whispered to Marissa, "You don't have to stay if you don't want."

"As long as I don't have to eat it," she said.

I watched him with fascination as he expertly sliced the fish and rolled and cut the maki.

"You make it look so easy," I gushed.

He continued to work, but smiled. "It's easy with practice. You want to learn?"

I nodded enthusiastically. "Yes."

He glanced over my head at the crowd forming, probably because the shop was going to close soon for the night. "Maybe someday, we'll open the store after hours for lessons."

"I'd sign up for sure," I said.

"Your friend too?"

Marissa shook her head. "No offense."

The guy laughed. "None taken."

Twenty minutes and only twenty dollars later, I left with a smile on my face. "How cool would it be to learn to make sushi?" I asked Marissa as we walked uptown.

"As cool as Las Vegas in August," Marissa said dryly.

"More like as cool as a dip in the lake on a summer day."

Marissa snorted. "You're a fool for food, aren't you Jane Frank?"

"Better than a fool for men." Somberly, I added, "Although I'm both right now."

Draping an arm around me, Marissa said, "Forget Jim. You said yourself he was jerk."

I had said that. I only wished I'd convinced myself it was true.

# Chapter 14

The following Saturday night, I was sitting at my parents' favorite Italian restaurant celebrating their anniversary, along with Claire and Kevin. I had just taken the last stuffed mushroom from the hot antipasto appetizer when Claire clinked her knife against her full wine glass. "I'd like to make a toast, if you guys don't mind."

We all turned our attention away from our food and toward Claire.

My mom laughed. "I'm having déjà vu. Remember the speech you made at your father's fiftieth birthday party? We thought it was going to be how lucky you were to have such a great father, and instead you told us you were engaged. Way to steal our thunder."

Turning red, Claire released Kevin's hand. "Well, I *do* feel lucky to have such a great father." Her eyes on our mom, she said, "And a great mother too. Together you've set a wonderful example of what a good marriage should look like, and I hope you'll be at our dinner table when Kevin and I celebrate our thirty-third wedding anniversary."

Raising his glass to his mouth, my dad said, "I'll drink to that."

"Me too," said Kevin.

"I'm not finished yet," Claire said.

"Keep going, dear. I'm liking it so far," my mom said.

Suddenly feeling sentimental, I glanced over at my smiling parents and back toward Claire, who was beaming. I took another sip of wine. "Me too."

Claire paused dramatically. "You've also been great role models for a mommy and daddy, and your example is finally going to be put to good use." Claire stopped talking and looked at us as if to make certain we were paying attention before saying anything else. Finally, she pushed her untouched wine to the side, raised her glass of water and squealed, "We're having a baby!"

My mother instantly bolted out of her chair and jumped up and down in a display of giddiness I hadn't witnessed since our Memorial Day picnic of 2008, when she was reunited with her best friend Barbara from college for the first time in twenty years, drank three frozen margaritas, and jumped in the pool with her clothes on.

She dashed over to Claire's seat on the other side of the table. By then Claire was also jumping up and down, and when my mom got to her, they embraced in a bear hug while rocking back and forth. Equally enthusiastic was my father who took hold of my elbow and do-si-doed me until I was dizzy and laughing tears of joy. As my dad spun me around, I caught a faint glimpse of Kevin grinning and shaking his head at our very rare display of public silliness. Finally, Claire and my mom noticed Kevin was not an active participant in the celebration and took him into their embrace.

Thirty minutes later, we had regained our composure and were sitting quietly at the table, talking in a much more socially acceptable tone. My dad had ordered a bottle of champagne, a glass of sparkling cider for Claire, and a family-style portion of tiramisu.

My mom clinked her fork against her glass. "Hush, everyone. It's Mom's turn to make a toast."

I had switched seats with Kevin so I could congratulate my sister. She had just apologized for not telling me sooner, and I was about to tell her no apologies were necessary, but when my mom demanded our attention, I turned away from Claire and waited for my mom to continue. I could tell she was tipsy, because her face was flushed and she hadn't bothered to smooth back the hair that had gone wild from dancing around the table.

"While I hate sharing the spotlight on my special day, even with my own flesh and blood, I'll gladly make an exception this time. I am so excited to be the hottest grandma on the block..."

Before she could finish, my dad piped in, "Hear, hear!"

My mom waved her hands at my dad, shooing him away, and kept talking. "And since the happiness of both of my daughters is important, I'll be equally excited to be the mother of the bride once again when my beautiful daughter Jane finally ties the knot." Beaming at me, she said, "Jim, perhaps?"

With all of the festivity, I had actually put Jim out of my mind. But with a few simple words from my mom, there he was. I released a chuckle when my dad muttered, "Not until she makes partner." I faked a smile when Kevin whispered, "Just don't be a bridezilla like your big sis."

Realizing no one even noticed I hadn't actually responded to my mom's comment, I took a spoonful of tiramisu as a tear dropped down my cheek. When I looked up from my plate, Claire was studying me with a furrowed brow. "Come with me to the bathroom, Jane?"

I nodded and followed Claire to the bathroom, torn between the need to release pent up despair over being blown off by another guy and guilt for potentially ruining one of the happiest nights of her life.

The bathroom appeared to be empty and, after bending down to check the stalls for pairs of feet, Claire leaned against the sink. "Spill."

"I'm sorry, Claire. I don't want to ruin your night."

"Stop it, Jane. I'll still be pregnant tomorrow. Besides, seeing you cry makes me upset whether you like it or not."

I stared at my reflection in the mirror. Looking at myself, I had no idea what I lacked to keep a guy's attention. I had nice wavy hair that glowed blonde in the sun. I didn't even need to pay for highlights. I had big brown eyes with speckles of green and orange. Bob used to say he could get lost in them. *Amber. Damn that Randall.* I was also thoughtful, kind, and a great cook. Sure, I could stand to lose five pounds, but women much more voluptuous than I had boyfriends.

I was still pondering my invisible anti-boyfriend gene when I noticed Claire staring at me.

"Well?" she asked.

"It's Jim."

"I gathered as much. What happened?"

I told her.

"Why don't you call him?"

"Shouldn't he call me? Andrew said when he's into a girl, he reaches out to her first." I couldn't bear if he screened my calls like Randall did.

"You're probably right. I don't want you dating a guy who doesn't call you after sex. Was it good at least?"

I was so over that question already. "No! It sucked."

"Really? Then good riddance."

Scanning the room to avoid eye contact, I said, "I don't know if it was that bad, actually. I was kind of drunk."

Her eyes widening, Claire said, "You were? You never get drunk."

"I made an exception. I was terrified."

Claire laughed. "Of what?"

"I don't know. Being awkward and uncomfortable?"

"So instead you got sloppy drunk? I'm sure you were graceful like a ballerina, little sister."

I brushed the top of my hand against my lips to stop biting them again. "I vaguely recall giving him a striptease."

"You gave him a..." Claire's shoulders shook. "You gave him a...striptease?" Shaking and holding her stomach, she said, "Priceless."

"Shut up." If the tables had been turned, I knew I'd be much more supportive and at least wait until Claire left the room to laugh my ass off at her expense.

Tears streaming down her cheeks, Claire continued to clutch her stomach.

"It's not that funny," I insisted. "Really, it's not..." Feeling my mouth start to quiver, I placed both hands on my hips and gave

Claire my most serious lips-pursed expression to avoid my own unwanted laughter. But as my body began to spasm, I lost the stubborn grip I had on my facial expression and soon we were both keeled over in hysterics.

When I finally regained control of my vocal chords, I punched Claire in the arm. "Why didn't you tell me dating was this hard."

"I did, little sis. I did," Claire said, a fat tear of laughter still lodged in the corner of her left eye.

Conceding, I said, "I suppose you did."

Finally serious, Claire said, "I'm sorry you found yourself another loser, Jane. But at least you learned a lesson, right?"

"What? Don't expect a guy to call after sex?"

Claire shook her head.

Maybe there was a bright side after all. "What?"

"If you don't want a guy to call, just give him a striptease. So far it's got a hundred percent success rate."

No longer laughing, I said, "Not funny, Claire."

"Just kidding." Claire kissed me on the cheek. "You'll get through this. I promise. And besides, you're going to be an aunt!"

I draped my arm around Claire, putting my head on her shoulder. "Best news I've heard all year."

# Chapter 15

I glanced around the majestic Rose Main Reading Room of the New York Public Library where grand chandeliers hung from the high ceilings, and wondered how many of the other people occupying the wood tables were studying for the LSAT exam. There were men and women of all ages, some sitting alone and others in groups. One couple was holding hands across a table even while diligently reading from two different books. I looked at them longingly and wished I was with a boyfriend instead of chewing over a practice exam all by myself. I was bored, but promised myself I'd study for at least two hours to make up for the time I missed moping over Randall and then Jim. It had been two weeks since my train wreck of a date with Jim and it was time to dig deep and focus on the big picture—getting a high enough score on the LSAT to win acceptance to a top tier school and make my parents proud. One of the articles I read online for prep advice suggested I find a place to study that was conducive to test taking. My bedroom didn't qualify since I kept falling asleep. The post also advocated finding a spot that was quiet but not completely free of distraction since the day of the exam there would be sounds I'd need to drown out, like other students coughing or pencils tapping against desks. The reading room was quiet, which was to be expected at a library, but almost eerily so. Next time I'd try my firm's library where the silence was peppered with hushed conversations among the attorneys doing research.

The ringing of my phone startled me out of my comfortable seat and after I saw it was Claire, I ended the call and mouthed "I'm sorry" to the patrons who'd glared in my direction. I asked the older man at the table next to mine if he'd watch my stuff for a few minutes and hurried to the bathroom to call my sister. When she answered, I said, "Sorry I hung up on you. I'm at the library where causing a raucous with a ringing phone might get me beat up."

Claire chuckled. "I've heard the library attracts the most violent of scholars. Where are you now?"

"Bathroom. What's up?"

"What are you doing tonight?"

"I have no plans. Marissa has a first date and I...don't."

"Want to come to a party with Kevin and me? One of his friends is having it." Before I had a chance to respond, she added, "You never know who you'll meet."

Claire's comment didn't inspire much enthusiasm given my success rate with dating lately and I tried to stall. "Um..."

"Please, Jane. I can't drink and am afraid I'll be so bored while Kevin gets loaded."

I bit my lip. I hated to leave Claire alone and sober at a party. Picturing the loving couple holding hands in the library, I also knew I needed to put myself out there to avoid spending the rest of my Saturday nights alone. "I'll go with you guys."

"You're the best. Come over to our place around eight and we'll leave from there."

"Sounds good."

After we hung up, I returned to my table and thanked the man for not letting anyone steal my stuff. I doubted LSAT practice exams were a hot commodity for thieves, but they weren't cheap. A glance at my watch revealed I'd been at the library for almost two hours. Since the article I read also cautioned against setting unreasonable studying goals, I figured I'd done enough for one day. The exam was still four months away. I packed up my belongings and headed home.


"I need to use the bathroom. You?" I asked Claire.

Claire turned her eyes away from where Kevin was getting

creamed by another guy at foosball. "Surprisingly, no. I thought pregnant women always had to use the bathroom."

"It's still early on. I'll grab some snacks for you on my way back."

"I'm not hungry."

"It's not for you. It's for the little one. You're eating for two, remember?" I made my way through the crowd of people toward the bathroom. The party was pretty tame—just a bunch of people standing around and drinking from red Solo cups. Out of loyalty to Claire, I didn't drink, but I'd eaten my fair share of snacks. In case no one thought to bring food, I'd even made deviled eggs and a spinach artichoke dip in a bread bowl.

After I used the bathroom, I washed my hands and smiled at my reflection in the mirror. I was glad Claire convinced me to come. Even though I hadn't met anyone interesting, hanging out with Claire was more fun than staying at home watching television. I did a nice thing for her while distracting myself from my single relationship status, but it was time to go home. I opened the door and jerked back when I came face to face with a redheaded guy blocking my exit. "Excuse me," I said.

He looked up from his plate and opened his blue eyes wide. "Oh, sorry. I was lost in this dip."

I look at his plate and saw the heap of spinach dip and several chunks of pumpernickel bread. "You like it?" I asked, gesturing at his platter.

He wiped his mouth. "Understatement of the century. I don't usually bring food with me to the bathroom, but I was afraid it would be all gone by the time I finished."

"I made it," I said with a grin.

His freckled face lit up. "Nice. It was the highlight of my night until now."

"What happened now?"

He smiled. "I met you. I'm Cory."

# Chapter 16

I glanced at my watch and hoped Cory would get there soon. His text twenty minutes earlier said he was leaving his office in five minutes.

"I can't wait to meet your man, Jane," Marissa said.

"Yes, we'll try not to embarrass you too much," Lainie said. "But, if we do embarrass you and he still calls tomorrow, you'll know you've finally found a good one."

I hadn't planned on asking Cory to meet my friends so soon, but when I told him that Katherine had bailed on our reservation at a new Mexican restaurant downtown, he offered to take her place.

"Just don't bring up sex."

"I would never," Marissa said.

Pointing at Lainie, I said, "I was referring to her."

Her lips on the edge of an overflowing margarita, Lainie took a sip and carefully put the glass down. Feigning innocence, she asked, "Who, me?"

"Yes, you," I said.

"Couldn't be!"

Laughing, Marissa said, "Then who?"

Just then, I felt a hand on each of my shoulders and, startled, turned around to face a smiling, freckle-faced Cory. I greeted him, touched the seat next to me, and said, "Sit."

Cory kissed me on the cheek before sitting down. After brief introductions, we each looked at the menu. Cory gently placed his hand over mine and asked, "You guys want to share an order of guacamole first?"

Marissa looked up from her menu. "Sounds good to me."

"Me too," said Lainie.

Squeezing his hand, I said, "Me, three," and smiled at him.

I'd been reluctant to give Cory my phone number at first. I was hesitant to go out with him, not because I didn't find him attractive—he was a cross between Prince Harry and Richie Cunningham from *Happy Days*—but because I was afraid he'd be like Randall and Jim. But we had fun on our first date to Dave & Buster's, and so when he asked me out for Indian food later that week, I agreed. And when he asked if I was up for a third date, I said yes again.

But I was determined not to get caught up in any rules, like having sex on a third date. I would have sex with him when, and only when, I was ready—as it should be. When I wasn't ready on our third date, it wasn't even an issue. After dinner and a stroll through the park, Cory walked me home, kissed me goodnight, and went on his way. He called me the very next day. On our fourth date, we ordered in Chinese and watched a movie at his apartment. When the kissing got heated and Cory's hand roamed to the button of my jeans, I calmly brushed it away and told him I wasn't ready yet. He said he was in no hurry, but when he put me in a cab later that night, I was certain I'd never hear from him again. I was wrong. We were now on our fifth date, he was meeting my girlfriends, and he hadn't seen me naked yet. I really liked him. Unlike Randall, he wasn't "Rico Suave," but he didn't act all googly-eyed and mushy like Jim either. Like Goldilocks searching for her perfect bowl of porridge, I was looking for the guy who was just right, and I thought I might have found him in Cory.

Admiring the way he took charge and placed our order for the guac with the waiter, I felt butterflies and wondered if he might actually be the one.

About an hour later, I gazed at the remaining flour tortilla on my plate with disappointment. I didn't have enough steak left to fill it. Cory still had some of his, I noted with envy.

"Take it," Cory said.

I glanced at him in surprise. "How'd you know?"

Cory shrugged. "I had a feeling."

"You must be psychic, but on second thought, I'm not hungry anymore."

Cory nodded, his face serious. "You say that now, but if you skip the chocolate churros for dessert, you'll regret it."

Smiling, I said, "You're right. You really *are* psychic."

Outside the restaurant after dinner, Lainie said. "Is everyone taking the subway?"

"I'm going to cab it," Cory said.

"I'm going to go back with Cory." I turned shyly to him. "Assuming you want me to."

Opening the door of a cab, he said, "No brainer."

I hugged the girls goodbye and slid into the cab. When Cory sat next to me, I snuggled close to him confident I'd gotten it right this time.


A few days later, I was over at Cory's apartment. I had my head against one end of his couch with my legs extended across his lap. He sat forward and absently stroked my knee while fully engrossed in the television show we were watching. I wasn't even sure what it was—some sort of paranormal reality show. I sat up, leaned forward, and gave Cory a soft peck on his smooth cheek. He smelled like orange-scented soap. "You mind if I grab some water?"

Cory muted the television and looked at me. "Of course not. There are water bottles in the fridge. I have other stuff too. Beer, soda, snacks. *Mi casa es su casa*," he said, smiling.

I stood up. "Water's good. I'm parched." I walked over to his small kitchen.

"Rock climbing will do that to you," he called after me.

"I still can't believe you talked me into indoor rock climbing. My sister will be shocked. I always sucked at gym class in school." I opened the refrigerator and sorted through the contents. "You want anything?" I asked as I felt arms embrace me from behind.

"I bet you're much more athletic than you give yourself credit for," he whispered in my ear.

I turned around to face him, my back against the refrigerator. "You think so?"

Tucking a hair behind my ear, he said, "I know so." Then he took my hand and led me out of the kitchen. He stopped to turn off the television. "If you join me in my bed, I'll prove it to you."

I took his hand and shook it firmly. "You've got yourself a deal."

# Chapter 17

Cory brushed my arm as he walked from Claire and Kevin's living room to the bathroom. After stuffing ourselves with delivery pizza and the garlic bread with cheese I had made, we were too tired to tear ourselves away from the couch and late-night television. Kevin had just confided his jeans were unbuttoned underneath his sweatshirt, and we were laughing about it when Cory came back in the room.

After plopping down on the couch next to me, he asked, "Did I miss something?"

"I asked Kevin why he wasn't as forthcoming with information when my parents are around," I said.

Kevin stood up and stretched his arms over his head, revealing some of his bare belly which had grown considerably over the past month. "I wouldn't unbutton my pants in your mother's presence, much less tell her about it. I swear Mrs. Frank has X-ray vision. She'd know."

"That's nuts," Cory said. "How would she know?"

All at the same time, Claire, Kevin and I replied, "She'd just know."

Running a hand through his thinning light brown hair, Cory said, "Yikes. She sounds scary."

I scooted closer to him on the couch and kissed his cheek. "No worries. She'll love you. You're a catch."

Winking, Kevin said, "Yeah and she's kind of a M.I.L.F."

Claire, who had gotten up to gather the empty beer bottles

drunk by the boys, playfully swatted Kevin's head before walking to the kitchen. "So gross, Kevin." When she returned to the room, she wagged a finger at Cory and me. "By the way, she's been asking when you're inviting Cory over for Sunday brunch."

"What did you tell her?" I asked.

"I told her to keep me out of it."

I turned to Cory. "No pressure. You don't have to meet my parents if you don't want. At least not until she asks me directly. For now, I can play dumb." As excited as I was about my new relationship, I didn't want to scare Cory away with my parents, particularly my mother.

Cory squeezed my knee. "Set it up for whenever you want."

"Really?" I asked.

"Really?" Claire repeated.

Laughing, Kevin said, "No. Really?"

"How bad can it be? Free brunch, right?" Cory said, laughing and kissing me on the cheek.

"Well, if you don't bring cake or something, she'll talk about you behind your back, so it won't be completely free," Kevin said.

Grinning, Cory shook his head. "I can handle it. Besides, I'll have to meet the folks eventually, right?"

My face beaming, I said, "Right." I should have known Cory wouldn't be freaked out about meeting my parents. My mom would love him and I welcomed the chance to show him off.

Just then Cory's cell phone rang and he whispered, "Crap. It's work. I have to take this."

As he walked to the hallway to talk in private, I looked over at Claire. She gave me the thumbs-up sign and mouthed, "A keeper."

I was thinking the exact same thing.


"Claire said you've been asking about Cory," I said to my mother a few days later.

My mom said, "I don't know what you're talking about."

"She said you want to meet Cory."

"Only if you plan to keep him around. You tossed the others aside pretty quickly."

I'd been too embarrassed to admit to my mother that I was on the receiving, not giving, end of the rejections, and I'd sworn Claire to secrecy. "The others weren't right for me."

"So you say. I still hope you won't regret breaking up with Bob someday."

"We've been over this before. I love Bob, and I know he loves me too. But we're not in love anymore. And besides, he's happy with Trish." Now that I was with Cory, I felt much better about the Bob/Trish situation. I was even kind of excited to meet Trish.

"Yes, although Arlene isn't thrilled they're moving in together without getting engaged first. I wouldn't be happy either."

"Then it's a good thing you don't have to worry about it. Mom, please. I don't want to move in with Cory. Let's change the subject. He wants to meet you and Dad."

"Who?"

"Cory! When do you want us to come over? Is brunch good? I'd like Claire and Kevin to be there. He gets along great with Kevin."

"Well, then I guess you don't need my blessing. You have Kevin's."

I removed my phone from my ear and rolled my eyes at the air. "Do you want us to come for brunch on Sunday or what?"

"Yes. But I told your sister that dad and I will come into the city and have brunch at her place. We'll get lox from Zabar's."

The conversation was becoming more puzzling than the questions in the LSAT practice exams I had every intention of taking after Cory and I exited the honeymoon stage and settled into a routine. "You discussed this with Claire already?"

"Yes. I spoke to her yesterday."

"When were you going to tell me? I still have to ask Cory if he's free."

"Claire said she'd tell you. If Cory is serious, he'll make sure he's free."

"He's serious. It was his idea."

I heard my mom sigh into the phone. "Calm down. I didn't mean to get you so wound up. It's not good for your skin."

Noticing I had been scrunching my face, I relaxed my facial muscles and took a deep breath. "Then stop stressing me out. Please."

"I have to run out for an errand."

"Okay."

Her tone gentler, my mom said, "I'll talk to you later in the week."

"Sounds good. I love you."

"I love you too. Now go call Cory."

As soon as we hung up, I called Cory, but not because my mother told me to. I wanted to make sure I got to him before he made other plans for Sunday. We'd been dating for a couple of months and had spent at least part of every weekend together pretty much since the beginning, but I was still afraid he'd made other plans. If I told my mom he wasn't coming to brunch, she'd hold it against him forever.

His phone went directly to voicemail, so I left him a message saying he was invited to brunch with my family on Sunday. I figured he'd be happy we were having it at Claire's, since it was a more neutral location than my parents' house. "I hope you can make it. Sorry for the late notice, but that's my mom. Let me know as soon as you can. My mom is sort of a nightmare about this stuff and will probably ask me every five minutes if you'll be there. Sorry in advance and, by the way, I think you're super sweet for being so agreeable about this. Talk to you in a bit. Bye."

After I hung up, I was hyper on nervous energy and knocked on Lainie's door, hoping she could distract me until Cory called back.

"Come on in. What's up?" Lainie was stretched out on her bed reading a gossip magazine. "Guess which two extremely popular singers are now dating?"

I sat on the edge of her bed. "Don't know."

Tossing the magazine at me, Lainie said, "I'll let you read it for yourself."

I lacked the focus to read, so I said, "Thanks" and put the magazine on the floor in front of me.

"What's going on?"

"Cory's meeting my parents this weekend."

Sitting up straighter, Lainie said, "Wow. You nervous?"

"Yes, but I'm also excited. It's a big step."

Lainie laughed. "I should have known you'd be 'committed' quickly. You definitely lack the gene to play the field."

"Not true. I just got lucky. The whole point of playing the field is to find the right guy, right? I've found him so I can stop playing now."

Scrunching her nose, Lainie said, "Not everyone plays the field with the sole purpose of meeting the right guy, Jane. Some of us actually do it because it's fun. Meeting lots of guys, fooling around with them—it's fun."

Doubtfully, I said, "I suppose for some people."

"Ah, Jane, we're apples and oranges, I guess. It's a good thing you met Cory. You're not meant for dating in the big bad city."

It occurred to me I knew very little about Lainie's relationship history. "Have you ever brought a guy to meet your parents?"

"Aside from my dates to homecoming and prom? No."

"Really? Haven't you ever had a real boyfriend?"

Lainie twirled a hair around her finger. "I've gone through periods when I only dated one guy at a time, of course, but nothing significant. In my family, bringing a boy home means serious business, and serious business involves touring trunk shows for designer wedding dresses, reserving the church, and making sure my alcoholic aunt Desiree doesn't cause a scene at the reception." Lainie rolled her eyes. "Trust me, my family wants nothing more than for me to settle down with a polite southern boy. Unfortunately for them, my taste is more outside of the box." Smiling at me, she said, "My mom would be thrilled if I brought home someone like Cory. Only with a southern drawl and a Bible in his desk drawer. Cory doesn't have a Bible in his desk drawer, does he?"

"I have no idea what Cory has in his desk drawer. I'm not a snooper. But even if he does, he's mine."

Lainie leaned forward and removed the magazine from her bed. Swatting me lightly with it, she said, "You can have him. Not my type. Too perfect."

My heart filled with joy at her words. Cory was perfect and he was mine.

# Chapter 18

I still hadn't heard back from Cory when my mom called later that night. I never spoke to my mom more than once a day, so I knew she was calling about Cory and screened the call. I felt my heart in my throat as I stared at the phone and waited for her to leave me a message. I was irritated at Cory but didn't want to admit it to my mom, because anything negative I said about him now would be held against him until the end of time. My mom would make an instant judgment that Cory was either not good enough for me or didn't like me enough to treat me better. If I fibbed and said I'd heard from him, somehow she'd know I was lying. Or, if he'd previously made plans for the day, I'd have to lie again to explain why he suddenly wasn't available. Maybe he was working late or out with his guy friends, but I was irked he couldn't take two minutes to return my call, especially since I told him how annoying my mother was. I thought about calling him again but decided to give him the benefit of the doubt and wait until the morning. He might call me later or email if he got home too late.

When I woke up the next morning, I immediately checked my phone to see if he'd called during the night. I felt a pit in my stomach when I saw I had no new text or voicemail messages or even a missed call. Cory had always returned my calls pretty quickly until now. I was sure he had a good reason, but it was totally annoying that he waited until now to leave me hanging.

In the shower, I rehearsed what I would say when I finally spoke to him. Absent a good excuse, I wanted him to know how hurtful it was to repeatedly ignore my calls. But I didn't want to attack him or make him feel emasculated. I'd learned how to communicate with Bob to get my needs across without alienating him, but all guys were different.

I didn't feel like talking to Lainie in case she asked whether Cory was coming to brunch, so I left my yogurt in the fridge. I'd pick something up for breakfast on the way to work instead. Walking briskly past the kitchen where she was drinking a cup of coffee, I waved and said, "Gotta be at work early. Have a good day," and hurried out of the apartment before she could say more than, "Bye" in response.

By lunch time, I was thoroughly pissed off. Each time my phone rang, I banged my fist on the desk when it wasn't Cory.

Finally, at 3:23, the alert of a text message sent me flying out of my seat, and I rummaged through my handbag to find my phone. At that hour of the day, it made more sense for him to text since he probably didn't have the time to call.

Relief washing over me, I excitedly checked my phone. It was Marissa. One of her favorite authors was giving a talk at the 92nd Street Y that night and she wanted to know if I was around after work.

Angry, I tossed the phone back in my bag and muttered, "Call me back. C'mon already."

The wait was killing me. I could only avoid my mother, roommate, and every other person who might ask about the upcoming brunch for so long, so I called Cory. When I got his voicemail again, I groaned knowing I'd be back at square one, waiting for him to return my call. I considered hanging up and trying again later, but felt the urgent need to remind him he hadn't confirmed his availability for Sunday. I took a deep breath and tried to sound calm. "Hey Cory, it's me again. Just wondering where you are. Can you please call me back as soon as you get this? I really need to know if you're in for Sunday. My mom will probably reschedule the trip into the city if you can't make it, since I think the real reason they're coming in is to meet their youngest daughter's new boyfriend." I paused and bit down on my lower lip. We hadn't officially settled on the boyfriend/girlfriend titles yet. Too late now. "So please call me back. I know you're busy, but I'd appreciate it. Thanks. Talk to you soon."

It was possible there was a reasonable explanation for why he hadn't called me back. Maybe something happened to him. What if he got hit by a city bike or was pummeled by falling scaffolding and was in the hospital? I called Claire, figuring Kevin might know since they had mutual friends, and asked her to check on Cory's whereabouts. I urged her to be subtle so I didn't come off looking like I was checking up on him. She promised she'd be discreet. I hung up the phone and stretched my arms over my head. Glancing at Andrew, who was carefully scrutinizing an Excel chart he had just printed out, I said, "Guys are infuriating."

Andrew put down the chart and winked at me. "But you love us, don't you?"

I didn't answer.

"Right?" Andrew said.

I sure didn't love men at the moment. "Need you. I need guys, I suppose. But you can be so annoying, stupid, and downright heartless sometimes."

Andrew laughed. "You know what your problem is, Jane?"

I didn't have a problem. Cory had a problem. Exasperated, I said, "What?"

"You take it all so seriously. It just leads to pain. You should learn to date like a guy."

Rolling my eyes at Andrew, I said, "And how do guys date?"

"Love 'em and leave 'em, babe."

"That's dumb."

"Why? It works for me fine. You don't hear me whining about how girls are infuriating, do you?"

"If you really loved someone, Andrew, you wouldn't want to leave her."

Andrew looked at me thoughtfully. "Okay, scratch that. Slight amendment to the plan, 'Nail 'em and leave 'em.' Is that better?"

As I wondered where the hell Cory was and when he planned on calling me back, I shouted, "You're a pig" to Andrew, who responded by tossing a box of condoms he apparently kept at the office onto my lap. "Nail 'em and leave 'em, Jane. Trust me."

# Chapter 19

The work day ended and the sun set without a return call from Cory. I had a sick feeling Cory was never going to call and needed a distraction from staring at my phone. A distraction in a place loud enough where I wouldn't mistake every sound for my phone ringing. Listening to an author speak at the Y didn't qualify. I called Marissa and asked if she wanted to get a drink. Lainie heard me talking to Marissa and invited herself along. I didn't mind, since she always managed to spice up the conversation.

We found three red plastic-covered stools and leaned over the faded wooden bar to get the bartender's attention. I needed something stronger than wine, so I took Lainie's suggestion and ordered a vodka tonic with very little tonic. The strength shocked me and I almost regurgitated the first sip, but it went down easy after that. I was feeling much better by the time the glass was half empty. I raised my drink slightly off the table and took a sip. "Cheers! To friendship. Better than men."

"Cheers," said Marissa, taking a sip.

"Not sure I can toast to that, but I'll make an exception," Lainie said. "And by the way, you're supposed to drink after you toast, not before."

Giggling, I said, "Oops!" and took another sip. I called out to the bartender, "Another round, please."

A couple of hours later, we were on our third or fourth round, and I was feeling good. "Cory who?" I asked before downing the rest of my drink, slamming the glass on the table and raising my hand in the air to catch the bartender's attention.

Grabbing the twenty-dollar bill from my hand, Marissa said, "Maybe you've had enough."

Protesting, I jerked the bill out of her grasp. "Don't think I've had nearly enough."

Laughing, Lainie said, "Let her be. She's having fun."

"Exactly." Looking over at Lainie, I realized how much I appreciated her and felt a wave of guilt for taking her for granted. "I love you, Lainie. You're the best roommate ever." I reached over to hug her and nearly fell off the barstool. Deciding it would be smarter to hug her standing up, I climbed off the stool and chanted, "So drunk. *So* drunkey." Attempting a group hug, I put one arm around Lainie and one arm around Marissa. "My best friends!" After I kissed them each on the cheek, I turned around to tell everyone how lucky I was and saw the bartender from my second date with Randall—Cassandra. I remembered how chummy she was with Randall. What kind of bartender ruffled the hair of another girl's date right in front of her and practically shoved her boobs in his face?

Disgusted, I turned back to the girls. "Ugh. Not a fan of that girl."

Not bothering with subtlety, Lainie whipped her head around. "Which one?"

Refusing to turn around, I muttered, "Long blond hair, blue skinny jeans. Behind you."

I observed Lainie give Cassandra the once-over but still refused to look. I took another sip of my drink and waited for her reaction.

Shrugging, Lainie said, "She's okay, I guess. The guy she's with has a great ass though. I love a guy in cords."

When I heard the word "cords," curiosity got the best of me. I finally turned around and sucked in my breath when I saw who Cassandra was with—Randall—and she was kissing him. I placed my hand on the back of Marissa's barstool for support. I needed a toilet and choked back a sob when I saw the line for the bathroom. It was a blurry line, but a line all the same, and I wasn't going to make it. Grabbing Marissa by the arm, I muttered, "I'm gonna hurl. Gotta get out of here." Then trying not to fall, I ran out of the bar and onto the sidewalk. I felt someone hold my hair away from my face and pat my back as I puked four vodka tonics while moaning, "Randall the Rat."

I didn't remember how I got home, but as I lay in my bed and watched the ceiling spin, I heard Andrew's voice. Over and over again, he said, "Nail 'em and leave 'em, Jane. Nail 'em and leave 'em."

When I woke up the next morning, the first thing I remembered was seeing Randall and Cassandra kissing at the bar. I grabbed my phone from my nightstand—still no call from Cory. If he didn't want to meet my parents, he could've just said so. What was wrong with guys in this city?

"Aren't there any normal ones?" I asked Lainie that morning. She was getting ready for work. I was taking a mental health day. Although it could technically be called a sick day, since I was still dry heaving every half hour.

Lainie shut off her blow-dryer and turned away from her vanity to face me. I was lying stomach down on her bed, my head toward the edge. "I think normal has a different definition when it comes to guys in New York City," she said. "There are so many girls here, it's like eating at a Chinese buffet. They want to sample everything."

I fought the urge to dry heave again and buried my head under one of Lainie's throw pillows. I mumbled, "Isn't anyone actually looking to meet one special person?"

Lainie pressed her lips together and gave me a soft smile. "Sadly, not really."

I threw the pillow off the bed, sat up and pouted. "I can't stand guys. Such dicks."

Laughing, Lainie said, "Jane! Not used to the negativity from you. Or the profanity."

"How am I supposed to remain positive? It's not like this is a one-off occurrence I can explain away. It's become a pattern. First it was Randall, then Jim, and now Cory And it all started with Nate."

"Who's Nate?"

"The eHarmony guy—said we had different values. We hadn't even emailed yet."

Lainie joined me on the bed to pull on her boots. "Sorry, Jane. Have you told your mom yet?"

"Not yet." Noticing a box of condoms on Lainie's dresser, I thought of something. "My friend Andrew said I should date like a guy to avoid being hurt. Nail 'em and leave 'em."

"Smart guy, that Andrew, but he clearly doesn't know you very well."

I wished Lainie a good day at work and went back to my room, making a pit stop at the bathroom. Kneeling on the cold tiles with my head over the bowl, I had a feeling if I had taken Andrew's advice, I'd be going about a typical day at work instead of praying to the porcelain God.

When I woke up from my nap and had managed to go twelve straight hours without dry heaving, I reluctantly called my mom to tell her Cory wouldn't be coming to brunch. I was fortunate in that I knew she played Bunko on Wednesdays and wouldn't pick up the phone. I was certain she'd press me for details eventually, but I wasn't ready to face her head-on yet. I honestly didn't know what to say.

Since I didn't have other plans for the evening and didn't want to mope about Cory, I dragged my sorry butt to the computer desk and vowed to buckle down on LSAT prep for at least an hour. I hadn't made much progress since I'd met Cory, and although I still had almost three months before the exam, I knew it would go by fast.

Stubbornly gripping whatever was left of my trademark optimism, I first checked to see if Cory had sent me an email. No email from him, but about ten from various social groups regarding

New Year's Eve parties. When I had started dating in September, I was positive I'd have a boyfriend by the end of the year. Now it almost January 1st and I had no idea what I was doing to ring in the new year or with whom.

My phone rang—Claire. "Hey," I said before returning to my bed.

"I have some bad news."

I sat up. "Is Cory in the hospital?"

There was silence on the other end and my heart raced.

"Claire? What happened to Cory?"

She sighed loudly. "I wish I didn't have to tell you this, but Kevin's friend was out with Cory last night. He's fine."

I was thoroughly confused. "So why hasn't he—?

In the background, I heard Kevin say, "Want me to kick the piece of shit's ass for ghosting on you?"

"Our future child's father is not kicking anyone's butt," Claire said. "Sorry, Jane. He's a jerk and you deserve so much better. Brush it off."

I wondered why I wasn't crying. Instead, I felt numb inside.

"Are you going to be all right?"

"Yeah. I've gotta go. Thanks for letting me know." I hung up the phone and stared straight ahead.

I went back to my desk and read the next reading comprehension question in my practice exam. Eight camp counselors were assigned different activities and they had to conform to certain conditions. One of the activities was rock climbing. I let Cory talk me into rock climbing—a decidedly non-Jane activity—and he'd ghosted me. Whatever that meant. Curious, I Googled it. According to the Urban Dictionary, "ghosting" was when a person ceased all communication with someone they were dating instead of telling them they were no longer interested. I let out a breath. I'd been ghosted all right. No longer in the mood to study, I got in my pajamas and went to bed hoping thoughts of my new niece or nephew would lull me to sleep. I hoped Claire would have a girl. A nephew would be fun until he got his first erection, and then he'd be like the rest of them. Starting now, I wanted no part of the male species. Except my dad. I wondered how my mom had managed to make an honest man out of him. She was my mom—that was how. Claire was more like her than I was, which explained why Kevin hadn't flown the coop. If he ghosted on her and my niece, I'd kill him. I'd put arsenic in his beer.

Wondering how I could get my hands on arsenic, I fell asleep.

# Chapter 20

I now understood the appeal of *The Walking Dead*. Zombies were dead inside and incapable of breaking hearts. It was more uplifting than *Say Yes To The Dress*, so when Marissa asked if she could still watch it at our apartment even though Lainie had a date, I said yes and watched it with her. Dressed in two-piece fish-printed pajamas from Old Navy, I stretched my body across the entire length of our cushy caramel leather couch. My legs were buried under one of the larger throw pillows and my arms were locked behind my head.

From our reclining chair, Marissa said, "My product manager left notice today."

"Is that a good thing?" I asked.

"She was nice, but Katherine thinks it's the ideal opportunity to ask for a promotion. What do you think?"

Yawning, I said, "I think you should do what you want and not just what Katherine says."

Marissa sighed. "Of course I want to be promoted, Jane. But do you think they'd give it to me? I only have a couple years of experience. And if they didn't want to promote me, I'm afraid they'd hold it against me for asking."

"What do we have here?" I asked as Lainie walked in the room, dressed to impress in a zippered denim dress over tight black pleather pants and pointy-heeled black leather boots.

Marissa whistled. "Sexy, sexy."

Lainie shrugged nonchalantly. "It is what it is."

"You do look sexy," I agreed. "Who's the guy du jour?" Unlike me (in my previous life—the one that included men), Lainie wasn't one to eagerly discuss her manly pursuits.

She walked over to the couch and patted my legs with her hands in a gesture to make me sit up and let her share the space. I was reluctant to give up the comfort of my position but begrudgingly complied.

"I met him at an underground after-hours lounge earlier this week. He's a record producer. Chocolate brown eyes, midnight black long eyelashes, and sun-kissed skin. And a well-travelled tongue that took me places I'd only read about in..."

I raised my hand in the air and interrupted. "We catch your drift. Details not necessary."

"Speak for yourself." Marissa was now sitting up straight, her eyes opened wide in interest.

"He sounds just your type. Hot, sexy, and temporary. Perfect." The last word had formed as an expression of sarcasm, but as I heard it leave my mouth, it rang more sincere than I expected.

"I don't know. I might keep him around for a little while."

I turned to Lainie in surprise to see if she was joking, but she was leaning over, lacing up her boots, and her curly hair blocked her facial expression. When she sat back up and stood, there was no hint of jest on her face.

Walking briskly to the front door, she grabbed her keys from the hook and called out, "Later, girls." She glanced back at me one more time. "Don't wait up."

As the door closed and I heard Lainie's footsteps down the stairs, I yelled, "Nail him and leave him." Under my breath, I added, "Before he leaves you first."


I spent the next few weeks avoiding eye contact with anyone who was likely to have a penis—in the island of Manhattan, you never really knew for sure. I walked the city streets briskly, eyes focused straight ahead. I scowled at the construction workers who dared to whistle and refused to acknowledge the less obvious corporate types who gave me a quick once-over as our paths crossed. I didn't want to be noticed and stopped trying to disguise my plumper lower half. I also packed away my V-neck, cleavage-enhancing sweaters and opted for looser tops like button-downs. During nights out with the girls, I feigned exhaustion and excused myself early if we were approached by single guys. When Lainie caught on and questioned why I was so tired lately, I stopped pleading sleep deprivation in favor of needing to study for the LSAT. I'd cancelled my eHarmony subscription and suspended my membership in the Meetup singles group. The fees seemed a waste of my hard-earned dollar.

I gave Bob a reprieve from my hostility toward testicle-bearing beings. Even I had to concede he had been a good boyfriend. Although he found someone else to remind him to get a haircut, we still spoke every couple of weeks.

I had just spent ten minutes feigning interest in his purchase of an "off the hook" fifty-two-inch flat screen TV and how watching the Syracuse games on that piece of plasma would be "legendary." Bob and his buddies described anything slightly more interesting than the eleven o'clock news as legendary. I wasn't really listening. I was wracking my brain for an excuse to bail on my plans with Marissa to go to Katherine's tree-trimming party that night. Apparently Katherine's husband had a friend they thought would be compatible with me. A couple of months ago, being set up with a lawyer would have thrilled me, but now I feared the higher I allowed my hopes to soar, the farther I would fall if it blew up in my face.

"You'll be there, right?"

"Only because Marissa begged me," I wailed.

"Huh? You lost me at 'Marissa,'" Bob said.

Realizing Bob wasn't privy to the internal thoughts in my head when I was supposed to be conversing with him about his "legendary" flat screen, I said, "Never mind. What are you talking about?"

"Mine and Trish's housewarming next Saturday night. You'll be there, right? Feel free to bring a date," he said. "Or Marissa. Word on the street is you're not really dating right now."

I wasn't aware my relationship status was worthy of street talking. "I'm not bringing Marissa. I'll bring a date. Don't know who your source is, but she doesn't know what she's talking about." I immediately regretted this statement since whoever told Bob I wasn't currently dating was right.

"Sweet," Bob said. I could almost see the gleam in his super straight teeth as he said it.

"Yeah. Sweet," I repeated as an idea came to me. Through the wall of my room, I called out, "Lainie? Can I borrow that denim zip-up dress? The pleather pants too?" With any luck, I'd hit it off with Katherine's lawyer friend and he'd stick around long enough to be my plus one to Bob and Trish's party.

# Chapter 21

I dipped a baby carrot in hummus and popped it in my mouth before scoping out the room. To Katherine's credit, there were a lot of attractive, professional-looking people in attendance. When I caught her eye, she frantically waved me over. By her side was a guy with his back to me. He wore a backwards baseball cap with a red sock logo on it and I assumed he was the attorney she wanted me to meet. I said a silent prayer there would be a mutual attraction between us, sucked in my stomach, and walked over to them.

"Katherine, hi." I gave her a kiss on the cheek and turned to smile at the guy who was now facing me. My stubborn hopes for an instant love connection plummeted when I felt no immediate attraction to him, but he had nice blue eyes. "Thanks so much for having me."

"So glad you could make it. The exciting life of a single girl. Ah, the good ol' days," Katherine said.

I bit my tongue to keep from debating the definition of good. "I can always make time for friends." Glancing over at Marissa deep in conversation with her brother and sister-in-law, I said, "Marissa was so excited about it too." Remembering my mission, I smiled shyly at the guy. "Hi. I'm Jane."

Before he could respond, Katherine put her hand on his shoulder. "Oh how rude of me. Jane, this is Todd. He's a lawyer. Could probably give you advice on law school."

"You're in law school?" he asked.

Shaking my head, I said, "Not yet. I'm studying for the LSAT."

Todd laughed. "Good times. Almost as good as studying for the bar."

Katherine excused herself, claiming she needed to get back to her hostess duties and that Todd and I probably had a lot to talk about.

"Great hat," I said.

Todd grinned. "Are you a Red Sox fan?"

"I usually stick to black socks. Or white if I'm working out, but red socks are certainly interesting."

"Ha! Good one," Todd said. "Want to try it on?"

I doubted he had lice, but the thought of wearing a strange guy's hat grossed me out. I absently ran a hand through my own hair trying to come up with a way to say no without insulting him.

He removed the cap from his head of too-long brown hair and I instinctively took a step back. But then he put it back on—this time in the right direction—and frowned. "Pretend I didn't make the offer. I'm very superstitious. I let my ex wear it once and the Red Sox lost their first place position in the division. No one but me is wearing the cap ever again."

I said, "I understand completely" even though I had no idea what he was talking about.

"Do you like sports?" he asked.

"No," I answered honestly.

"What do you do for fun?"

"I cook and bake. Are you a foodie?"

"I'm allergic to shellfish, fish, and peanuts, and I'm lactose resistant. I also have a weak palette. Food doesn't wow me." He took a sip of his beer as if not at all burdened by what would be my worst nightmare.

I had no idea how to respond. "I can't even imagine."

He shrugged. "Some folks live to eat, and I eat to live."

We stood in silence for a few seconds during which I suspected we had nothing in common besides a mutual interest in a legal career. Doubtful he'd be escorting me to Bob and Trish's party, I glanced around the room hoping to spot another eligible bachelor.

"Do you like to bowl? My firm is hosting a bowl-a-thon on Monday night and we need cheerleaders."

My eyes opened wide at his unexpected invitation. I was hesitant to accept his offer since I was pretty certain there would be no love connection between Todd and me.

"If you go with me, maybe we'll get you your own 'Schwetty Ballz' team hat. I bet you'd look real cute in it."

I pictured myself at Bob and Trish's housewarming party—the sad and lonely ex-girlfriend. Since I was desperate to keep that from becoming reality, there was only one answer. Smiling at Todd, I said, "I'd love to."

# Chapter 22

Exhausted, I fell back on my bed, still dressed in my souvenir "Schwetty Ballz" t-shirt. Todd was a decent guy, but he was a Chatty Cathy who had a one track-mind—all sports all of the time. I didn't contribute much to the conversation, but he didn't seem to notice. In fact, he asked me on another date. I didn't think it was fair to rule him out simply because I found our conversation lacking while bowling with all of his colleagues. There was more kissing than talking on my second date with Randall and I wanted to go out with *him* again. I didn't hold Jim's love of football against him either. It was only fair to give Todd another chance too.

When Todd's idea of a second date was sitting at a local bar watching UCLA take on Arizona in college basketball, I knew it was hopeless, but by then I'd made up my mind to ask him to Bob and Trish's party that weekend and there was no going back. On a commercial break, Todd turned his attention to me. "Thanks for agreeing to watch the game with me. I'm usually more creative on a second date, but the Bruins and Wildcats are major rivals. Like the Yankees and Red Sox. Or the Giants and Eagles. This game is a must-watch."

I got the distinct feeling Todd was way more passionate about sports than torts. I flipped my hair and placed my hand over his. "No worries. This is fun."

Todd grinned. "Great. I'd hate for my addiction to ruin my chances of a third date."

"I'm happy you want to go out again," I said. The sweetness of my voice contrasted with the sour feeling in my stomach from lying.

The game had resumed and so, with one eye on me and the other watching the screen, Todd nodded. "Totally. The sooner the better."

Crossing the fingers of my left hand under my thigh, I said, "I was wondering if you wanted to come to a party with me on Saturday night. A friend of mine just moved in with his girlfriend and they're having a housewarming party." I didn't have it in me to tell Todd who Bob really was.

Todd removed his attention from the game and angled his body toward mine. He grabbed my hand. "I'd love to, Jane." Jutting his head in the direction of the television set, he said, "Any chance these friends of yours follow college basketball?"

"Totally. Bob played basketball in college. He's practically addicted." An embellishment more than a lie, since Bob was on the basketball team in high school and even got to play a few games.

Beaming, Todd exclaimed, "Then it's a date."

I beamed back.

A moment later, Todd was again entranced by the game. He was still smiling and, although he only spoke to me on commercials, he would occasionally squeeze my hand. I squeezed it back, and while the tall men in red came back in the last twenty-eight seconds to score the winning point, I prayed Claire would agree to do my hair and makeup the night of the party. As the ex-girlfriend of the host, I knew there would be silent comparisons between me and Trish, and couldn't bear the thought of people saying Bob had upgraded.

# Chapter 23

It was Saturday night at seven forty-five and I was perched on my bathroom counter, legs dangling over the edge, while Claire applied my makeup. "So this makeover has nothing to do with impressing your date?"

Claire applied a second coat of mascara, and I nodded my response. When the rod was no longer in danger of poking me in the eye, I said, "We're not a match, Claire."

"How do you know?"

"He eats to live. 'Nuff said."

"Yikes." With a damp cotton swab, Claire removed excess mascara from my eyelids. "If you're not into this guy, why are you going out with him again?"

With a pained expression, I said, "I tried to like him, Claire. I gave it two dates hoping I missed something on the first, but there's nothing there and the party is tonight. I can't go to my ex-boyfriend and his new girlfriend's housewarming shindig alone." I felt my eyes well up. "Am I a horrible person?"

Claire took a step away from me and studied my face. "First of all, don't cry or you'll ruin the hard work I've done to get the smoky eye effect."

I swallowed hard. "Okay."

"What you're doing is not nice, but you're not a horrible person. You don't have it in you. You went in with good intentions, right?"

I nodded like an eager puppy. I had.

"You didn't intentionally set out to play with his feelings and you're not going to lead him on after tonight or use him to try to make Bob jealous are you?"

I shook my head vigorously. "No way."

Claire gave me a kind smile. "Then cut yourself some slack. You're human and this is a difficult situation."

"Thank you," I said, before taking what felt like the first breath of air I'd inhaled in an hour.

"Do we know what Trish looks like?" Claire asked.

"Mom said that according to Mrs. Krauss, Trish looks like she could be in a Ralph Lauren ad, except she's barely five feet tall. She's got a sleek blunt haircut—a brunette, wears big round sunglasses all year round and a lot of polo shirts. Sounds like a freak to me, but it's Bob's life."

Snorting, Claire said, "Not for nothing Jane, but you're not exactly a hip dresser either. You always look like you just walked off of an Ann Taylor catalog." After swiping my face with translucent powder, Claire put the big brush down and took a step back. "Voila. Makeover complete."

I jumped off the counter and peered closely at my reflection. Claire had used just enough bronzer to give me a naturally sun-kissed look and my complexion looked flawless. I reached over and hugged her. "I love it. Thank you."

"You're so easy to please, little sister," she said. "You look pretty. Todd will be blown away. Too bad you're going to break his heart."

I felt a renewed twinge of regret in my belly. "I promise to be really nice to Todd, okay? And besides, I don't want you worrying about me." I pointed at her not yet growing belly. "You should be focusing on my unborn niece or nephew."

Claire raised an eyebrow. "So it's fine for me to spend my evening doing your makeup, but showing concern about your love life is harmful to my pregnancy?"

"First of all, I don't have a love life, and second of all, exactly."

Laughing, Claire gave me a light push out of my bathroom. "Hurry up and get dressed. You're gonna be late."

\*     \*     \*

The first thing I noticed about Trish's apartment—correction—Trish and Bob's apartment was how white everything was. White walls, white leather couch and love seat, white porcelain countertops in the kitchen. Sure, there were pops of color here and there—red throw pillows on the couches, black wooden coffee and end tables, dark blue area rug—but pretty much everything was pristine white. Even the paintings were black and white Ansel Adams knock-offs. At least I hoped they were knock-offs, considering the only artwork in my apartment were ten-dollar landscapes I picked up at the Second Avenue Street Fair the summer before. As I imagined Bob trying to eat a slice of pizza in front of the massive flat screen television set without staining the couch, I laughed out loud.

Todd whispered, "What's so funny?"

Bored with him but happy to have survived the cab ride from uptown listening to him brag about how the Red Sox's acquisition of some ace pitcher from the LA Angels during the off season would totally give the Sox an edge over the Yankees, I whispered back, "Nothing. Just thought of something silly." I took Todd gently by the elbow and led him toward the back of the living room where I easily spotted Bob since he was a head taller than most of the people at the party. His gaze was focused downward and he was hunching slightly. I assumed Trish the midget was at his hip. I licked my dry lips, ran my free hand through my hair, and stood quietly while I waited for Bob to notice me. I didn't want to interrupt and used the free moments to inspect Trish. She was slender and toned, and I reluctantly concluded that, despite being vertically-challenged, she had a better body. My eyes focused on her boobs, hoping with less body fat she'd be flat-chested. They looked about the same size as mine, which might have been the only thing we had in common, at least appearance wise. I noted her nose was slightly long relative to her tiny face and her dark eyes were kind of small and unimpressive, which might explain her propensity to wear sunglasses. I definitely had a prettier face so, all things considered, it was a tie.

I was searching for a tie-breaker when Bob called out, "Janey!" and pulled me into a hug. As I embraced him, I looked at Trish to gauge her reaction to seeing her new live-in boyfriend with his arms around his ex-girlfriend of nine years. She was smiling and, although I looked really hard, I saw no jealousy or insecurity behind her eyes.

When Bob and I separated, Trish jumped up and down. Clapping her hands excitedly, she came barging at me, squeezing me with full force. Although her mouth was eye level to my neck, I was able to make out her muddled version of, "I'm so happy to finally meet you."

Taken aback, and somewhat frightened, I pulled away and straightened the top of my scoop neck sweater. Offering my hand, I forced a smile. "Hi. I'm Jane."

Trish squealed, "I know. Bob's told me so much about you. And I've seen all of Arlene's photo albums. Love the ones from the high school prom." Winking at Bob, she said, "He looked so cute in his tux."

I glanced at Bob, hoping he'd roll his eyes and we'd share a silent laugh, but he had his hand on Trish's shoulder and was beaming as brightly as she.

While I counted the number of tiny freckles on her nose, Trish continued, "Looking at the pictures, part of me wished I knew Bob back then. But you were such a great girlfriend to him. Thanks to you, I got him unjaded. Unlike some of these other NYC guys."

When I heard a cough in the background, I remembered Todd was next to me. "Oh, I'm so sorry," I said. Gesturing toward Todd, I said, "This is Todd. My, uh, my—"

Interrupting my eloquent introduction, Todd nodded at Bob. "Todd. Jane's lucky date. Nice to meet you. Jane baked this potato soufflé for you guys."

Taking the platter from him, Trish said, "Thanks so much. Bob said you were a really good cook. Me, not so much." Her eyes dilating in interest, she looked from me to Todd. "How'd you guys meet?"

I started to explain. "Todd's a lawyer, and my friend Marissa's sister thought we'd—"

"At a party," Todd cut in.

"Cute. When was the party?" Trish asked.

Wanting to keep the duration of my relationship with Todd vague, I started to answer, "I don't really remember—"

"Last Saturday," Todd said. "Jane liked my Red Sox hat."

"That's funny, since Jane has zero interest in sports," Bob said, laughing.

"Bob told me about the time his boss got tickets to a Ranger's game and you fell asleep in the second half." After she said this, Trish covered her mouth with her hand. I wasn't sure if she was regretful for embarrassing me or trying to contain her laughter. The former would mean she was nice, so I hoped for the latter. But I guessed the former.

"Yeah, well. It was a weeknight game. Long day of work."

Patting my back like a child would a pony, Todd said, "Aw, she's a good sport. Watched basketball with me this week and even accompanied me to my firm's bowling tournament. And we've only been dating a week."

Feeling busted, I reluctantly met Bob's glance. His eyebrows raised, he nodded, "A great sport indeed."

"I'm gonna get another beer. Anyone want anything?" Todd asked.

In unison, all three of us replied, "No, thanks."

After Todd was out of ear shot, Trish said happily, "He seems nice. There are too many people here tonight for us to really talk, but you guys should come over for dinner sometime. Bob speaks so highly of you. I would truly like us to be friends."

I examined Trish's face again for some sign she secretly hated my attendance at her party. Some indication that late at night when Bob was asleep, she stuck needles in a Jane-inspired voodoo doll wishing my existence would be removed from Bob's memory and all pictures of me would magically disappear from Mrs. Krauss's photo albums. But what stood before me was a truly nice person who was neither fat nor ugly and seemingly not fatally flawed in any way. Trish was sincere. She was not threatened by me. She was not jealous. She was not insecure. She was in love, she was happy, and she wanted me to be happy too. And she actually wanted to be friends.

My whole charade was failing miserably. It was obvious Todd and I were not on our way to cohabitated bliss like Bob and Trish, and worse, pretending to be right behind her in the line to romantic happiness was pointless and would only serve to make me look even more pathetic than I already did. I had to change directions and fast.

I leaned in toward Bob and Trish and motioned with my finger for them to close the space between us. When they moved in, I confided, "If you must know, I don't think Todd is the one."

Bob laughed. "Oh, really?"

Trish frowned. "That's too bad."

"Nah. As you know, I had the same boyfriend for nine years. My first and only boyfriend, if you know what I mean." I gave Trish a knowing look, but she stared back at me blankly. "Bob was a good lover and all, but I've got serious oats to sow before I settle down." I did a turn of the room as if making sure no one could overhear my next words. "All the guys I'm dating now? Using them," I whispered. "For sex."

Bob let out a loud guffaw while Trish stared at me, her mouth agape. I knew Bob was waiting for me to say, "Just kidding" and I half wanted to, but the words didn't come.

"Okay then," Trish said, her face red. After a minute, she recovered. "Good for you, Jane. Might as well take advantage of your independence while you're still single." Then she gave Bob a pleading look. "Help me in the kitchen, sweetie? I want to warm Jane's soufflé in the oven."

Trish kept her distance from me for the remainder of the party. Bob tried to corner me a few times, but when I saw him coming, I made sure to be on my way to the bathroom or in the foyer taking an urgent call from the dial tone.

I had no idea what had come over me. "I'm using them for sex." I felt as if a piece of my sanity was slowly chipping away, yet I also felt empowered.

It was all a matter of perspective. Jim hadn't dumped me after we had sex. I had taken what I wanted and moved on. Cory hadn't disappeared on me seemingly for no reason. I was no longer interested in what he had to offer. Randall hadn't kicked me to the curb because I wouldn't sleep with him. I wouldn't sleep with him because I didn't want him.

It occurred to me, while sitting on the cold white toilet seat pretending to pee in order to avoid Bob, that I much preferred having the power over the man and deciding when to cut the cord, over being on the receiving end of the silent fade away.

With my newfound philosophy firmly in place, I was ready to leave and spotted Bob laughing with a few guys from his accounting office. I walked over to them and when there was a pause in the conversation, I coughed. "Bob, we're gonna leave now. Thanks so much for having us." I glanced at Todd, who was standing quietly behind me.

Bob eyed me suspiciously but just said, "I'm really glad you guys could make it. I'm so happy you finally met Trish." He turned around and called her name.

Trish looked to be in a dynamic conversation with an older woman but smiled brightly when she heard Bob call out to her. Then she looked over at me and frowned.

"Come say goodbye to Jane," Bob said.

Trish looked at Bob and then back at me and slowly walked over. "It was nice to meet you, Jane," she said flatly. "You too, Todd. Good luck to you." Then she stood on her tippy-toes and tousled Bob's hair before walking away without another mention of us coming over for dinner.

Bob turned back to us. Extending his hand to Todd, he said, "Nice meeting you."

"You too," Todd said. "Thanks for having me. I totally forgot to talk to you about basketball. Jane told me you played."

Bob muttered, "Of course she did. Next time."

When Todd walked away first, I caught Bob's eye and he gave me a questioning look. I winked in response and followed Todd out the door.

Todd and I didn't talk much during our walk to the 6 train after the party. My epiphany made me want to skip down the cobblestone village streets and nod knowingly at all of the girls I saw holding hands with some guy to see if they were in on the secret. But Todd was dragging his heels with his head bowed. I remembered what Claire said about not purposely hurting his feelings and stopped in my place. Todd walked a few steps before realizing I was no longer by his side. He finally stopped, turned around, and asked, "What's wrong?"

"I was going to ask you the same thing. You've been so quiet. What's up?"

Todd led the way to the steps of a brownstone and motioned for me to join him.

I was reluctant. The steps were part of someone else's property. I really wanted to go to bed, but instead I sat down and patted the concrete step next to me. "Sit."

Todd sat down and I waited for him to speak his mind. "How come you didn't mention Bob was your ex-boyfriend? You said it was a friend's party, not an old boyfriend and his new girlfriend's party."

"I didn't think you'd want to go if I told you the truth." This was true, but I left out the part about desperately needing a date.

"Do you still love him? I know it's only our third date, but I need to know if you're still pining over an ex before proceeding to a..."

Interrupting him, I put my index and pointer fingers on his lips. "I'll always love Bob, but we're not in love and haven't been in a long time. I've moved on. I wouldn't watch college basketball for just anyone, you know." Claire had also said I shouldn't lead him on, but it seemed kinder to make him think we had a future than dump him right there on someone else's stoop. I probably didn't need to lay it on so thick, but at least he'd go to bed happy.

When Todd's lips parted in a smile, I kissed him softly. We kissed for a few minutes before I claimed an upset stomach from too much red pepper and garlic hummus, and, promising a fourth date soon, asked if he'd walk me to the subway.

I lay in bed alone twenty minutes later and, as my head hit the pillow, I knew one thing for certain:

There'd be no fourth date. But this time, it would be on my terms.

# Chapter 24

The next morning, I woke up at my weekday time without an alarm and felt so rested I made it to the eight a.m. spin class at the gym. Energized and famished, I walked through the entrance of H&H bagels, thought better of it, then walked back out and stepped to a corner to call Lainie.

When she greeted me with a frog in her throat, I said, "Wanna go out for breakfast?"

After yawning loudly into the phone, she answered, "Calling me from the next room is really lazy. You could've just knocked on my door, Jane."

Laughing, I said, "I'm so lazy, I just finished a spin class. It's beautiful out. Feels like Spring in December. Get up and meet me at EJ's. I'm all sweaty, so no need to shower. I'll call Marissa and reserve a table."

After a brief hesitation, Lainie said, "Okay, but pick me up a coffee somewhere first. The wait will be long, and I need coffee to deal with a perky Jane."

Very happy to be "perky Jane" again, I agreed. "Sure thing. See you in a few."

By the time I convinced Marissa to skip the shower, picked up coffees for all three of us, pushed my way to the hostess to put our names in for a table and returned to the waiting area, Marissa and Lainie had arrived. Forty-five minutes later, we were seated at a corner table by the window, the huge menus stretched out in front of us. I took a quick look and slammed the menu shut. "Blueberry pancakes. No brainer. Just don't tell my mom."

Looking up from her open menu, Marissa asked, "Why not?"

"Let me guess," Lainie said. "She thinks protein is a better way to start the day?"

"And the winning answer goes to the curly-haired southern belle in the pink hoodie," I said cheerily.

"That's why you should order a side of bacon with the pancakes," Lainie said matter-of-factly.

"Another brilliant idea from Lainie."

Just then, my cell phone rang. Before I could remove it from the table, Marissa looked over. "It's Todd," she said. "You can answer it. We won't be mad."

"Speak for yourself," snorted Lainie.

I turned off the ringer and tossed the phone in my gym bag. "Thanks, but I'm busy with my peeps."

Marissa nodded. "I suppose that's the way to go. Don't want to appear too available. You can call him back later."

"Or not," I muttered under my breath.

"Katherine told me he really likes you. She's happy to have fixed him up with a nice girl. He's had some bad luck," Marissa said.

"Haven't we all," I said. "But no matter." I glanced out the window at the exact moment a lanky, dark-haired guy, probably about five foot seven, sporting black jeans, a white t-shirt, and a sexy five o'clock shadow was peering in. Catching my eye, he smiled.

Despite skin sans makeup and my unwashed hair being up in a bun, I felt endorphins from my earlier workout and smiled back. He motioned at me to come outside. When I shook my head and motioned for him to come inside instead, he disappeared out of sight. I assumed he continued to his original destination and giggled at Lainie when she gave me a high five for my flirting effort.

I felt a tap on my shoulder and turned around. Standing over our table was the guy from outside, lugging a bag of CDs. Smiling brightly, he said in a British accent, "I told the waitress my friends were already in the back. Mind if I join you?" Not waiting for an answer, he sat down in the booth next to Marissa and across from me and dropped his bag on the floor.

Marissa stared at him open-mouthed while Lainie looked out the window and snickered. Nonchalantly, I motioned to the bag. "What's with the CDs?"

He looked from me to the bag. "Oh, those? I was bringing them across the park to Westsider Records when I saw you and realized how hungry I was for..." Removing a piece of bacon from my plate, he winked at me and took a bite. "Bacon."

"So, buddy," Lainie interrupted. "Got a name?"

He flashed her a straight-toothed smile. "Buddy will do." Directing his gaze back at me, he said, "More importantly, what's yours?"

"Frankie." I ignored the questioning looks from Marissa and Lainie.

"Well, Frankie. I really do need to get these CDs off my back. But what do you say to a rendezvous in the park, maybe the volleyball courts in Sheep's Meadow, in an hour?"

"Make it two and you've got yourself a date, Buddy."

"Brill." Standing up, he waved to the girls. Winking at me, he said, "Cheerio. See you in two hours," and walked away.

After watching him make his way to the exit, I continued eating my pancakes. When I looked up from my plate, Marissa was looking at me wide-eyed. "You're not seriously gonna meet that guy, are you?"

"Why not? He was cute."

"I guess," Marissa muttered. "But you don't even know his name. And what about Todd?"

"He doesn't know mine either. That's the fun of it. And Todd isn't my boyfriend." I would tell Marissa why I wasn't interested in Todd later. Right now, I wanted to bask in the anticipation of my spontaneous date with Buddy.

Lainie laughed. "Not sure what's gotten into you, but I'm digging this new Jane. Or shall I say, Frankie."

"Just having some fun, girls. Never killed anyone."

Clinking her glass of orange juice against mine, Lainie offered an enthusiastic, "Amen to that."

Shaking off Marissa's furrowed brow, I smiled at Lainie and repeated, "Amen, sista."

# Chapter 25

Two hours later, after finishing my breakfast and taking a long, hot shower, I crossed the 72nd Street transverse, zigzagged out of the path of the many runners taking advantage of the unusually warm temperature for December, and walked west toward the volleyball courts in Sheep's Meadow. Buddy was leaning against a tree. I only got the side view but could see him take a deep drag of a cigarette and blow the smoke skywards. I felt the pitter-patter in my belly as I wondered what the day would bring for Frankie. I anticipated far more excitement would ensue than in the typical Sunday of one Jane Frank.

To start, Jane would have chosen her outfit based on how well it camouflaged her backside, but Frankie was wearing tight black skinny jeans with a cropped soft pink sweater emphasizing her rear-end in all its squeezable/biteable glory. Jane would spend the afternoon outwardly making entertaining conversation with Buddy while inwardly wondering how her first name would sound before his last and worrying how many dates she should wait to sleep with him. But Frankie would toss all that nonsense aside and enjoy the ride in full certainty there was no point worrying about a future that would never unfold. Frankie would live for today.

Finally, Jane would have done an about-face the minute she spotted Buddy smoking. She hated smokers and didn't want to raise children in a smoking environment. But Frankie had no desire to procreate with Buddy and couldn't care less if he was a pack-a-day kind of guy.

Buddy didn't seem to see or hear me approach, so I leaned

against the other side of the tree, stretched out my hand, and lightly jabbed him in the side, forcing his feet to lift slightly off the ground in surprise. He turned around and smiled when he saw it was me. "Blimey, Frankie, I didn't even see you coming."

Keeping my hand on the tree, I pivoted so I was standing in front of him. "Didn't mean to scare you."

He nodded. With a quick glance at his black leather cuff watch, he said, "You're right on time."

Jane would've purposely arrived five minutes late, but Frankie had no interest in playing games.

I noticed his bag from earlier was not in sight. "Any luck selling the CDs?"

Buddy raised his eyebrows. "Depends on your definition of luck. I sold them all but for sod all."

Knowing Jane would have pretended she had the slightest clue what that meant, I said, "No comprende British-speak."

Laughing, Buddy explained, "I sold them, yes, but I might as well have given them away." He motioned west toward the expanse of greens. "Shall we walk?"

I nodded and accepted Buddy's hand as we strolled through the park. Buddy, who had only been in New York for six months, was decidedly enthusiastic about the beauty of Central Park. We walked up to the Belvedere Castle, through the great lawn and ended our tour watching the model sailboats at the Conservatory. Our legs heavy as tree stumps from our scenic explorations, we left the park and headed to Baker Street Pub where we sat at the bar with Scotch Mist whiskey cocktails before us.

Buddy was sitting sideways, his long legs crossed and resting on the foot of my bar stool. I was initially facing forward and turning only my head toward Buddy, but after the second drink, I mirrored his body language.

Buddy trapped my legs between his and traced his palms up and down my thighs. As the warmth from the alcohol coursed through my loins, I leaned over and kissed him. When I felt his tongue gently massaging mine, I moved so I was standing between his legs. I held his stubbled cheeks in my hands as the kiss grew more passionate.

Buddy pulled away, bringing me back to reality. Feeling otherworldly, I looked at him confused. "Is something wrong?"

Buddy shook his head. When his black eyes pierced into mine, I felt like he could see through my clothes. "Nothing's wrong, Frankie," he said. "You're a dish, that's all. And it's not just because I'm sloshed."

I leaned over and nibbled on his soft earlobe. Blowing in his ear, I said, "You're a dish too. Not sure if it's because I'm sloshed, but I don't really care."

"Not to sound cliché, but should we take this someplace more comfortable?"

I nodded my response.

He nodded back. "Your place or mine?"

As if injected with an anti-drunk remedy, I was immediately bolted back into the real world as I thought about how to answer his question. Even with my new philosophy toward men, going to his place was not an option. I had been Jane for far too long to trust going to some strange guy's apartment. If I wanted to keep my identity a secret, bringing him to my place was out of the question as well. Besides, he'd be bored to death with all of the LSAT prep books occupying the small space of my bedroom. My mind racing, I flashed back to my bathroom the previous evening, when Claire was doing my makeup. She mentioned something about leaving for Philadelphia early the next morning to visit Kevin's parents and how he'd bribed her into it with a promise to stop for a cheesesteak on the way home. Claire reasoned it was acceptable to consume a cheesesteak after eating dinner with her in-laws because she was eating for two.

I surmised that even if they ate dinner at five p.m., they wouldn't be home until at least nine, which meant I could use my spare key to get inside, have my fun, and leave without anyone knowing, and without giving away my true identity and complicating things.

Returning my attention to Buddy, I said, "My place."

Buddy called out "Cheers" to the bartender, tossed some cash on the bar and winked at me. With a glance at the exit, he said, "Shall we?"

I collapsed onto my back, my body glistening with sweat after the best sexual experience of my life. Well, the best sexual experience I ever had on my sister's living room floor. (There was no way I could do it on her and Kevin's bed, so I told Buddy the walls of the bedroom were being painted and the fumes were dangerous).

I turned my head toward Buddy, who was leaning on his elbow and facing me. I peered over his head at the grandfather clock behind him. It wasn't even eight p.m. but I wanted to get him out of the apartment soon, just in case my sister decided to skip the cheesesteak on the way home.

Running his hands gently up and down my arm, Buddy smiled. "I suppose now that we've shagged, you should know my name is not really Buddy."

I bolted up and, realizing I was naked, wrapped my hoodie around my lower half, ironically self-conscious after sleeping with a stranger. "Buddy works for me. Let's not ruin the mystery. You—Buddy, Me—Jane." I pounded my fists on my chest Tarzan-style until I realized my slip. "So, I totally forgot I need to do some grocery shopping, but this was fun."

Buddy, also buck naked, stood up and stretched his arms above his head. I glanced at his fair-skinned body, slender and hairless except for a small patch on his chest. I avoided gazing downwards, again ironically, since his privates had been in the most intimate quarters with mine mere moments ago. He drew me into an embrace, our nude bodies once again pressed together until I moved away. He looked me up and down and flashed me a devilish grin. "Jane, huh? Fair enough. I'm sure there's more mystery to you than a fake name, and I want to solve it." He gazed into my eyes. "Slowly."

I slipped on my jeans, not even caring I wasn't wearing panties. Concentrating on checking the rug for the used condom so I didn't have to make eye contact, I said, "That's sweet, Buddy. Really. But, to be honest, I'm not looking for anything long-term. Like more than one day." My heart was pounding in the aftermath of my first one-night stand, and I wondered who had taken control of Jane.

Buddy leaned over to pull up his black jeans. He had stopped smiling and his lower lip protruded almost in a pout. He looked genuinely disappointed, although I doubted he really cared that much. He was hot and could easily pick up a girl at the corner diner next weekend for another Sunday Funday if he wanted. He turned his back on me as he put his shirt on and we stood there in silence until he faced me again.

"Wow, Jane. I'd heard you New York City girls were a ruthless bunch, but, blimey, I wasn't expecting it from you." With that, Buddy grabbed his wallet and keys and headed to the front door of Claire and Kevin's apartment. With a quick glance behind him, he muttered, "Thanks for the shag" and walked out.

I quickly got dressed, took a cursory look around the room, and hightailed it out of the apartment. I didn't breathe until I turned the corner of my own block ten minutes later. I wondered what time Claire and Kevin would be home and was relieved they'd never know what transpired on their living room floor. Buddy was in my sights the entire time so I knew he didn't steal anything, and we hadn't been there long enough to make a mess. As far as I was concerned, no harm was done, but I wasn't sure she'd support my foray into meaningless sex or even believe me. Jane Alexis was not the type to have sex with a random stranger anywhere, much less in her sister's apartment.

Giggling as I headed for my walk-up, I thought to myself, apparently such activities were not out of the question for Frankie. Ruthless New York City girl indeed.

I was anxious to share the events of the day with Lainie, but when I saw she wasn't home, I jumped in the shower instead. As the hot water cascaded over my body, I thought about how good a bubble bath would have felt instead and questioned my quick escape from Claire's apartment since she had a Jacuzzi tub. After I toweled off and put on my pajamas, I checked my phone. Among two text messages from Marissa, the first asking if I was alive and the second demanding I text her back, was a text from Todd saying, "Hi" and a voicemail asking if I wanted to grab wings at Manny's and watch the game. As if I was supposed to know to which game he was referring. Since none of the guys I'd dated since Bob formally broke up with me, I figured ghosting was how it was done these days and I deleted both his text and voicemail. I assumed he'd get the hint eventually. After confirming to Marissa that I was alive and well, I opened up my LSAT practice exam book. I hadn't spent nearly as much time focusing on the upcoming test as I'd promised my father. If I didn't study more, I was afraid I'd only get into a third-tier law school. I answered two of the questions and was reading the third when there was a knock on the door. Before I could answer, Lainie barged in and jumped on my bed. "So?"

I folded the page of the book and tossed it onto the wooden floor next to my bed. I took a deep breath.

"I thought about what you said about the fun in playing the field." I paused dramatically.

Lainie's lips curled up as she nodded. "What did you decide?"

My facial expression serious, I stood up on the bed with my hands on my hips and looked down at Lainie, who was sitting on the edge awaiting my reply. Not able to contain myself any longer, I jumped up and down, clapped my hands excitedly, and exclaimed, "It's awesome. Who needs one boyfriend when you can have several?" Noticing Lainie's amused reaction, I grabbed her hands and pulled her up so she was standing too. Holding hands, we jumped up and down until, exhausted, we both collapsed onto the bed.

Lainie started to speak, but whatever she said was muffled by her hysterical laughter. With one hand holding her stomach, she raised the other in the air with a finger pointing up. Then she put her hand to her mouth and took a deep breath. Finally composed, she said, "I guess Frankie and Buddy had fun today, huh?"

I nodded. With a sly smile, I said, "Frankie was a very bad girl today."

Her mouth dropped open. "You didn't."

Bobbing my head and up down, I confirmed, "Oh, yes, I did."

"Well, I'll be damned. Jane Frank had sex on a first date."

"It's only worth counting if there's gonna be a second date," I said matter-of-factly.

"And the jury says?"

Shaking my head, I said, "No. Not interested."

Lainie frowned. "Sex sucked, huh? What? Too small?"

"No and no. Just not interested."

With her brow furrowed, Lainie asked, "Was he not nice?"

She appeared to be genuinely concerned, and I was afraid she thought Buddy forced himself on me. To defend my ability to horde off an inappropriately aggressive guy, I insisted, "No, he was super nice."

"Not enough attraction?"

"No. Did you see him? I could never sleep with a guy I wasn't attracted to. I've only been with three other guys in my life." Two of them in the past five months, I noted to myself.

Lainie leaned in toward me, as if preparing for a heart to heart chat. "What's the issue? Is it Todd?"

I was thrown by Lainie's failure to appreciate the beauty of my one-night stand and no longer enthused by the conversation. I stood up, grabbed my facial moisturizer from my vanity and began applying it, my back to Lainie. "There is no issue. Just not interested in seeing the guy again." I turned back around and faced Lainie. She was frowning at me. "What? I thought you'd be my biggest cheerleader for playing the field."

"I am. It's just...you're different." She studied my face as if searching for answers in my pores.

I nodded. "I suppose I am."

She opened her mouth as if poised to say something else, but I cut her off. "I'm really beat. Long day for Jane. Or shall I say, Frankie."

Taking the hint, Lainie stood up and walked out of my room. Hesitating at my bedroom door, she said, "Night, Jane. Sweet dreams."

I had to brush my teeth, so I walked past her on my way to the bathroom, said, "You too," and closed the door behind me.

That night I dreamed about my wedding dress. Well, wedding dresses. I was shopping with my mom and Claire at Kleinfeld, where Claire had bought hers. I tried on all sorts of dresses in varying styles including the sexy body-clinging silk dress with a scoop neckline and low back, the more traditional strapless A-line with beaded train, and even the gaudy gown with the puffy sleeves that I wouldn't wear in real life even if all of my guests were legally blind.

The reception was being held at the Water Club on the East River and the ten-day honeymoon was booked for New Zealand for reasons I couldn't fathom, since I had no desire to go there. My mother's face was beaming as she exclaimed, "That's the one. That's the dress." And then I woke up with a jolt before I even learned who I was marrying.

I lay awake looking up at the ceiling, replaying the dream for a few minutes, before I moved to get out of bed and log onto the internet. I searched my memory for the password I hadn't used in well over a month and logged onto eHarmony. I had eight un-viewed profiles waiting for me. With shaky hands, I moved my mouse over the first thumbnail picture. His name was Neil and his longish curly dark hair was peeking out of a Mets baseball cap. I inhaled, highlighted the picture, ready to right click.

Then, as if a sign from God, the faces of Randall, Jim, and Cory flashed before my eyes one after the other, each smiling but dead in the eyes. Slowly, I slid the mouse to the upper right-hand corner of the screen, exited the page, and got back in bed.

# Chapter 26

"Frank!"

I looked up from my computer and over at Andrew, who had his legs stretched out on his desk and his arms locked behind his head. "This is your office, Andrew," I said. "Not your living room."

Andrew said, "Yes, Mom" before removing his legs from the desk and giving me an amused smile. "Coming to happy hour?"

One of our vendors was treating the paralegals to a happy hour later at Opal. I scrunched my nose. "I don't know."

"C'mon, Jane. Let your hair down for once."

I chuckled. It had been a couple of weeks since my one-night stand with Buddy, but I was still enjoying the after effects.

"And that made you laugh, because...?"

"Fine. I'll stop by. Who else is going?" I no longer expected to meet my soul mate at the neighborhood pub but hoped there would at least be other people I knew besides Andrew.

"The regulars. And I told a few of my non-work friends. Sean is usually good about guests."

Sean was the vendor, a nice off-the-boat Irish guy who always made sure the paralegals were good and drunk by the time they left one of his happy hours. It was one of the reasons I rarely attended. "Count me in."

Andrew turned to his friend Brandon, a blue-eyed, fair-skinned stocky guy in a gingham button-down shirt and dark brown cargo pants and gestured his draft of Guinness in my direction. "Jane shares my office," he said.

I motioned my appletini in Andrew's direction. "Correction. Andrew shares *my* office." I smiled at Andrew. "He's a good tenant. Keeps his work space clean and is relatively quiet."

Andrew finished his chicken wing, dropped the bone on his plate, and wiped the excess blue cheese dressing from his mouth. "And I frequently offer my therapy services," he said

Brandon raised one eyebrow.

I glared at Andrew as I felt my face get hot, but he kept talking. "Jane's dated a bunch of douche bags."

I smirked. "Takes one to know one. Anyway, I won't be needing your services anymore."

"Why's that?" Andrew asked. "Going lesbian?" Before I could say anything, Andrew said, "Because girls can be just as douchey as guys."

I rolled my eyes.

"Just saying," Andrew said.

I shouted, "Not going gay."

Brandon scooted his chair closer to mine and looked me deep in the eyes. "Well, that's good news."

"Why? Lesbians are hot," Andrew said.

"I prefer girls who'd rather go out with me than my twin sister, Brandina," Brandon said sheepishly.

I smiled shyly at him, thinking he had a cute baby face. Andrew glanced up from his depleting plate of wings and shook his head in Brandon's direction. He removed his phone from the table and stood up. "Reception sucks in here. Going outside to call Don." Don was another guy on the soccer team and I hoped he was as cute as Brandon. I debated inviting Marissa and Lainie to join us, but decided against it.

An hour or so later, I had switched my beverage of choice to water and my attention to Don, a shaggy-haired guy with kind brown eyes and a dimple on his left cheek. He wore white jeans that I thought, until I met him, only worked on rock stars and Daniel Craig in *Casino Royale*.

Don ran his hands through his hair and grinned at me.

"You've got a great head of hair," I said, smiling back.

Seemingly reluctant to accept credit for the attribute, Don shrugged. "Genetics, I guess. Hopefully, I have time before it starts receding."

"How old are you?" I asked.

"Thirty-one. You?"

"How old do I look?" I asked flirtatiously.

Don examined my face for a few seconds before guessing, "Twenty-eight?"

Pretending to be hurt, I pouted. "Twenty-six. Should I be insulted?"

Defending himself, Don said, "Not like I guessed forty-eight." He added, "Besides, twenty-eight and twenty-six are practically the same. But I apologize if I hurt your feelings."

Shaking my head, I said, "Nah. Just busting your chops."

Don let out an exaggerated breath of relief. "So I didn't blow any shot I had of you going out with me sometime?"

I glanced over at Andrew on the other side of the table playing quarters with two of the other female paralegals and wondered how he'd feel about me dating his friend. Turning back to Don, I said, "Sure, I'd go out with you. Andrew has my number." The article I read in *Cosmopolitan* was wrong—confidence wasn't the biggest turn on to men, indifference was. The less I cared, the more attention I got. I bit back a laugh at the irony. Chances were, he wouldn't call anyway.

I stood up. "Gotta go to the ladies' room. I'll be back."

After washing my hands, I flipped my head upside down and shook out my hair. Staring at my reflection, I reapplied a shiny muted red gloss that came in a sample packet Marissa had given me. I smacked my lips together, smiled at myself, and walked back out into the bar. I didn't want to go back to the same table, so I scanned the room until I spotted Brandon standing in the corner with Bethany, our firm's librarian and probably the only law librarian with a purple streak in her hair and five studs running along the lobes of both of her ears. Brandon seemed to be enjoying their banter, but then we met eyes and he gave me a come-hither gesture.

I reluctantly joined them. The only time I'd spoken to Bethany was when I first started at the firm and she trained me to use the Lexis/Nexis search database. She was twenty-nine and known for coming to work straight from after-hour raves and doing lines of cocaine in the bathroom to stay awake. I wasn't sure I believed the rumors, but she did wear dark sunglasses inside a lot, and I had caught her rubbing her nose a few times.

Bethany's back was to me, but when I reached where they were standing and Brandon greeted me, she turned around, smiling brightly. "Hiya, Jane. What's going on?"

Nervous, feeling not nearly as badass as her despite my recent torrid fling, I self-consciously flipped my hair. "Not much."

"Do any interesting research on Lexis recently?"

I figured Bethany was equally aware we had no other common ground. "Nope," I said, shaking my head. As Cory's freckled face popped into my head, I recalled his sudden disappearing act. "Although I am tempted to check whether my last boyfriend has a criminal record. Or has ever been admitted to an insane asylum."

Bethany put her drink down on the floor and clapped her hands together, laughing. Then she looked at Brandon. "I like this chick." After picking her glass back up, she said, "Off to make rounds. Later, folks." As she walked away, she tapped my shoulder and said, "If only we really *could* bill clients to conduct background information on potential boyfriends. Good one!"

I watched her walk away, still chuckling, and turned back to Brandon who was subtly shaking his head at me, but who I could tell was smiling behind his pursed lips. "Are you really that jaded?" he asked.

"No," I lied. "Was just being funny. Or trying to."

Brandon looked at me doubtfully. Finally, he said, "Not sure I believe you." He whipped around and pointed to a laughing Andrew still surrounded by females and engaged in drinking games. "He did say you dated a lot of douche bags."

I sighed. "It is what it is." I had no desire to revisit the stage in my life when I gave guys so much power over me.

"How about you let me take you out to prove not all guys are douche bags."

"Sounds good," I said, giving him my finest toothy smile to emphasize my eagerness. As I saw Andrew walk in our direction, Don in tow, I whispered, "Andrew has my number." Then I walked away calling behind me, "Gotta go to the bathroom."

Since I didn't really have to pee, I gripped the sides of the sink and frowned at my face in the mirror, hoping no one would come in needing to wash her hands. Brandon had looked so sincere when he asked me out. For a moment, I doubted a guy with such a baby face could tear my heart into shreds. I would not judge a book by its cover, I vowed. No matter how cute he was, I would not be made a fool again. Holding hard to my virtual handle on reality, I exited the bathroom, contemplating whether it was time to go home.

When I returned to our table to grab my coat and say my goodbyes, no one was there. Confused, I looked around wondering if everyone was going to jump out from under the tables, screaming, "Surprise!" After a moment, I sat down to check my cell phone, thinking Andrew might have texted me where they went. But I had no messages. "I guess they ditched me," I muttered.

From behind me, I heard a girl's voice say, "No, they didn't." I turned around and faced Bethany. "They went to Press Box across the street. Wanted me to tell you to meet them there."

"And you stayed behind to tell me?" I asked, surprised.

Bethany laughed. "Not quite. I'm waiting for a friend to confirm the location of the next stop on my bar crawl this evening. I figured I might as well stick around here."

"You're not going to Press Box with the others?"

"Not my style. But I figured I'd take advantage of the free cocktails now to get my buzz on for the main event later."

I visualized Bethany donning a blond wig like Lady Gaga and dancing to the latest house music with a bunch of coked-up rock stars.

"Wanna come along?"

Assuming she was joking, I laughed out loud. "Yeah, I'm sure I'd fit right in."

Smiling brightly, Bethany said, "Sweet. I'll text my friend and tell her to add your name to the list. You should text Andrew and let him know."

Was she serious? Did she just invite me to a party when the only words we'd ever exchanged prior to that night were "Lexis" and "Nexis"? Did I really say I'd go? What if I was the only one without bright streaks of color in my hair? My blond lowlights certainly didn't count. What if they started discussing recreational drug use? Would it be uncool to admit the strongest drug I'd ever ingested was doctor-prescribed Tylenol with Codeine? I had at least a hundred more "what-ifs" to run through and hadn't yet reached the double digits, but before I even had a chance to let Andrew know I wouldn't be joining him at Press Box, I found myself speed walking to keep up with Bethany as she raced to the downtown 6 train on Lexington Avenue. I'd text Andrew later.

The subway was surprisingly packed for a Thursday night at ten thirty, but Bethany and I squeezed into the subway car, our hands practically touching as we and about three strangers gripped the same pole for balance. I looked over the other passengers' heads through the dirty train windows and watched the train across the platform leave a few seconds before us.

I felt a twinge of envy at the people on that train since it was headed uptown, in the direction of my apartment. But I'd humor Bethany by having a drink before leaving. At least it was a Thursday night and work the next morning was a built-in excuse not to stay out all night.

Bethany shouted over the rumbling of the train, "We're going to Lex Bar. It's in Murray Hill."

We were standing uncomfortably close, and I leaned my head back to tease myself into thinking I had any semblance of personal space. "Cool." I was relieved we weren't headed to a more exotic neighborhood off the grid and completely unfamiliar to me.

"It's cool if you like frat boys and girls who shop in Banana Republic," Bethany said, laughing.

As the doors of the train opened, I crossed my arms over my down jacket, which was hiding my Ann Taylor blouse. Uncertain whether Ann Taylor was better or worse than Banana Republic, but confident that it didn't make much of a difference either way, I followed Bethany onto the street.

# Chapter 27

I had no idea Bethany was so smart. When I told her I was trying to lose five pounds and didn't want to use up all my calories on fruity drinks, she told me about the vodka shot diet. She'd lost thirteen pounds the year before simply by doing a shot of vodka once every half hour instead of ordering full drinks. Although I wasn't a big drinker anyway, I figured I'd give it a shot. *No pun intended.* I was on my second one and felt great. I didn't even miss the soda or cranberry juice.

I was sitting on a red velvet couch in the dimly lit hotel bar with Bethany, her friend Anne, and two guys, one tall and round with black hair and one short and round with blond hair—like Fred Flintstone and Barney Rubble. I wondered if any of them were dating. When the boys got up to order another round of drinks, I took it as my opportunity to ask over the blasting house music.

Bethany and Anne exchanged a glance before laughing. "No way. We've all been friends since college," said Bethany.

I figured as much. Bethany and Anne were way more physically attractive than Fred and Barney. But not everyone cared about looks. "Where did you go?" I figured it was NYU or maybe some fashion or artsy school.

"SUNY Buffalo," Bethany said.

Anne nodded. "We were in the same sorority."

"That's so funny," I said.

Bethany and Anne exchanged another look. "Why is it funny?" Anne asked.

Suddenly feeling stupid, I shook my head while wishing I

could take a sip of a drink to bide time. "Not funny really. It's just that..." I looked at the girls who looked back at me expectantly. Directing my answer at Bethany, I said, "I didn't picture you as a sorority girl. You seem more, well, independent. It's a compliment."

Bethany smiled. "I'll take it as one. Can't judge a book by its cover."

I smiled back, happy I hadn't offended her. "Totally."

When the boys returned with our drinks, I did my shot like a pro, barely flinching, and pulled out my wallet to give them money.

Fred—I didn't catch his real name—pushed my hand away. "I've got this one. You can pay for the next round. So long as I get to go up to the bar to order them."

When I put my wallet back in my bag, I noticed my phone was flashing. I didn't want to be rude to the others, so I ignored the call, but placed the phone in my lap to check later. "Why do you insist on going to get the drinks? Not that I'm complaining."

They all laughed, confusing me even more until Bethany said, "Have you seen the bartenders here?"

It was my first time there, and I hadn't been up to the bar yet. I sort of hoped I wouldn't have to since it was packed, and if all the bartenders were female, they'd probably ignore me anyway. I shook my head. "No."

Bethany motioned her hands over her chest area. "Holy tits behind the bar."

"Oh," I said, gazing down at my own bosom. I was a small C.

Catching me check myself out, Anne said, "You have a nice rack, Jane, but the bartenders here are super endowed, most of them artificially enhanced, if you know what I mean. Why do you think we're here?" Gesturing toward Bethany, she said, "Let's just say it was not our idea."

The same guy who refused my money sat down next to me. "Yes. We're here for the boobage behind the bar, but you girls make the time between rounds very pleasant."

Giggling, I said, "Gee, thanks. By the way, I don't think I got your name."

Bethany said, "Charming guy over here is Andy." Pointing to Barney, she said, "And this guy, who is less charming and more of an ass man than a breast man, is Arthur. We call them 'the A team.'" Glancing at the phone on my lap, she said, "Anyone interesting?"

I listened to the voicemails. Both from Andrew, one asking if I was joining them at Press Box and the other telling me they were all going home. "Nothing interesting. Just Andrew."

Bethany bit her lip. "Crap. Weren't you supposed to text him you were coming with me instead of meeting them? We distracted you with shots."

Anne snorted. "And boobies."

Laughing, I said, "Andrew's my officemate, not my keeper. I think he'll get over it."

"I think his friend Brandon had the hots for you," Bethany said, winking.

I nodded. "I think so too. So did his friend Don. Whatev. Hoes over bros."

Anne stood up, her hands on her thin hips. "You calling us hoes, girly-girl?"

Andy (or was it Arthur) muttered, "She said it, not me." Extending his hand to me, he said, "Time for more tits. I mean drinks. Hand me some cash, little girl."

Vastly entertained by these virtual strangers and ready for a fourth shot, I gave him a wad of cash. "Make mine a double."


The last thing I remembered before my head hit the pillow was the time on the clock-radio: 3:11. I had exactly four hours and thirty-four minutes before the alarm would sound. I was surprised I was capable of doing the math after all of those shots. I decided I wasn't really that drunk, and while I would be tired the next day, the hangover would be minimal. I only had to get through one more day of work before the weekend.

\* \* \*

I didn't understand why my brother-in-law kept kicking me on the side of my head. I shouted for Claire, begging for mercy. Claire smiled, her teeth so white I wondered if she'd been using Crest White Strips and whether they were good for the baby. I was flat on my back with my knees pulled to my chest to protect myself from further flogging by Kevin. When Claire bent over me, I turned to my side, my head pounding, and opened my mouth to whisper, "Help." At the precise moment I straightened my legs, Claire flashed me an evil grin and kicked me forcefully in the stomach. As I heard a police siren in the background, I felt the bile rise to my throat and sat up.

My alarm clock was sounding. It was all a bad dream. Except I felt like my head was being squeezed by a pair of pliers, and if I didn't get to the bathroom in the next ten seconds, I would puke all over my soft pink area rug.

As I leaned over the toilet bowl, the stains on the bottom turned my dry heave into a full-blown regurgitation of the vodka ingested the night before. Vomiting temporarily reduced the stirring in my stomach, but the pain was instantly transferred to my head. I felt like someone was hammering a nail into my temples. I cursed Lainie. It was her turn to clean the bathroom, and she had conveniently skipped the toilet.

A sick day was clearly in order, and when I was convinced I had rid my system of the poison, I got back in bed, dragging my garbage can with me just in case. First, I removed the pink and green beaded decorative cover my now-deceased grandmother had made back when I was a baby and threw it across the room to avoid accidentally puking on it. I curled myself into a ball and whispered a desperate plea to God to make the pounding stop. Then I realized I had to call in sick. I begrudgingly sat up and reached for my phone. As I dialed the paralegal manager's number, I remembered the mandatory legal assistant meeting for that morning, lay back in the bed, and sobbed.

I cried for about three minutes, eyes closed, feeling the pressure in my head slowly ease. Approximately twelve minutes later, I forced myself out of bed, cried again on the way to the bathroom, and took two aspirin and a long, scalding hot shower. With a quick wave to Lainie thirty minutes later, I left my apartment with a wet head and no makeup. I hid my bare face with black wide-rimmed sunglasses. I wrapped my head in a black scarf to protect my face from the cold. In my black wool sweater and matching pants, I wondered if I looked like a woman who was trying to discreetly follow her husband to see if he was going to a business meeting, as promised, or to meet his mistress at a hotel. But I had no husband to stalk, just the nearest coffee cart. Preferably one that would also sell me a bacon, egg, and cheese sandwich.

I assumed Andrew would give me crap for being late and tease me about my hangover, but our office was empty when I arrived. Still in my scarf and sunglasses, I inhaled my sandwich before logging onto my computer, and had my head on my desk when I heard someone come in. I sat up and looked over at Andrew who was already leafing through a handful of documents.

Weakly, I said, "Hey."

Without turning away from the papers in his hand, Andrew said, "Have fun last night?"

"I feel awful." It was the truth, but I wanted to share the details of my night with Andrew anyway. He'd be impressed I'd let my hair down and engaged in some chicanery, especially with the resident "druggie" (who I'd learned last night had never even tried cocaine. Just mushrooms—once—back in college).

"About what? Being a tease?"

I jerked my head back, surprised by Andrew's accusation. Swallowing hard, I whispered, "I was referring to my hangover. I had less than five hours sleep last night." I frowned as Andrew turned back to his papers. "Are you mad at me or something?" I held my breath.

Andrew put down his papers and stared at his desk for a

moment before turning to face me again. "Brandon told me he was going to call you, which I thought was great. But then Don said you told him to get your number from me. He's a great guy too, but one of them wasn't enough for you?"

I released my breath, relieved it wasn't anything serious. "I was just being friendly. I didn't mean to piss you off."

"Is everything all right with you?"

"I've never been better. Aside from this hangover. Why?"

"Your behavior last night was unlike you."

I groaned. "You're the one who told me to date like a guy and not take it all so seriously, remember? I was only trying to follow your advice. I'm sorry if it seemed I pit one friend against another or put you in the middle. It wasn't my intention. Satisfied?"

Andrew rolled his eyes.

"I was enjoying the attention. Since when is that a crime?"

"It's not," Andrew muttered before focusing on his computer.

Smiling, I said, "So we're good now?"

"We're peachy," he said, still not facing me.

"And it's not like either of them was really interested in me anyway so no harm done."

Andrew whipped his head toward me and opened his mouth to say something. Seeming to change his mind, he glanced at his watch, grabbed a legal pad and a pen, and stood up. "The paralegal meeting starts in five minutes. Are you coming?"

# Chapter 28

"It's between me, my teammate Pam, and a woman from a different department," Marissa said before breaking off a small square of banana nut bread and putting it in her mouth. "Are you sure you don't want a piece?"

I grimaced. "The baked goods at Starbucks aren't worth the calories."

"This is low fat."

"Which means it will taste even worse. What makes fattening foods taste good is the fat. Take it out and you might as well be eating a piece of fruit."

Marissa rolled her eyes. "More for me then. Anyway, since Pam and I have the same background, Katherine suggested I emphasize qualities I have that she doesn't to make me stand out." She pulled a notepad out of her purse. "Help me?"

I glanced around the Starbucks. We were at the expansive Union Square location and it was packed with hipsters. I motioned with my chin to couple at a neighboring table. "She's way more into him than he is into her."

"How can you tell?"

"She's looking right at him while he is looking everywhere except her."

"Interesting." Marissa glanced down at her pad. "The only thing I have so far is that over the last two years, I'm the one who covers for our boss when she's out of the office. I've already done the job at least temporarily. But what else?"

Twisting my mouth in thought, I said, "How about you're organized?"

"I am, but so is Pam."

"When are they deciding?"

Marissa crinkled her nose. "Not sure. The job hasn't even been posted yet, but I don't want to be caught off guard."

My face breaking into a smile, I said, "Now she trained her boyfriend well." I pointed to a girl with brown curly hair. She stood off to the side reading from her phone while her boyfriend, holding both of their coffees, walked around to find a table.

"How do you know he's her boyfriend?"

"You can tell."

"Oh. So back to my list. We both started at the company on the same day, but you think my prior experience at Sephora will put me over the edge?"

As another couple—a tall skinny guy with unruly hair and a tiny girl with a sleek brunette blunt cut—stepped off of the line, my body froze in place.

"Jane. What do you think?"

Out of the side of my face, I said, "Bob and Trish are here." Bob caught my eye and waved before nudging Trish, who did a double take before nodding a hello. They approached our table and I stood up.

"What a small world," Bob said giving me a kiss hello. "Hey, Marissa," he said.

"We were at Burlington and craving coffee. Do you guys want to sit with us?" I asked.

"I...um..." Bob glanced at Trish as if asking her permission.

"Sure," she said, but I could tell she didn't want to.

Bob pulled up chairs for both of them and said, "How's Todd?" with a sly smile before bringing his cup to his mouth.

"Yeah, I've been meaning to ask how things were going with you guys," Marissa said.

"It's fine," I said before taking a sip of my coffee and avoiding Trish's curious look. I reached across and tapped my hand against Bob's. "How's the new pad?"

"It's great," Bob said.

"We're really happy." Trish smiled and took Bob's hands in hers. "Aren't we, sweetie."

"Never been happier," he said beaming at her.

Trish glanced at Bob. "We should get going." To us, she said, "We weren't planning on sitting for more than a few minutes. Bob has so much stuff to unpack and we need to organize everything."

"Remember when we helped Claire and Kevin move into their new place. What a mess," I said.

Bob grinned. "I remember you carried that queen-sized mattress all by yourself."

I laughed. "Yes. I became the Bionic Woman for just long enough to carry the mattress from the moving truck to the entrance of the apartment."

"And then you dropped it in the lobby." He shook his head at me. "We told you to let someone help."

My cheeks flushed in embarrassment at my stubborn and stupid behavior. Still, it was a good memory. I wondered what kinds of memories Bob would make with Trish. Did she have siblings? I opened my mouth to ask as Trish stood up.

With a hand on Bob's shoulder, she said, "Honey, we really should head out."

Bob glanced at his watch. "Trish's right," he said standing up.

"It was good seeing you both," I said with a smile.

"Nice meeting you," Marissa said to Trish.

The two of them waved goodbye, and I watched their backs get smaller and smaller as they reached the entrance. "What did you think of Trish?" I asked Marissa.

"She seemed nice. Didn't say much."

"Do you think she's prettier than me?"

Marissa narrowed her eyes. "No, but you can't even compare you guys. You're on the tall side and she's tiny. Her hair is almost black while yours is more of a golden brown. Totally different. Do you think my attendance at more industry conventions will work in my favor?"

"We must have something in common if he chose her after me.

Maybe I should look for guys who are more like Bob." After I said it, I remembered, I was through searching for love. "Never mind."

Marissa giggled. "Enough about Bob and Trish. You probably shouldn't try to find another guy like him considering you're not in love with each other anymore. What do you think about the conventions?"

"What conventions?"

"Are you even listening to me?"

"Of course I am." I took a last sip of coffee. "Let's head out soon. I'm beat."

Marissa groaned. "We didn't even work on my list."

"You said yourself the job wasn't posted yet. Seeing Bob and Trish together really wiped me out. And, besides, you came up with a bunch of them by yourself. You don't even need me."

"Not like I have a choice," Marissa muttered before standing up and shrugging on her coat.

Wrapping my scarf around my neck, I said, "A choice about what?"

Marissa secured her winter hat on her head. "Never mind. Let's go."

# Chapter 29

A few days later, Andrew remained distant, only speaking to me to ask or answer a work-related question. I didn't understand why he was so upset. It wasn't as if I'd done anything wrong.

"I replaced the paper in the printer," I said, motioning to the printer we shared. "That thing eats paper like it's an all-you-can-eat buffet. We barely print anything and it's always empty."

Andrew nodded. "Thanks."

I watched him as he stared intently at the inside of an open manila folder. "Whatchya doing?"

Without looking up, Andrew said, "Work. It's what they pay me for."

I muttered, "Okay then," as my phone rang. "Jane Frank."

"Hi. You have a minute?"

"Of course, Marissa. I always have time to talk to my friends." I glanced at Andrew and, raising my voice, said, "Even when I'm working. What's up?"

"I just got off the phone with Katherine. Everything's fine. Except..."

"Did something happen? Are your folks okay?" There was silence. "You're scaring me."

"What's up with Todd, Jane?"

Confused, I said, "Huh?"

"He told Katherine you've been ignoring his calls. He said you told him you really liked him and then blew him off. He's upset, Jane."

I rolled my eyes. "What? Is he five years old?"

"Is it true?" Marissa asked.

I blew a stream of air out of my mouth. "Yes."

"Why?"

"The truth is I don't like Todd. I tried, but I just didn't feel anything."

"Why didn't you say anything when I asked you about it in Starbucks?" She sounded hurt.

"I didn't mean to keep it from you. We only went out three times and I didn't think it was a big deal. And besides, I didn't want to talk about it in front of Bob and Trish. I'm sorry."

"You should have said something when I asked, but what's done is done. You might want to tell Todd though."

"The last three guys I dated dumped me silently and I got the hint eventually. I figured Todd would too. Isn't that the way it's done these days?" It occurred to me I'd been spending a lot of time justifying my actions to other people lately and I didn't like it. Raising my voice, I said, "What's the big deal?" I could feel Andrew looking at me. *Oh, now he's interested.*

Marissa sighed. "I thought you'd be more old school. It's not like you to be so insensitive."

I sighed. "For the love of God. It didn't work out. Life goes on. I've certainly been on the receiving end of less consideration than I afforded Todd."

"Two wrongs don't make a right," Marissa said.

I mimicked, "Two wrongs don't make a right."

"I'm just saying," Marissa said.

"What do you want me to do about it? Should I call Todd and apologize for my heartless behavior? How about I bake him cookies? Or does Katherine want me to clean her apartment in repentance for my bad deed?"

"Don't be ridiculous."

"Well, this entire conversation is ridiculous. I think you, your sister, and good ol' boy Todd need to lighten up. I love you, Marissa, but c'mon."

"Katherine said if she'd known how rude you were, she wouldn't have set you up in the first place."

"Did you ask her why she didn't set him up with you instead? She's so involved in your life, you'd think it would extend to your love life."

"Katherine specifically chose Todd for you because of the law thing." I heard Marissa exhale deeply into the phone.

I thought about my conversations with Todd. Interestingly, none had involved law. "You're not smoking are you?"

"No," Marissa said. "But I'm glad to hear you're concerned about my well-being at least. I'll talk to you later."

I hung up and put my head on the desk, exhausted from the conversation. I heard Andrew get up and walk out of the office whistling. I noticed I had a missed call and voicemail from Claire and felt a pang of guilt I hadn't checked up on her in a while. I listened to the message.

"Hey little sister. I haven't heard from you in a while and wanted to check in. I assume between work and studying you've been too busy to call your pregnant sister. Funny thing, Kevin was mopping our living room floor and found a random red lace panty. For a second, I wondered if he was cheating on me, but as he so wisely reminded me, most cheating husbands would hide random underwear from their wives, not bring it to their attention. I didn't look too closely, because...gross...but they're Hanky Panky and I know you love that brand. What gives with you leaving undies at my place? Did you do laundry when we were away or something? Anyway, call me back. I haven't seen you since the whole Cory mess and want to catch up. Bye."

I lowered my head to the desk. I was quickly running out of time to study for the LSAT, but right now, I had too much on my mind to focus. I wanted to call Claire back, but had no desire to hear another person tell me what a horrible person I'd become. Especially not her.

# Chapter 30

"I'm bored," I said to Lainie, who had just walked out of her bedroom into the living room. "Let's go to Mad River and get a drink."

Looking at me through the mirror over the mantle, Lainie smiled. "I love the spontaneity, Jane, but I have plans already."

"Really? Now?" I checked the time on our cable box. It was almost ten p.m. "It's kind of late on a school night." Hoping to get in on the action, I said, "Can I come?"

Lainie peered at her reflection from all angles before turning to me with a sly smile. "You're cute, Jane, but I'm not into the ménage à trois."

Sitting up straighter, I said, "Oh, really. *Those* kinds of plans. Who's the guy?"

"Antoine."

Scanning Lainie's virtual black book, my memory drew a blank. "Who?"

Lainie put her hands on her hips and looked at me like I was a clueless intern at work. "The record producer? The only guy I've been out with in over a month. Remember?"

So that was the guy I'd seen going in and out of Lainie's bedroom the past couple of weeks. I never imagined it was all the same person. Smirking, I said, "Well-traveled tongue man, right? I understand why you'd keep him around."

Shaking her head at me, Lainie said, "That's not the only reason I keep him around."

Still laughing, I said, "Well-hung too?"

Lainie let a small smile escape. "Yes, that too. But, the truth is,

I just like him." Her face turning red, she said, "I think he's a keeper."

I stared at Lainie, my mouth open. In the two years I had lived with her, I could count on one hand, with fingers to spare, the number of guys she hung out with more than twice. And she always referred to those guys as "fuck buddies."

"Maybe you should study for the LSAT. Isn't the exam coming up?"

Waving my hand at her, I said, "Hold on. A keeper? What happened to playing the field?"

"Been there. Done that. Besides, I recall being told the only reason to play the field is to find the right guy." Lainie removed her coat from the hall closet. After putting it on, she turned to me. "Maybe Antoine is the right guy."

Dragging my slippers along the wood floor as I walked back to my room, I mumbled, "Doubt it," under my breath. Loud enough for Lainie to hear, I said, "Have fun. Tell Antoine I said hi."

After Lainie left, I flopped on top of my covers and thought about what she had said about Antoine being the right guy. The more I thought about it, the angrier I became. Lainie was such a hypocrite.

I recalled the many times I'd sat on the edge of her bed and told her about a great date with Jim or Cory and she'd accused me of gushing. Suddenly Antoine was a keeper?

I climbed out of bed and ran a brush through my hair, remembering her telling me I was wasting my most attractive years dreaming about a happily-ever-after with one guy when I should be exercising my sex muscles on the freeway of love that was New York City while I still could—before the wrinkles and gray hairs made their appearance. Now she wanted to be in a monogamous relationship?

As I puckered my lips and applied plumping lip gloss, I remembered one time, when she was standing particularly high up on her soapbox, she actually had the nerve to say I was taking up prime real estate in Manhattan when I'd be just as happy in small town America, barefoot and pregnant. I bet she already had a name picked out for her and Antoine's first-born child. I slipped off my pajama pants, pulled on a pair of blue jeans, and threw a deep V-neck royal blue sweater over my white lace camisole. Deciding against wearing a jacket, I walked briskly around the corner to Mad River.

It was crowded for a Sunday night, but bars were almost always packed in New York every night of the week. I saw one empty bar stool next to two twenty-something guys and, happy for the opening line, smiled. "Is this seat taken?" I stood up straighter hoping my chest would entice them to engage me in flirtatious banter.

The guys turned away from the television set above the bar and, without so much as the "Manhattan once-over," the less attractive of the two said, "Don't think so" before turning back to the screen. Basketball. I was through pretending to like sports for a guy. Let the guy pretend to like chick flicks for me instead.

Figuring there had to be guys at the bar who would rather talk to a pretty girl than watch tall, gangly, sweaty men shoot hoops, I ordered a glass of water and swiveled my bar stool so I was facing the crowd. I quickly dismissed the pockets of girls and those boy/girl combinations that were probably on a date, until my eyes focused on a group of three guys laughing amongst themselves. One was significantly taller than the others and, with his unruly brown hair, reminded me of Bob. I left my glass on the bar and headed in his direction. As he came closer into my view, I noticed his shirt and had second thoughts about approaching a guy who would be seen in public wearing a shirt emblazed with designs of foreign currency. By the time, I removed my focus away from his shirt, I realized I was busted.

His significantly better dressed friend poked him in the arm and, grinning at me, said, "Can you please tell my friend he's wearing the ugliest shirt in the bar?"

By now, I no longer cared what he was wearing and was simply appreciative of the attention. I pretended to examine his shirt to consider how tacky it was, even though I already had a strong opinion. Very tacky. "Well, I can't imagine male models will be strutting down the runway in that particular shirt anytime soon."

Tacky Shirt Guy looked down at his shirt and back up at me with a twinkle in his dark blue eyes. "But it's a great conversation starter, ain't it? You wouldn't be talking to us otherwise."

Whatever worked. I raised my eyebrows.

Chiming in, Significantly Better Dressed Guy said, "What brings you here tonight? You here with anyone?"

"Nope. Just me." Not wanting them to think I had no friends, I said, "My roommate was supposed to come but didn't feel well, and I was really thirsty." I hoped I sounded casual and relaxed.

Tacky Shirt Guy glanced at my empty hand. "Where's your drink?"

"I guess I forgot to buy one." Hint hint.

"Can I buy one for you?"

I held his eye contact a few seconds longer than normal. "That would be nice."

He motioned for me to follow him to the bar and we stood behind the two guys who had ignored me earlier. They were still watching basketball. I wanted them to turn around and see I had found more interesting guys to talk to, but they remained entranced by the game.

Tacky Shirt Guy maneuvered his body to face me while keeping his eyes on the bar to catch the bartender's attention. "I'm Steve, by the way."

"I'm Jane."

"So, Jane, do you go to bars by yourself often? Not that I'm complaining, mind you."

"Actually, I've never done this before. I was bored at home."

Steve looked at me doubtfully. "Sure. I bet you use that line all of the time to get free drinks."

I felt my face get warm and defensively said, "No way."

Steve shook his head. "Whatever you say." But the twinkle was back in his eyes and I knew he was teasing me.

I playfully pushed him in the arm. "Whatever *you* say."

"I say, what are you drinking?"

"Do they have cider?" I watched Steve survey the beers on tap before turning back to me. "Yeah, they have Magners."

I gave him a thumbs up, even though I'd never tasted it before. I was psyched to tell Lainie I had met three guys, one of whom bought me a drink. Although she probably wouldn't care now that she had *Antoine*.

Steve handed me my drink. I followed him back to where his friends were standing, leaning over the Touch Tunes digital jukebox.

I took a sip of my cider, totally psyched to have the attention of three cute guys. Steve smiled brightly, and I decided he was seriously adorable despite his ugly shirt. I was pleased he was the one who seemed to take the most interest in me, although the attention of three men was three times better than the attention of just one.

Steve said, "What? Was there a sale somewhere? It's about time you guys got here."

After a confused moment, I realized Steve wasn't talking to me. Three girls had walked over and he had pulled one of them into an embrace. I observed the six individuals pair off into couples of two, and suddenly it was like I wasn't in the room. I took another sip of cider, not sure what else to do, and hoped someone would remember I was standing there.

The fingers of his free hand now laced with the fingers of a petite and pretty blonde girl, Steve pointed at me. "Meet Jane, girls. She looked lonely all by herself, so we bought her a cider."

The girls smiled at me. "Hi Jane," they said in unison.

One of the girls, who I thought I recognized from the gym, except her shiny black hair now cascaded down her shoulders instead of in a long, smooth ponytail, looked at me with pity. "That's so sad. You can totally hang out with us if you want."

"Yeah, definitely," Steve's girlfriend agreed.

I dropped my gaze to the dirty bar floor, focusing on a cocktail napkin that looked like it had been stepped on repeatedly but still hadn't attached itself to anyone's shoe. I took another sip of cider, felt it starting to go to my head, and willed myself to look up and fake a confident smile. I nodded in Steve's direction. "I appreciate it, but I'm going to call one of my friends. We planned to maybe meet later. Thanks for the drink. Nice meeting you guys." I calmly walked back to my old spot at the bar where I planned to pretend to text a friend in case Steve and his posse were still watching me, but the space was now occupied by a couple. The girl was sitting on the bar stool, her body angled toward her date who was standing between her legs. His back was to the two guys who were still riveted to the basketball game.

Uncertain as to my next move but not ready to end the night on a sour note, I headed to the bathroom line to pass the time and hopefully flirt with a guy on his way out. There was one girl already waiting. I smiled and asked, "Someone in there?" just as her phone rang. She nodded to me before raising the phone to her ear and saying, "Where are you?" Then she rolled her eyes at me and mouthed, "Boyfriends."

I gave her a sympathetic smile, although it was obvious she was not looking for pity and more likely bragging about her attached romantic status.

She was still on the phone when the bathroom became available and while she and her boyfriend probably engaged in phone sex in the women's room, at least six guys went in and out of the men's room. I smiled at each of them. When one came out and saw me still standing there, he grinned, showing a mouthful of yellow teeth. "You're still waiting? So glad I'm not a chick."

He was unattractive, but at least he was speaking to me. "If she doesn't come out soon, I might have to pretend to be a guy for a few minutes." I looked at him from underneath my lashes. "Think anyone would notice?"

Scratching his bald spot, he laughed. "We'd notice. But we probably wouldn't mind."

"I'd mind though. He's taken," said the girl who suddenly

appeared by his side. Her mouse-like black eyes darted up and down the length of my body. She kissed him on the cheek, and said, "C'mon, honey" before dragging him away with her chubby hands.

I left the bar without peeing. I didn't have to go that bad anyway.

# Chapter 31

I wished I hadn't gone out. I'd been hoping for some harmless male attention to boost my ego. Instead I'd been reminded that virtually every other female in my age range was part of a couple while I stood alone in a bar packed with people, feeling invisible and unlovable. I had two voicemails, so apparently two people cared I was alive. Unless both calls were from the same person. Or wrong numbers.

Alone in the apartment, I sat on my bed and dialed into voicemail, feeling tears building behind my eyes and hoping for some good news. The first message was from Bob asking me to call him back as soon as I got the message. I listened to the second message. It was my mom asking if I'd heard the news about Bob and Trish.

I felt the color drain from my face and the hairs stand up on the back of my neck. I had a feeling I knew exactly to what news my mom was referring. I was glad I only had one drink at the bar, because otherwise I might have thrown up. I felt like someone had punched me hard right in the belly, even though Bob's good news technically had nothing to do with me. Instead of being happy for Bob, all I could think about was whether I'd ever get married. I'd die if they had a short engagement and I wasn't with someone by the wedding. There was no way I was going to my ex-boyfriend's wedding stag.

With a pit in my stomach, I contemplated who to call first, Bob or my mom, since I knew both calls would leave me equally miserable.

It was past eleven, but I knew under the circumstances they'd both be awake. I made my choice.

"Hi, Mom," I said, faking cheeriness.

"Did you hear the news?"

"About Bob and Trish? Yes. Well, kind of," I mumbled.

"What do you think?"

"About what?" What thoughts was I supposed to have about my ex-boyfriend of nine years proposing to his "rebound" girl?

My mom said, "They're thinking next spring. How do you feel?"

"I'm happy for them." I really was. Sort of. I just would have preferred they be happy for *me* first.

The remainder of the conversation consisted of me responding with "uh-huh" or "yup" whenever there was a pause in the conversation, and I assumed my mom was waiting for me to say something. She might have suggested I jump in a cab and head over to Bob's place to fight Trish to the death for all I heard. I stopped listening after she said, "next spring," and felt pangs of nausea like I guessed some of my single friends felt senior year in high school when talk turned to the prom and they didn't know who, if anyone, would ask them. I never had those concerns. I always had a boyfriend. I always had Bob. Soon I'd receive an invitation to his wedding and worry about who to bring as my date. Maybe I'd find an excuse to decline the invitation. Or maybe I'd be practicing law pro bono in some underprivileged country. I could defend innocent people who were wrongly accused of crimes. Or I could prosecute the men in Guyana who brutally raped women without repercussion. The assistant DA on *Law and Order: SVU* took a leave of absence to do that.

Back in my room, I refocused on the conversation.

"Your father and I will buy them something off of the registry on behalf of the family, but under the circumstances, it would be nice for you to give them a gift from just you."

"Mom?"

"Yes?"

I wanted her to tell me I'd done the right thing. Bob was my first love, but not my great love. I needed her to tell me it would be okay. "Is Dad there?"

"Yes, it's late though. He's in bed."

I heard my father say, "I'll take it" in the background and then, "Hiya, Pumpkin" into the phone.

My voice quivering, I said, "Hi, Daddy."

"Crazy news about Bob, huh?"

*Not as crazy as going to a bar by yourself and accepting a pity drink from a guy in an ugly shirt.* "Yeah, it is."

"Between you and me, munchkin, he's making a mistake." Whispering, he said, "No one should get married before thirty. We'll get you on partnership track, and then you can focus on getting married. Don't tell your mother."

A small smile escaping, I said, "Sounds like a plan."

"Bob wasn't the one for you anyway. I'd prefer you choose a guy who is shorter than your old man for one."

"I'll do my best. I love you."

"Love you too, sweetheart. How's the studying going? Only a few weeks away from the big day."

"It's going great, Dad." I closed my eyes and bit back a sob.

After we hung up, I searched for Bob's number on my phone. I had my finger on the call button but hesitated to press it. I glanced at my clock radio. It was almost midnight. Too late to call an ex. Even if it was to congratulate him on his engagement. I put the phone down, removed my jeans and sweater, and got into bed. I stared at the ceiling, thinking I should get up and study. As my dad reminded me, I was running out of time, but motivation was outside of my reach. I turned onto my stomach, my head pressed into the pillow. I replayed in my mind the moment I knew Bob and I were no longer in love—when he told the story of how we got together for the umpteenth time, and instead of laughing and looking up at him lovingly, I made a quick getaway to the ladies' room and splashed cold water on my face. It was my decision to break up, but he didn't fight me on it. Would he have fought for

Trish? And if so, was it because she was the right girl? Or was Trish simply the type of girl men fought for while I was the type of girl men left without looking back?

Desperate for comfort, I went searching in the only place that never let me down—my food pantry. I headed to the kitchen and removed a large stock pot, a frying pan, and a soup pot from the cabinet above the sink. Then I collected my ingredients and placed them on the counter. Leeks were notoriously sandy and dirty, and very good at hiding it, so I washed them thoroughly before cutting off and discarding the root ends and the thick dark green parts. I melted butter in a large soup pot while I chopped the leeks and some garlic, added the potatoes, chicken stock, bay leaves, thyme, salt and pepper. While waiting for them to boil, I fried up strips of bacon and basked in the smell of them crisping to a delicious finish. By the time I was through, I'd made enough potato leek soup to feed Lainie and me for the next few days and found enough peace to finally fall asleep.

# Chapter 32

I stared at my computer screen where I had typed "Hi Bob" in the text of a new email. I pressed the delete button until the screen was blank. It wouldn't be right to congratulate him in an email. Especially since he had called me personally to break the news.

I took a deep breath, placed a hand over my rapidly beating heart, and picked up my work phone. As it rang, I silently prayed for voicemail.

"You've reached Bob."

I mouthed "thank you" to my office ceiling and waited for the beep.

"Hello?"

"Bo—Bob?"

"Nope. Just Bob," he said laughing.

"I thought it was your voicemail," I said in dread.

"Nope, I'm here. Hey Jane."

"Uh, hi." Remembering the point of my call, I said, "Congratulations! My mom told me."

"Thanks. I figured you were out last night with one of your new boyfriends."

Nope, just Tacky Shirt Guy, Yellow Teeth Dude, and *their* girlfriends. "Yes, I was out. Sorry I got home too late to call you back."

"No problem. Thanks for calling."

"Of course." I scooped a handful of paper clips from the holder on my desk and began separating the large ones into a separate compartment. "You guys must be super stoked. Send my best wishes to Trish."

"I will. We're planning to have an engagement party."

*Great.* "Great!"

"Did your mom tell you how I proposed?"

"No. Tell me."

Speaking quickly and enthusiastically, Bob said, "I told Trish I needed new cuff links and asked her to help me pick them out. I had already told the jeweler to place the engagement ring in the center of the container with the cuff links. When the jeweler asked if I wanted to take a closer look at any of them, I gestured to the ring, and when he gave it to me, I got down on one knee and proposed."

I bit my lip to stop it from trembling. "Wow." I tried to form other words but gave up and said, "Wow" again.

"Yeah, it was legendary," Bob said proudly.

"Epic," I agreed.

"Anyway, thanks for calling, Jane. Wish I had more time to talk, but I'm slammed and we have dinner with both sets of parents tonight."

"Then I'll let you go. Congratulations again."

After we hung up, I stared at the phone and ignored the tears making their way from my eyes down to my chin.

"Jane? Are you all right?"

I absently looked over at Andrew, who was wide-eyed with concern. "No," I said. I had completely forgotten he was in the room.

"What's wrong?"

Wiping my eyes, I swallowed back my tears. "Nothing." But the tears were stronger than my resolve not to shed them. I had to get out of there fast. I calmly stood up, straightened out my skirt, and walked out of the office. I looked both ways and, certain no one was in the hallway, ran to the bathroom.

Alone in the stall, I stood up and banged my head repeatedly against the door in frustration. In between gasps for air, I softly cried, "What's wrong with me? Why doesn't anyone want me? Why? Why? Why?" until someone joined me in the bathroom and I willed myself to keep quiet. I waited patiently, biting my lip again to keep silent while my bathroom buddy did her thing. I stood still while she washed her hands. It wasn't until I heard the door of the bathroom close that I finally opened the door of my stall and walked to the sink. My face was blotchy like I got a bad sunburn and my eyes and lips were swollen. Since I didn't have any makeup to apply, I lightly tapped on my cheeks, hoping the swelling would go away, and I removed the excess makeup from the corners of my eyes. I hoped Andrew had taken his lunch hour so I'd be alone in the office to compose myself.

He hadn't. He had pulled his chair closer to my desk and was reading Christopher Moore's *Island of the Sequined Love Nun*. I stood next to him and coughed until he looked up.

"Can I help you, Andrew?"

Andrew dropped the book in his lap and pursed his lips. His head was cocked to the side and he was looking at me strangely. Finally, he said, "Nope. But if you tell me why you're crying, I might be able to help you."

I walked around his chair and sat down in mine. I was locked out of my computer, so while I reinserted my password, I told him, "Thanks, but no thanks. Besides, I thought you didn't like me anymore."

"Of course, I like you, Jane. You've just been strange lately..." Andrew sighed, "...not acting yourself."

Still unable to look at him, I continued to focus on my computer screen. "Not this again. Being myself has gotten me nowhere. At least Frankie was having fun."

"Frankie?" Andrew shook his head. "Strange. See what I mean?"

"If you must know, I was trying to do what you said. Nail 'em and leave 'em. And it was working."

Andrew's mouth fell open. "Really?"

Heat rose up my neck as I clarified my previous statement. "Well, not nail 'em, exactly. Just that one time. But, you know, not care so much. Be in control for a change."

"I'd love to hear about that one time." Standing up, Andrew said, "First things first. I'm starving. Let's go out to lunch—Cafe Europa. You can get one of those 'make your own salads' you girls cream over."

I rolled my eyes. "Nice, Andrew."

Andrew gestured to the door. "Coming?"

I grabbed my purse from behind my chair. "I'm right behind you."

Twenty minutes later, Andrew and I were seated at a table in Cafe Europa. I was eating a mixed green salad with tomato, cucumbers, carrots, mushrooms, chicken, and some blue cheese and Thousand Island dressing to add actual taste. Andrew was having a buffalo chicken wrap, a bag of salt and vinegar potato chips, and a can of Dr. Pepper.

As I observed him swallow half of his wrap in three bites, I marveled at how some people could eat whatever they wanted and not get fat, while even when I religiously worked out five times a week and starved myself on salad, I still had to wear Spanx and lie on my back to zip up my size-eight jeans. If I was PMSing and bloated, forget about it. Sure, I could nix the blue cheese and substitute fat-free dressing, but I'd probably not fit into a size six anyway and, instead, would be miserable, hungry and wind up with my head in a bag of mini Three Musketeers bars three hours later. So I was stuck with my, in online dating terms, "about average" body.

I waited until Andrew finished chewing. "My ex got engaged."

Andrew put down his soda can and pushed his plate to the center of the table signifying he was finished. "Ahh. So that's what the tears were about."

"It's not because I want him back. I don't."

Andrew nodded. "But you didn't want him to move on before you."

"Exactly. I always thought I'd get married first. I'm so ready. He's so immature. Like a little boy." I glanced down at the remnants of my salad. I wasn't hungry anymore.

"Men are boys 'til the day they die, Jane. Doesn't mean they're not capable of getting married and having kids."

I recoiled at his last words. "Kids? Don't even go there. I'll die if he has kids while I…"

"While you what, Jane?" Andrew held my gaze as if willing me to try to turn away.

I reluctantly answered, "Don't even have a boyfriend."

"You're not gonna get a boyfriend if you jerk guys around like you did with Brandon and Don," Andrew said matter-of-factly.

I slammed my fist on the table. "That's what you told me to do."

Andrew shook his head. "I meant you should stop taking it all so seriously and not think of every guy as 'the one.'"

"No. My sister used those words. You told me to, and I repeat for all the kids watching at home, 'nail 'em and leave 'em.'"

Andrew raised his chin defiantly. "You're preaching to the perverted, babe, and I stand by my advice. But I didn't mean you should toy with other people to build your own ego, which, let's face it, is the only reason you pretended to be interested in Brandon and Don."

"I wasn't pretending, Andrew. They're really nice guys and I liked them both, but I was acting in the moment and didn't give any thought to what would happen next. I was enjoying the attention because they made me feel pretty and wanted, and…" My voice dropped off as I realized I'd proved Andrew's statement.

He raised an eyebrow.

"It's not like guys have never flirted with me for the fun of it with no intention of asking me out. Tacky Shirt Guy bought me a drink even though he had a girlfriend."

Andrew blinked at me. "You lost me at Tacky Shirt Guy."

I sighed. "My point is why do guys get to play with my feelings, but I can't play with theirs? Kind of a double standard, don't you think?"

"Those guys you dated last year who blew you off were jerks, Jane. You deserve better than them, but you shouldn't hold their behavior against the entire male gender." Andrew stacked my tray on top of his, stood up, and walked to the garbage can with both of them.

When he returned I said, "I think I'm done with dating. Guys are assholes. I'm just going to be the best lawyer ever and live man-free."

"Do what you need to do. But, so you know, not all guys are assholes."

Throughout the remainder of the day, I kept hearing Andrew's words, "Not all guys are assholes." As I rode the subway home later, I glared at the cute corporate guy reading the *Wall Street Journal* directly across from me and thought about the guys whose acquaintance I'd been unfortunate to make over the last six months. They'd certainly done little to support Andrew's statement. Randall was an asshole supreme, and Cory was definitely in the same category. As Corporate Guy looked up from his paper and glared back at me, I quickly looked away. He was probably an asshole too, but even men, I guessed, should be seen as innocent until proven guilty. In truth, there were some decent men in my life. I had to admit, Bob was not an asshole. Score one for men. Claire's Kevin had, so far, been nothing but loyal and sweet. My heart warmed, remembering the picture Claire had emailed me earlier in the week. Apparently, Kevin had been kind enough to match Claire's weight gain, pound for pound. If that wasn't anti-asshole behavior, what was? And, of course, my father was a shining example of non-asshole-like men. So score two and three for men.

I stood up in anticipation of the train's arrival at 77th Street. So did Corporate Guy. The stop was popular for guys in their twenties and early thirties. Maybe he added to the decent men quota too. I attempted to make eye contact to silently apologize for the dirty looks I gave him earlier, but he rushed off the train and was up the stairs before I had a chance. On my walk home, I tried to think of other good guys and immediately remembered Andrew. Despite telling me to date like a man, I got the feeling he was something of a romantic. Maybe I shouldn't have flirted with both of his friends in the same night when I had no intention of going out with either of them. If I'd met either of them before being blown off by Randall, Jim, and Cory, I would have been happy to go on a date with either of them. At least if they ghosted me, they'd have to answer to Andrew.

It was kind of him to treat me to lunch and try to convince me not to hold bad behavior by a few rotten apples against the entire male race. I now understood why all of the female paralegals flirted with him. I always thought he was a bit goofy, but his concern was sweet and sexy. I peeked in the window of Pick-a-Bagel, contemplating whether to buy something for dinner. I really had to study for the LSAT and reluctantly decided it was more efficient to pick up food than waste precious study time cooking. I'd buy a sandwich for Lainie too. Maybe I'd ask her to tell me more about Antoine, since it seemed her interest in him extended beyond that of a carnal nature.

I scooped out the insides of my bagel and tossed them in the garbage. I sat back down at our kitchen table and, while spreading low-fat vegetable cream cheese on both sides, I said to Lainie, "I think my officemate Andrew at work might have feelings for me."

Lainie looked up from her bowl of potato leek soup. She opted to save the turkey sandwich I bought her for lunch the next day. "Did he say something?"

Shaking my head, I said, "Not exactly." I paused while trying to find the best words to describe it. "It's just he's...well, he's a guy's guy, totally crude, and he definitely plays around. But he's so nice and patient with me. He's always telling me I'm better than these losers who keep blowing me off."

Lainie got up and grabbed a large bottle of Snapple iced tea from the fridge and two glasses. After she sat down and poured us both a glass, she said, "I keep telling you the same thing."

I smiled at Lainie, who had surprised me more than once with her pep talks. "I know. But you're my friend. You have to say those things. Andrew has nothing to gain by being sweet."

"Do you like him?"

I tried to picture Andrew moving in to kiss me and was able to visualize myself leaning into him. "I never thought about it until now. Since we share an office, it could be awkward. But, yeah, maybe I do. I don't know. It's worth exploring, right?"

Lainie raised an eyebrow. "That's what dating is about Jane. Go for it. But don't get your hopes up."

"I won't. By the way, how do your parents feel about Antoine? Is he the 'eligible bachelor' they had in mind? Have they reserved the church?" I joked.

Lainie shook her head. "The folks are still on a need-to-know basis."

"Gotcha," I said, taking a bite of my bagel. "Your secret is safe with me."

Later, as I searched my closet for something flattering to wear to work the next day, my phone rang—Claire again. I'd completely forgotten to return her message from before, but I wasn't in the mood to talk to her tonight. Better I wait to see how things played out with Andrew. Last time I spoke to my sister, I was in a bad place after being dumped by Cory for no reason whatsoever. I'd rather wait until I felt better about things so I could give her good news for a change. It was time I stopped trying to protect myself from getting hurt by pretending not to care. I wasn't fooling anyone and, Andrew was right, the guys who had hurt me were jerks, but not all guys were. As soon as I got my love life back on track, I'd call Claire back and fess up about my one-night stand with Buddy.

# Chapter 33

When I arrived at work the next morning, Andrew was already sitting at his desk. I smiled brightly at him. "Good morning." He waved and motioned to the cell phone he was holding against his ear.

I mouthed, "Sorry" and logged onto my computer while trying to overhear his conversation. All I got was, "Sounds good. Talk to you later" before he hung up, turned to me, and said, "Feeling better today, Jane?"

"Much. Thanks so much for lunch yesterday. I needed that."

"No problem. I wasn't sure if I'd made you feel better or worse."

"Better. Definitely better. It just took a few hours for your words to sink in."

"So I don't have to worry about you studying law from a convent?"

I felt my face flush, which I hated. "No. I've decided giving up on men would be a premature decision."

Andrew winked. "Good. The male race thanks you."

Feeling my blush deepen, I said, "Speaking of thank you, I'd like to take you out for drinks to express my appreciation for being so nice to me."

"Totally not necessary, Jane. But who am I to refuse drinks?"

Figuring I would seem too anxious if I pushed him for a date, I just laughed and turned toward my computer, trying to force the smile off my face.

"I'm free Thursday."

I looked over at Andrew and beamed. "Thursday it is."

# Chapter 34

Andrew didn't come to work on Wednesday. I worried he was sick and we'd need to postpone our drinks for the next day. I was also nervous about how to broach the subject of kicking our relationship up a notch. I didn't think he'd reject me, but I also knew he wouldn't make the first move, and why should he? He knew I dated a lot, and I'd even flirted with two of his friends. He probably had no idea I liked him. I wished I hadn't wasted so much time on other guys when Andrew was there the entire time, but I wouldn't look backwards—onward and upward.

I would wait until we'd had at least one drink, so I'd be less tense and it wouldn't come out rehearsed. But I'd rehearsed it, make no mistake. My father always said, "Chance favors the prepared mind."

I had planned to go shopping with Marissa after work for an anniversary present for Katherine and Katherine's husband, Martin, but I called to see if she'd come over to help me pick out an outfit for my date with Andrew instead. It was almost five p.m. I was still at work and supposed to meet Marissa at six outside of Crate & Barrel.

Marissa said, "I really need to get going on this. The entire family is getting together on Sunday to celebrate. Our parents, his parents, Katherine, Martin, and, of course, me." Attempting a laugh, she added, "No date, of course. Anyway, I really need your help. My idea of domesticity is Ramen noodles in a hot pot. I have no clue what to buy a couple on their first anniversary."

I pondered sending Andrew a text to make sure he was okay.

"Jane!"

Startled, I said, "I'm here."

"You promise if I come to you tonight, you'll shop with me on Friday after work?"

"Promise." I decided not to text Andrew and hope for the best.

Later that night, Marissa and I rummaged through my closet for the optimum outfit.

Marissa pulled a pair of black dress pants from my closet. "What about these with your white silk blouse and red patent pumps? Katherine suggested wearing high heels so your legs would look longer and slimmer, but I told her Andrew wasn't that tall."

Shaking my head, I said, "Too corporate. We'll probably go someplace more casual. Andrew likes pubs. And why did you tell Katherine about my drinks with Andrew?"

"Where do you think you'll go?"

Aware that Marissa conveniently ignored my question, I scratched my head and scrutinized the pile of clothes in front of me. "I don't know. We haven't discussed it." Neither of us had mentioned going out since Tuesday morning when we'd agreed on Thursday. I was worried he'd forgotten and hoped he'd bring it up first so I wouldn't have to. I picked my gray pants off the floor. "Screw it. I'll just wear these pants and my black cashmere sweater and boots. It's not like Andrew doesn't see me every day. He either likes me or he doesn't."

"You're right." Marissa paused and then said, "But wear your pushup bra anyway."

"Couldn't hurt. And my sexiest thong." I grimaced when I remembered I'd left my favorite one at Claire's apartment and still hadn't called her back.

Looking at me questioningly, Marissa said, "You're not planning to sleep with him on the first date, are you?"

I'd known Andrew for years, so it wasn't really a first date, but I hadn't thought about having sex with him. It might be weird since we'd have to work with each other the next day. Although it could also be a sexy secret, like Meredith and Derek on the first season of *Grey's Anatomy.*

Interrupting my thoughts, Marissa said, "It's kind of premature to think about sleeping together, since you haven't even told him how you feel yet. Have you thought about what you'll say if he doesn't like you back?"

"Of course," I lied. "But I can't see this going badly. Andrew flirts with a lot of girls, but he's different with me. More caring. Each time I imagine the conversation, he's relieved and laughs at me for being so blind. The only thing I can't picture is what happens next. Do we just kiss and make plans to hang out again or do we move right to boyfriend and girlfriend?"

Marissa bit her lip. "I don't know. I always think it's smart to plan for the worst-case scenario." She bent down to fold some of the sweaters I had thrown from my dresser drawer onto the floor. Looking up at me, she said, "I have a date next week too. A guy from Match. I broke down and joined one of the paid sites like you suggested."

I held a hot pink sweater against my chest. "Or should I wear this one instead?" Marissa stared at me blankly. "What?"

She put her hands on her hips. "Did you even hear what I said? About my joining Match?"

"Oh, sorry. That's great. I hope the online dating thing works better for you than it did for me. I didn't go on a single date from eHarmony."

"He's thirty-one, a trader and looks cute. I prefer the creative type, but you never know."

"At least you're used to being disappointed."

Marissa frowned, her naturally full lips protruding in a pout that could rival Lisa Rinna, and slid to the floor. "What's that supposed to mean?"

Noting the defensive tone in her voice, I bent down next to her. "I mean, you've been single so long now, it probably doesn't faze you anymore. Unlike me who had an amazing boyfriend for nine years. He placed the bar very high, and I was completely blindsided."

Jerking her head back, Marissa said, "If I'm hearing you

correctly, you're saying it's okay for my dates to lead nowhere because I'm used to being disappointed, but things should work out for you because you're not?"

"No. I..." I was getting flustered. "But I wasn't expecting to meet one jerk after another when my only experience before was so great."

Marissa looked at me with her forehead scrunched. "I could easily argue that I deserve to fall in love more than you because after all of my bad luck, it's my turn. But I wouldn't say that to my best friend."

"You're twisting around my words." I had no idea how we went from picking out my outfit for drinks with Andrew to fighting. Marissa's lips were quivering and I was afraid she'd cry. "I don't even know what I'm saying anymore, but I absolutely didn't mean to hurt your feelings or imply I deserved loved more than you."

Marissa nodded. "Okay."

"You're not mad?"

"I'm fine. How about tonight we focus on you and Andrew and Friday we can talk about my date?"

"Brilliant plan," I said with a smile. I held the pink sweater in one hand and the black in the other. "Which one?"

After Marissa left, I tried to come up with reasons Andrew might not like me. She was right. Over-confidence was dangerous. It would be embarrassing if he said he thought of me like a sister. Since he had coined the phrase, "nail 'em and leave 'em," maybe he'd say he wasn't looking for anything serious. Although I concluded it was entirely possible the night wouldn't go as planned, I decided I had to try—nothing ventured, nothing gained. Even after imagining the worst-case scenario, I felt strongly that by this time the following night, Andrew and I would be more than friends. And I'd never have to swim in the dating pool again.

# Chapter 35

I tried to cite check cases but kept losing track of what side the cases were supposed to support. So I gave up and organized some documents in chronological order. It was a good time sucker. I was painfully aware of Andrew's every move, from his hands shuffling through papers to his occasional cough to the sounds of him chuckling on the phone. Finally, my patience reached an end. Speaking over the beat of my heart slamming against my chest, I said, "So, where should we go tonight?"

My eyes remained focused on my computer monitor so Andrew wouldn't think I cared all that much. I'd confess my feelings soon enough. For now, I wanted to play it cool.

"How about a glass of wine at Hillstone?"

I was certain he'd suggest someplace fun and laid-back like Redemption or Opal or maybe something more intimate like Vero. The generic Hillstone right around the corner never even crossed my mind. And I hoped he wasn't being literal when he said "a glass" of wine. As in one. That didn't sound like the Andrew I knew. "Sounds good."

"Six thirty?"

"Works for me." I glanced at the time on my phone. Only six hours to go.

At five forty-five, I officially gave up working and went to the bathroom to pretty myself up. I decided early preparation would be less obvious than waiting until right before we were leaving and returning to the office with more volume in my hair and my makeup a little brighter. Especially since I'd never put much effort into looking good in Andrew's presence before.

Our office was empty when I got back. While I waited for six thirty to arrive, I checked my Gmail account. Among the email from eHarmony offering me a free communication weekend and a reminder from Meetup about a singles wine tasting event was an annoying chain letter from Marissa containing a Japanese proverb and instructions to forward along to at least five people to ensure good luck in my future. Normally I would have rolled my eyes and immediately deleted the email, but instead I sent it along to Claire, Lainie, Kevin, and my parents, adding in the text, "Sorry to be annoying, but I need all the luck I can get tonight!"

I hoped my good luck would start immediately and, after my night with Andrew, I would never have to read emails from online dating sites again. As I contemplated what to do with the remaining fifteen minutes, Andrew returned to the office, stood in front of my desk, and said, "Any chance you can get out of here now?"

I said, "Absolutely" while simultaneously closing out all of the windows on my computer.

As soon as I stood up, my work phone rang. Since we had caller ID at work, I knew it was Claire. I debated letting it go to voicemail, but when I remembered the other two messages I still hadn't returned, I picked up. "Hey. I'm sorry I haven't called you back, but I'm on my way out. I promise to call you tomorrow."

"I thought you might want to know the sex of the first person who will ever call you 'Aunt Jane,' but if you're in too much of a hurry, it can wait until tomorrow."

I raised my hand to alert Andrew I'd just be a minute. "Oh my God. What is it? Girl, right? No, boy. Girl? What?"

Laughing, Claire said, "You're going to have a nephew."

"A nephew." I said it slowly, letting the words sink in. My sister was going to have a son, and I was going to be his aunt. He wasn't even born yet and didn't have a name, but I already loved him. "I'm gonna have a nephew. Congrats, big sis!"

"Thanks, little sister. You've been MIA lately and we really need to catch up. Call me tomorrow. I mean it."

"I promise."

After we hung up, I said to Andrew, "Ready when you are."

Andrew grabbed his black messenger bag and walked to the door. He stepped to the side, waving his hand in the direction of the hallway. "Ladies first."

I took a few steps out the door, stopped, and turned around to let him catch up. Smiling, I said, "And they say chivalry is dead."

Andrew winked. "Not when I'm around, it's not."

On our way to the elevator, Andrew said, "So you're gonna have a nephew?"

"You heard, huh?"

"Sure did. Congrats, Aunt Jane."

Andrew stopped walking, so I stopped walking too. "What?"

"If you'd rather hang out with the mom-to-be, we can get a drink another time."

My heart beat rapidly. Was he trying to blow me off? "I'm sure she's busy making calls to everyone and sharing the good news."

Andrew nodded. "I'd hate to get in the way of sisterly bonding."

"Not a chance."

A few minutes later, we walked through the revolving doors of Hillstone, and Andrew pointed toward the couches in the back. Walking ahead of me to an empty one, he said, "No room at the bar, but this works, right?"

I sunk my body into the black leather seat cushion. "Very comfy."

Motioning to the bar, he said, "What are you drinking?"

"Riesling if they have it. Otherwise, Pinot Grigio." I started to get up. "But I'll go. It's on me, remember?"

Andrew shook his head. "I got it."

Feeling like we were on a real date, I nodded and gave him a soft smile.

I watched him walk to the crowded circular bar and patiently wait to get the pretty blonde bartender's attention.

At one point, he turned around and shrugged. I mouthed, "No worries."

At last, Andrew returned to our spot and placed our drinks on the table. He sat next to me on the couch. "Finally."

Sitting side by side that way made it impossible to talk to him comfortably unless I turned my head 45 degrees. So I angled my body to where my knees were level with his thighs. I raised my glass. "Thanks, Andrew."

Clinking his glass of red lightly against my glass of white, he said, "Cheers, Jane."

"What are you drinking?"

Andrew swirled his glass and brought it to his nose. "Argentine Malbec. Nice blackberry finish."

"Wow, you're a wine connoisseur, huh?"

Andrew took a hearty swig from his glass. "Nope. I'm full of shit. Just trying to impress you." He winked.

I blushed. "Mission accomplished."

"How are your cases? I haven't noticed you working crazy hours lately."

"I know. I'm torn between enjoying the stress-free environment and missing the overtime pay. How about you?"

"I billed almost three hundred hours last month." Andrew grinned. "So, not that busy by the firm's standards."

"Yikes."

"But let's not talk about work."

"You brought it up." I took a sip of my drink and felt the sweet liquid slide down my throat and start to warm my insides. I slid slightly closer to Andrew so my knees were almost touching his thighs. "What should we talk about then?"

Andrew appeared to contemplate. "How's your love life?"

I giggled. "Seriously?"

Andrew nodded.

After another sip of wine, my hands shaking slightly, I returned the glass to the table. "Well, considering you just talked me out of joining a convent on Monday, I can say with absolute certainty my love life is not very exciting. Currently." I gave him a meaningful look.

Andrew, wearing a closed-mouth smile, nodded again but didn't say anything.

I took another sip of wine and a deep inhale. I exhaled and with a controlled voice, asked, "What about you?"

Andrew quickly replied, "My love life is outstanding. I met someone I really dig."

I felt my pulse quicken and my mouth go dry. I slid my butt a little farther away from him and took a sip of my drink. Glad for the crutch, I firmly held my glass and took another sip. "I'm so happy for you. Tell me about her."

"We just met actually. But I've seen her every night since Tuesday."

"This past Tuesday?"

Beaming, Andrew nodded. "Crazy, right? She's the vendor for that new document retrieval company."

Still in a semi state of shock, I forced out, "Amazing. I'm thrilled for you."

"Thanks. Strange thing is, I wasn't looking for a girlfriend, but I met her and said 'yowza.' I think you just know when it's right."

Feeling deflated, I said, "I guess" and looked down at my drink. I only had about a quarter left in the glass.

"Your time will come too, Jane. You just have to stop putting so much pressure on yourself."

Averting eye contact, I said, "Easier said than done."

"Timing is everything," he said matter-of-factly.

Although my gaze was downward, with my peripheral vision, I saw him studying me. I faked a smile. "My timing sucks." *Evidently by a measly two days.*

Andrew took the last sip of his drink. "My advice?"

"What?"

"Let things come to you. Trying to control the who, what, and where never works."

"You're right." I finished my drink and raised my empty glass. "Care to share more wisdom over a second glass? This round on me." His relationship, if you could even call it that, was barely a fetus. Surely I could distract him for one night. Maybe he'd change his mind about his girlfriend of the week.

Andrew stood up and stretched. "Thanks, but I should really get going."

"Really? We've only had one. Is your girlfriend waiting for you at home?"

When Andrew raised an eyebrow, I worried I sounded bitter. Grinning, I said, "Just kidding" and pretended to adjust the back of my earring. I stood up and fidgeted with my coat. When I was ready to face him again, I said, "Ready when you are, my friend" as cheerfully as I could.

Andrew smiled and stepped aside to let me pass him. "After you."

Feeling nauseous, I walked past him. "Chivalry is still not dead." *But I wish I was.*

Standing outside of the restaurant, I felt like I was at the end of a really bad blind date. At a loss for more interesting parting words, I said, "How are you getting home?" I prayed he wasn't taking the 6.

Andrew yawned and raised his arms over his head. Stretching from side to side as if part of the cool down in an exercise class, he said, "I'm actually gonna grab a cab and head downtown to Farah's place."

I didn't ask him to confirm that Farah was his newly discovered soul mate.

"We're going to order in Chinese," he said.

"Sounds fun." I took notice of the mass of people walking past us in opposite directions on Lexington Avenue and felt my vision slightly blur. "I'm gonna jump on the subway. Thanks for the drink, Andrew." The ground beneath my feet felt unstable so I said bye and ran down the subway stairs, praying I wouldn't fall and that a train would come quickly. I heard Andrew call out, "See you tomorrow" but didn't stop to turn around.

As I walked toward the turnstile, I heard the recorded announcement, "The next stop is 68th Street," and the sound of the subway doors close. I muttered, "Shit," and tried to hold back my tears. The bench on the platform was dirty, but since I was afraid my legs wouldn't hold out, I sat down and willed another train to come soon. It did. Moments later, I exited on 86th and Lexington. I was afraid Lainie would press me for details if I went home, so instead I walked west toward the closest Williams-Sonoma store hoping to get lost in the aisles of cooking utensils and cutlery. I was examining a copper ten-piece cookware set, when a group of people brushed passed me.

"Great class," one of them said.

"My favorite part was the wine pairing," said someone else.

I put down the cookware set and followed them hoping to overhear more of their conversation, but they walked too fast for me. When I spotted someone wearing a Williams-Sonoma apron, I said, "Did I hear those people say they took a cooking class here?"

The guy nodded. "Yes, we offer weekly classes. You interested?"

I had no idea where in my busy schedule I'd possibly fit a cooking lesson, but for some reason, the possibility intrigued me. I felt a small amount of stress leave my body as I focused on an activity that didn't require a significant other. "Maybe," I said before thanking him and heading home.

# Chapter 36

Thankful Lainie was spending almost every night at Antoine's apartment, I began removing my clothes before I even got to my bedroom. I kicked my shoes into the closet, threw my sweater and pants in a ball on my floor, and tossed my bra across my desk chair. In just my Hanky Panky leopard-print thong, I went to the bathroom and washed my face. Back in my room, I removed my brush and phone from my bag, placed the brush next to my vanity, and checked my phone for messages. I had one voicemail. I sat on my bed with my feet dangling over the edge and listened to it. My dad. His voice made my heart ache. At least *he* loved me. I wiped tears away from the corners of my eyes. He wanted to wish me good luck on the LSAT on Saturday, just in case forwarding the Japanese proverb wasn't enough.

As my heart beat faster, I could feel the color drain from my face and a bead of sweat form under each of my armpits. How had I forgotten about the LSAT exam? It wasn't as if I hadn't known the date was approaching. It was right there in red ink on my desk calendar. But instead of buckling down, as I planned to do, something (or someone) else kept distracting me and now my time had run out. I could count on my hands the number of hours I'd studied since the one-year anniversary of my breakup with Bob and my disastrous reentry into the dating world, and I was as ill-prepared to sit for the exam in two days as if I hadn't taken a single practice test. My future as a partner in my father's law firm (or even an attorney for Legal Aid) was looking as bleak as my love life. I cried myself to sleep hoping I'd wake up and it would be January instead of March, but my luck was as thin as my time, and I woke up the next morning, the day before the test, just as unready as I was when I'd gone to bed. I pressed snooze twice before turning off the alarm and leaving a message with the head paralegal that I was not feeling well and wouldn't be in to work. I knew I had taken quite a few sick days in the past few months, but figured I had enough goodwill in the bank after a year of almost perfect attendance aside from vacation days. I went back to bed until three p.m. when my cell phone rang. Marissa. I let it go to voicemail, turned over on my stomach, and fell back asleep until my phone rang again. Marissa again. I reluctantly grabbed the phone from my nightstand.

"Can we talk later, Ris? I'm not up for a conversation right now."

"What's wrong? I tried you at work and the receptionist said you were out sick."

I buried my head under the pillow and mumbled into the phone, "Yes, sick. Sick and tired."

"What happened? Did you and Andrew get drunk last night?"

"Ha!"

"Huh?"

"No, we didn't get drunk last night." I sighed loudly and came out from under the pillow.

"Well, you can tell me all about it tonight."

"Tonight?" I flipped over and lay on my back, resting the pillow on my chest.

"Yes, tonight. When you help me shop for Katherine and Martin's anniversary gift."

I remembered. "Marissa, I'm sorry but I can't go anywhere tonight."

"Why not? Jane, you promised."

"The LSAT is tomorrow."

"It is? Why didn't you say something before?"

"Because I forgot."

"You forgot to tell me?"

"No, I forgot to study."

"How? Studying for the LSAT is all you've been talking about since you signed up months ago. Well, it was until recently. What are you doing to do? Are you going to take it anyway?" Marissa asked.

"I don't know how I forgot, and I don't know what I'm going to do aside from not taking the test tomorrow. Can we stop the question and answer session of this conversation?" I pleaded.

In a soft voice, Marissa said, "You can take the test the next time it's offered, right? When is that?"

"In four months," I mumbled into my pillow.

"It's not the end of the world. You'll study and take it then."

"And I'll have to delay enrollment in law school by a semester."

"On the bright side, at least you'll earn more money by working for an extra six months."

Her mention of work reminded me of what else had happened the night before. "And Andrew has a girlfriend."

"No way," Marissa said with a groan.

"He just met her on Tuesday. Can you believe it?"

"Oh, Jane, that sucks." She chuckled. "I told you to prepare for the worst-case scenario."

"So not funny." My head hurt like I had drunk a bottle of wine and not just a glass.

"Since you're not taking the exam tomorrow, why don't you let me cheer you up tonight? We can pick up Katherine and Martin's gift and then do anything you want. I'll even watch you eat sushi if it will make you feel better."

"Is that all you can think about? The stupid gift for Katherine and Martin? How selfish can you be?"

Marissa gasped. "*I'm* being selfish?"

"I've heard enough about Katherine and Martin's dumb gift. Isn't being married a good enough present for them?"

"Are you out of your mind? For the last few months, I've been a supporting character in Jane's world. All you do is talk about yourself. I let it slide because you've been going through some weird phase and that's what best friends do, but you can't do one favor for me and then have the nerve to call me selfish? It's obvious whose needs are more important in this friendship."

My mouth opened and closed like a fish. I'd never heard Marissa sound so cross before. "I'm sorry."

She sighed. "You've been saying that a lot lately. I'm beginning to think it's just words and I'm sick of it."

"It's not just words. I'm sor..." Assuming another apology wouldn't go over well, I changed direction and said, "How about we go to the mall tomorrow after I've had a chance to let this latest mess sink in?" There was silence on the other end of the phone. "Marissa?" It was pointless as she had already hung up. I knew I should call her back, but I couldn't bring myself to do anything but turn over on my stomach and go back to sleep.


I was thinking about how fantastic it would be if I could turn the men in my life into beady-eyed mice with the mere wiggle of my nose, when the sound of my phone ringing woke me from my *Bewitched*-imposed stupor.

Instantly nauseous, I picked up the phone. "Hi Daddy."

"Hey, Pumpkin. Getting ready?"

"Um-hmm."

"I think you should stop studying and just get some rest now. Probably not much more preparation you can do at this point. Better to relax."

Pulling the covers over my chin, I said, "If you say so."

"Knock 'em dead, kiddo."

"Will do."

"Call us tomorrow."

"Bye Daddy." After I hung up, I wiggled my nose wishing my dad would magically appear to tuck me in and make the last few months a bad dream.

# Chapter 37

By the time daylight peeked through my blinds early Saturday morning, my body was sore from having spent so much time in bed. The first thing I did was call Marissa to make good on my promise to go to the mall and pick up a gift for Katherine and Martin. When voicemail picked up, I left a message apologizing for how things went down the night before and asking what time she wanted to go to the mall. I took a quick shower and waited for Marissa to call me back. When I didn't hear back in an hour, I sent her a text that I was heading out of the city to avoid running into my sister or anyone else who might tell my parents they saw me when I was supposed to be taking the LSAT. Then I jumped in a cab and told the driver to take me to the closest PATH Station. I figured the likelihood of running into Claire or any other member of the Frank family in Hoboken, New Jersey was slim.

When the cab stopped at 33rd Street, I wished I had told the driver to take me to the less tourist populated 23rd or 14th instead. After weaving in and out of the Macy's traffic and fighting the urge to stop and buy a new bottle of my favorite Ralph Lauren Romance perfume from one of the many sidewalk vendors, I finally made it to the top of the platform stairs. As if I actually had someplace to be, I quickly ran down the stairs and followed the signs to the PATH train to New Jersey. I almost collided with a group of young guys, all dressed in green and wearing green beaded necklaces. As I walked past, one shouted, "Erin Go Braugh" in my face. I turned around to look at them, muttered, "What the hell," and quickly ran to the turnstile and swiped my Metro Card.

After I got my bearings, I scanned the various tracks. I had no idea which one went to Hoboken. I had never been there but was told it was only a mile from one end to the other, much smaller than my other option, Jersey City. I figured a mile of exploration plus the commute there and back would take me about as long as the LSAT.

Of the four tracks, two were closed, one was empty save for about ten people either sitting quietly on benches or intently looking at their phones, and one was jam packed with more people dressed in green screaming over each other. Hoping it was the empty one, I tentatively approached a mousy-looking woman sitting on a bench reading a paper. "Excuse me?" When she looked up, I said, "Is this the track for Hoboken?"

The woman shook her head, her frizzy dark brown ponytail bopping up and down, and pointed behind her. "This is Journal Square. That one is Hoboken."

I looked over at the mass of early twenty-somethings and frowned. "I was afraid of that. What's going on? Is it always like this?"

The woman laughed. "Thankfully, no. It's St. Patrick's Day."

"But it's not the seventeenth yet."

"In Hoboken, it might as well be. Today's the annual parade. Any excuse for these kids to drink beer all day." Scrutinizing me, she said, "You're young. You'd probably have a blast."

"I don't want to have a blast." Noting the woman's amused expression, I said, "I mean, I don't like beer. I guess I'm not going to Hoboken today after all. Thanks." I walked back to the turnstiles, wishing I hadn't wasted a ride on my Metro Card. I picked up the pace to get outside and away from the men in green. I heard someone call out my name and, startled, looked up into the smiling face of Bethany walking through the turnstile toward me.

"Hey. Small world," I said.

Twisting the green strand in her hair that had previously been purple, she said, "What are you doing here? More importantly, why are you headed in the wrong direction?"

"Hiding. Long story. I was hoping for an adventurous day in

Hoboken." I spun around and gestured to the ever-growing crowd of people waiting for the train. "I didn't realize the St. Patrick's Day parade was today."

"What could be more adventurous than the parade? Come with us. You remember my friend, Anne, right?"

I nodded and waved at her friend who I recognized from the drunken night at Lex Bar.

She smiled. "Come with us, Jane."

I glanced down at my outfit, which was desperately lacking the color green. "I'm not dressed for the celebration."

"Nonsense," Bethany said. She removed a strand of green beads and a four-leaf clover charm, one of her many necklaces, and put it over my head. "Ta da! Now you're aptly costumed."

"I don't even like beer though."

Anne laughed. "You'll learn to love it."

I rolled my eyes. "You guys are nuts." I pondered my next move while the two of them stared at me expectantly. Apparently not willing to take no for an answer, Bethany locked her arm with mine and dragged me back in the direction of the train, which was slowly making its way down the track.

Breaking into a jog, she tightened her grip on me. "Hurry!"

Since I'd already paid the toll and had nowhere else to be, I acquiesced and helped Bethany push our way through the crowd onto the train.

Trying to be heard over the rowdy crowd on the PATH train, I held the metal pole tightly for balance and loudly asked, "Where are we going?"

A guy pushed against me. "Black Bear, cutie, wanna come?"

I could smell beer on his breath and wondered what time he started drinking. The train was too crowded for me to move away from him so I muttered, "I was talking to my friends" and turned so my back was facing him.

I felt a tap on my shoulder and turned back around. "I can be your friend," said the drunk guy. He was tall and husky with dark, slightly unruly hair and a distracting beauty mark over his lip. I glanced over at Bethany and pleaded with my eyes for her to rescue me.

Bethany looked up at him and smiled. "Been to the parade before?"

"Yeah, I can show you the ropes." To me, he said, "What's your name?"

Wondering if Bethany misinterpreted my plea for help as a sign of interest, I stared up at his beauty mark and contemplated whether to use my real name or go with Frankie.

Before I could answer, he winked and said, "You're cute."

The train stopped and I took a step to the exit.

"Not yet," Anne said as even more green clad people entered the train, pushing me closer to Beauty Mark Guy. "Two more stops."

I sighed. "Where are we going?" I glanced at the guy who had his mouth opened to speak. "Besides Black Bear?"

Bethany and Anne laughed. "Actually, we're going to Black Bear."

Displaying a mouthful of straight, white teeth, our new best friend patted me on the back. "Lucky me."

Ten minutes later, we stood at the back of the very long line to get into Black Bear. I would have suggested going someplace else if the line for every other bar and restaurant we passed on the street was not equally long. Actually, I *did* suggest we go someplace else, to escape Beauty Mark Guy, but Bethany and Anne wouldn't have it. Apparently, Anne's friend from her book club said she'd heard from their mutual friend's cousin that a lot of people who graduated SUNY Buffalo their year would be at Black Bear.

It was cold out, which made the wait seem excruciatingly long. Shivering, I hugged myself to keep warm. "My God. How early do you have to get here to beat the line?"

Anne pulled her green ski hat over her ears. "Bars open at eleven, but the locals know to get in line early."

I looked at my watch in disbelief. "It's only eleven thirty. What time do people get in line?"

Applying lip balm, Bethany said, "Nine, maybe?"

"Nine last night?" I was only half joking.

"Ha ha." Bethany handing me her lip balm. "Want some?"

As I reached for it, I heard a guy say, "Good. Keep those red lips soft and moist for kissing me later."

I turned around and rolled my eyes at Beauty Mark Guy. He gave me a devilish grin and walked over to us. He was carrying a brown paper bag.

Trying to peek inside, Bethany said, "Whatcha got in there?"

"Milk. I'm a growing boy," he said.

"Yeah right," Anne said. "Got some for us?"

His eyes travelled between the three of us. "'Cause I'm such a nice guy..." he gestured toward me, "and you girls are so friendly. But be slick."

After Bethany and Anne each took a can of beer, he said, "If you see any sign of a cop, put the beer down on the ground and play dumb." He looked at me. "You can have one too."

Shivering, I spotted the Dunkin Donuts across the street and wished Beauty Mark Guy was offering me a thermos of white hot chocolate instead. "No thanks. I don't drink beer."

He shook his head and chuckled. "Why am I not surprised? Loosen up, Rainbow Brite."

In quick defense, I said, "I am loose." When he sneered at me, I dropped my gaze and corrected myself, muttering, "I mean, I don't need beer to loosen up."

Jumping to my rescue, Bethany put her arm around me. "Hey, be nice to my friend Jane here." But then she gave me a serious look. "Jane, maybe you should have a beer. I'm not even sure they'll have a full bar today. Might as well get used to beer."

Piping in, Anne said, "After the first few, you won't taste it anyway."

I reluctantly reached into the bag and grabbed a cold can, but only to prove I wasn't uptight. I didn't care what Beauty Mark Guy thought.

He grinned and tousled my hair. "There you go, Strawberry

Shortcake." He moved closer to me. "We should all huddle close to hide our beers."

"Nice try," I said.

Moving in to make our little circle smaller, Bethany said, "He's right, actually."

I pulled the tab off of my beer, praying it wouldn't spray all over my jacket, and took my first sip. I held my hand over my mouth so no one would see me snarl involuntarily from the sour taste.

"See?" Anne said. "It's not so bad."

I held my breath and took another sip, this one bigger. "Not bad at all." How many would I have to drink before I wouldn't taste it anymore?

About a half hour later, the line had moved maybe ten feet, and Beauty Mark Guy, whose name was actually William, was telling us how he ran into Paula Abdul in McDonald's the previous weekend.

"She was drunk off her ass. But I guess she was craving Mickey D's," he said as his friends, who had finally joined us, nodded in agreement.

"She was high on more than booze," one of them said.

I brought my almost empty can of beer to my mouth.

William nudged me and whispered, "Put your beer down."

Confused, I glanced over at Bethany as she slipped her can of beer into the arm of her bulky wool sweater. Then I felt a tap on my shoulder. In a slight daze, I turned around to face a blond-haired, blue-eyed guy, probably in his early thirties, in a police officer's uniform. "Can you come over here a second?"

I looked at the others who were watching me with concerned interest. "Uh, sure."

He stepped aside and I followed him, nervously biting my lip.

Ignoring the kids in line who had halted their own conversations to eavesdrop, he glanced at the can of beer still in my hands. "You know an open container is prohibited outside, right?" His eyes bored into mine.

I stared at the ground and watched my knees wobble. "Yes, officer. I'm...I'm sorry. I've never done this before, I promise." I looked up into his eyes again, afraid he was going to arrest me.

"I have to write you a ticket, and you'll have to appear in court." He removed the beer from my hand and tossed it into the nearest trash can.

I felt my lips tremble slightly and took a sideways glance at my friends who I could tell were trying to listen.

The officer removed the pen from his clipboard. "I need to take your information."

After I gave him my name, address, and birthday, he put the pen back and handed me the ticket. "If there is any incorrect information on this ticket, it will be thrown out of court. Do you understand?"

I nodded.

"Read the ticket carefully. Again, if anything is wrong, the judge has to throw it out." In a lower voice, he added, "I'm required to give out a certain amount of tickets today, but I was young once too." Then he lightly patted my shoulder. "You can go back to your friends now. Have fun. But remember, no more beer until you get inside the bar."

"I promise." I took a quick glance at the ticket and saw he had written my birth date to make me a year older, and looked at him again. He was smiling and his eyes were now more kind than disciplinary. I whispered, "Thank you," and returned to the line.

I sheepishly made my way back to my friends. "How does the girl who doesn't even drink beer end up getting the ticket?" Shaking my head, I said, "Where's the justice?"

"I tried to warn you," William said in a soft voice.

"Yeah, about two seconds too late." I pushed him lightly to let him know I was kidding.

With a wrinkled brow, Bethany asked, "What's gonna happen?"

"Well, I'll have to go to court. Can't wait to explain *that* one to my folks." Between this and missing the LSAT, they might send me for blood tests to confirm their daughter hadn't been abducted by aliens and replaced with a lesser, refurbished model—the anti-Stepford child. Choosing to leave the worrying for another time and place, I said brightly, "The good news is that, even though I have to show up at court, the ticket will be thrown out."

In response to a chorus of "Huh" and "Why" I said, "The police officer purposely wrote down my wrong birthday and said any incorrect information makes the ticket void."

"What a relief," Bethany said with an exaggerated swipe of her brow.

"Yeah, but why ticket her in the first place?" Anne said.

"He has to make his quota of tickets but probably knows drinking beers in line for a bar isn't the worst crime you could be committing," William said, smiling.

"Exactly," I said as the bouncer asked for our IDs. The smell of beer and sweat radiated from inside the bar, but it wasn't nearly as crowded as the long line suggested.

As if reading my mind, William said, "They must be managing the crowd due to fire department regulations."

When one of his friends said, "Beers, everyone?" I nodded. If the first beer resulted in a ticket, who knew what excitement would ensue after a second.

"Don't try to sweet talk me," I said to William an hour or so and two beers later. "I'm not buying it."

"Would you rather I be mean to you?" he asked, a smug smile on his face.

"On second thought, sure, whisper sweet nothings in my ear. But don't expect me to take you seriously. I don't take any of you seriously anymore."

William raised an eyebrow. "Any of you, who?"

"Boys."

"I see."

Pointing my finger at his broad chest, I said, "I know you just like the thrill of the chase. So chase me. But if I let you catch me, and that's a very big 'if,' I fully expect you to release me shortly thereafter." I took a gulp of beer. "I know the game."

"I can play by those rules." William grabbed my hand and shook it with a firm grip.

"Then it's settled. By the way, I need to do something." I removed my hand from his.

"What? Pee?" William pointed behind him. "The bathroom is in the back. I'm betting the line for the ladies' room is almost as long as the line to get into the bar."

"I don't have to pee." I sort of did, but only realized it that second. I stood on my tippy toes and leaned toward William, whose eyes opened wide, and I planted a soft kiss on his beauty mark.

"What was that for?" William asked.

"No reason. I felt like it. You complaining?" I could tell by his goofy grin that he liked it.

"Not at all," he said, lifting me off the ground and spinning me around. "You're a piece of work."

Pounding his back with my fists, I said, "Put me down. Don't know if my stomach can handle this on three beers."

William put me down. "You win."

"Remember, I don't want to be your girlfriend."

"Well I don't want to be your boyfriend."

I giggled, "Okay."

Bethany came over and handed me a white paper Dixie cup. "Green Jell-O shots."

I raised the shot in the air. "To missing the LSAT." I squeezed the alcohol gelatin from the cup and swallowed it in one piece. "Lunch is served."

"You missed the LSAT? What's that about?" Bethany asked. She detached herself from the grip of a short, stocky guy with a thick head of black hair, a five o'clock shadow, and a tiny leprechaun painted on his right cheek. I had no idea where he came from and wondered if she knew him from college. "Come with me to the bathroom," she said, grabbing me by the elbow.

I held out my glass while William refilled my beer from a pitcher. Before walking away, I looked at him. "Don't go anywhere."

He shook his head at me, and raised his hand in a salute. "Aye, aye, Captain."

I grabbed the back of Bethany's sweater and followed her to the bathroom line. "Who's that guy hanging on you?"

Turning halfway around while walking, she said, "My boyfriend, Phil. What's this about you missing the LSAT?"

Waving her away, I said, "Never mind about the LSAT. Not important right now. I had no idea you had a boyfriend. Everyone has a boyfriend but me. Not that I want one."

A girl ahead of us in line turned around. "Me neither. Men suck. But I wouldn't mind sucking face with someone today."

"Me neither. I'm gonna suck face with William when I get back," I said.

"Who's William?" the girl asked.

"A tall, obnoxious guy with a beauty mark." I shrugged. "He's grown on me."

Bethany laughed. "Beer will do that to you."

"Is he ugly?" Please don't say yes.

"No. He's not bad at all. But you had no interest earlier."

"That was then. This is now. And I'm not looking for a boyfriend. I just want to kiss him."

# Chapter 38

I woke up and turned over. Not expecting to see a man's bare back in my bed, I sat up and confirmed I was naked. I pulled the sheets over my body and muttered, "Holy shit." I reached down, grabbed a t-shirt that was conveniently at the foot of my bed, and pulled it over my head. Careful not to wake up William, I quietly stepped onto my floor and saw my phone sitting on my desk. I vaguely remembered posing for pictures.

I sat at my desk chair, stretched the bottom of my t-shirt over my legs and looked back at the pictures. Bethany and me with our mouths open showing green Jell-O on our tongues. Bethany leaning over her short boyfriend and kissing the top of his head. Bethany licking the leprechaun on her boyfriend's cheek. Me proudly holding up my ticket. *My ticket. Fuck.* William holding up my ticket. Me holding up the ticket with the group behind me. William kissing me.

"Morning, Hello Kitty."

I swiveled my chair so I was facing William, who was now sitting up in my bed.

"Morning. What's with you calling me all those names?"

William stretched his long arms over his head. "Terms of endearment, Peaches and Herb."

"You're strange."

"So are you," he said, smiling.

I tossed my phone on the bed. "We were way drunk yesterday."

"You sure were. I doubt I'd be here if the beer didn't succeed in loosening you up."

"No way," I quickly agreed. "I mean, no offense. I just don't usually bring strangers home with me."

Now sitting on the edge of the bed with his feet on the floor, William chuckled. "Good. I like to think I'm special."

I had to smile. "Special you are. But don't worry, I won't stalk you, and I don't expect to be your girlfriend just because we had sex."

"I don't usually do away games, even if it means I have to sneak out of a chick's apartment at four a.m. But you're a sweetie. And kind of fun after a beer, Little Red Hen."

I noted it was the best one-night stand of my life, a close race with the only other one I'd ever had. "Thanks. You're not so bad yourself," I said, adding a silent *Beauty Mark Guy* to the end of the sentence. Not quite as creative as him since one nickname was all I could handle after a day of drinking.

William got out of bed, and I turned away while he put his clothes back on. "I'll show myself out." Kissing me on the top of the head, he said, "Be good."

"I will."

After he left, I jumped back in bed, closed my eyes, and fell asleep alone. Just me, the biggest slut on the Upper East Side.

When I woke up a few hours later, I thought back to six months ago, when the only guy I had slept with was Bob, my high school sweetheart and the guy to whom I remained faithful throughout college and for years later. In a mere six months, I had multiplied my number by five. So much for sex being an intimate act meant to be shared between two people who actually cared about each other. I didn't even know William's last name. Or "Buddy's" first. What had become of sensible "Mary Jane" (my pledge name in college)? Who had replaced my white patent-leather Mary Janes with fire red "fuck-me" pumps?

My phone rang and I hopped out of bed. Claire. I tried to think fast, but the green Jell-O from the night before clogged my brain. I had no idea what to say to her. Chewing on my finger nail, I stared at the phone until it went to voicemail. I knew she was calling about the LSAT. Should I tell the family I thought I did well? That would make my dad proud. Or should I tell them I froze so I'd have an excuse to take them again?

I heard footsteps in the hallway. After slipping on a pair of sweatpants and my fuzzy slippers, I went into the living room where Lainie was sitting on the couch.

She saw me and quickly removed her feet from the coffee table. "I know. It's gross. I'm sorry."

I brushed her off with my hands. "No worries. Do what you want." Then I joined her on the couch, putting my own feet up on the coffee table. "Anything good on?"

Still staring at the television set, Lainie answered, "*My Fair Wedding* marathon on WE. Gotta support the hand that feeds me." She turned to look at me. "Why are you staring at me like that?"

"I feel like we're our own version of *Freaky Friday*."

Looking at me with interest, Lainie said, "Meaning?"

I somehow managed to make my cry sound like a laugh. "Just a few months ago, you loved to play the field and thought I was lame for wanting to be with one guy. Now you're exclusive with Antoine, riveted by a *My Fair Wedding* marathon, and I got a ticket for drinking beer on the street and brought a stranger home to my bed. Bizarro world."

A huge grin on her face, Lainie said, "A stranger in your bed, huh? I guess Frankie came out to play. Do tell."

"Yeah, Frankie had a blast. Apparently I'm better at being Frankie than I am at being Jane."

Lainie muted the television set, removed her legs from the coffee table, and angled her body to face me. "Did you ever think maybe there was always a little bit of Frankie in Jane just dying to come out?"

"Never," I said with certainty.

"C'mon, Jane. If you married Bob..." Lainie stopped speaking and gazed at the wall for a second before continuing. "Or even if you married whatshisname, Randall, after Bob, you don't think you'd ever wonder if you were missing out?"

"Easy for you to say," I mumbled bitterly.

"Why's that?"

I stared down at my slippers. "Nothing. Never mind."

"No. I'd like to know why it's easy for me to say. According to the gospel of Jane Frank."

"Because you have a boyfriend now."

"Yes, I have a boyfriend, but he's the only guy I've dated seriously. After catching a lot of fish and throwing them back, I was confident Antoine was different. You just need to play the field more."

"I've played the field. I dated Randall, Jim, and Cory." And had sex with Buddy and William. "I've played the field hard."

Lainie let out a chuckle. "Considering you can count the guys you've gone out with on one hand Jane, you're still a newbie to the dating scene. Give it some time so you'll be ready to settle down when the time is truly right. And don't punish yourself for the casual fun you have in the meantime. Enjoy it."

I was beyond tired of receiving unsolicited advice from folks with significant others. "Oh, and you're suddenly an expert on finding love just because you have a boyfriend? Thank you, oh wise one." I leaned over and turned the volume back on the television.

Lainie removed the remote from the coffee table and muted the television again. "Why are you getting so angry at me? I'm just trying to help, Jane. I thought my experience in the dating world might give you a different perspective. I'm sorry I bothered." She got up from the couch, tossed the remote at me, and said, "I won't make that mistake again" before walking out of the room.

I shouted back at her, "Maybe I don't want quite as much experience as you."

Facing me once again, her eyes wide open, Lainie said, "Excuse me?"

"Unlike you, I'd prefer to keep the number of men I've slept with lower than my age." My pulse instantly increased its pace in acknowledgment of how bad that sounded.

Lainie's mouth dropped open. "Wow, Jane. Getting laid is

supposed to make you a happier person. I think I preferred the Jane who was celibate for a year to the slut-shaming hypocrite you've turned into." With that, she turned around again and walked quickly to her room.

I turned off the television and walked to the kitchen. After grabbing a couple of Oreos and pouring a glass of chocolate milk, I headed to my room, stopping outside of Lainie's on my way. Even though Lainie was proud of her sexual freedom, my chest was tight with guilt for what I'd said. I gently tapped her door with the knuckles of my right hand. I thought I heard her on the phone and decided my apology could wait until we both cooled down.

I spent the rest of the day in my room, watching a *Top Chef* marathon and screening phone calls, one from my mother and another from Claire. My mom asked about the LSAT, but Claire didn't leave a message. I thought about asking Marissa if she wanted to go out for Chinese, but she stubbornly refused to respond to my calls or text and I didn't feel like being ignored again. I'd make something at home.

At about six thirty, I heard Lainie go into the kitchen and quickly followed her, hoping to butter her up with a home-cooked meal. When I got there she was sitting at the table with Antoine and they were eating directly out of containers of Chinese food. They were whispering, but stopped when they saw me.

"Hi, Jane," Antoine said in a soft voice.

"Hi there," I smiled before removing a frying pan from the cabinet. Hoping to ease the tension, I said, "I'm making a Croque Madame sandwich. Can I make one for you guys?"

Lainie stood up. "No thanks. We're going to eat in my room. C'mon, Antoine." She grabbed two containers of food and the plastic bag containing spicy mustard, duck sauce, and fortune cookies and walked through the archway that led from the kitchen out into the hall.

"Bye, Jane," Antoine said. Then he gathered another container of food and the bottle of Diet Pepsi and followed Lainie. I watched their backs as they disappeared into Lainie's room.

# Chapter 39

The next day, I put on headphones and listened to my iTunes at work to avoid overhearing Andrew's seemingly back-to-back telephone conversations with Farah. I realized I wasn't as into him as I was into the *idea* of him, but it pissed me off to no end that even the office flirt had tossed aside his playboy ways for a girlfriend. He was like the male version of Lainie—boasting about the pleasures of non-exclusivity and then opting for a committed relationship.

Ever since I was a little girl, all I ever wanted was to fall in love and get married. I wasn't naive enough to think simply wanting something made it so, but Andrew and Lainie's simultaneous conversion from terminally single (and happy about it) to blissfully attached while I was boyfriendless and without an LSAT exam under my belt, made me wonder if *not* wanting something was the key to making it happen.

When DNCE's "Cake By The Ocean" came on, I bopped around in my chair, singing. I hadn't been dancing in a long time, probably since Marissa begged me to go to Katherine's bachelorette party. Maybe Bethany would want to go dancing. She was currently the only friend still speaking to me.

"Jane!"

I removed my headphones and looked at Andrew. "What?"

Pointing at my office phone, he said, "Your phone is ringing."

"Oh." I looked at my phone. Claire again. I still hadn't figured out what I was going to tell her about the LSAT, so I let voicemail pick up.

"Screening your calls?" Andrew asked.

"Not all of them. Just my family."

Andrew raised his eyebrow at me.

"Don't ask."

Later that night, I was watching television in the living room when my doorbell rang. I muted the TV, got off the couch, and walked to the door, throwing the remote on the couch behind me. "Who is it?"

"Your sister."

I opened the door to see Claire with a small baby bump, hands on her hips, her lips pursed. "Hey," I said. "Unexpected surprise."

"Well, if you aren't going to return any of my calls, you leave me with no choice. I thought you might be dead."

I let out a laugh. "I'm clearly not dead. But thanks for your concern."

"That's what sisters are for. You might want to return the favor," she said, glancing over my head into the apartment.

I realized we were still standing in my doorway. Making room for her to walk past me, I said, "Do you want to come in?"

Her back to me as she entered the apartment, she said, "Thanks for asking."

I followed her to the living room where she sat on the couch and stared at me. "What's going on?" I asked.

"Why don't you tell me?" she said, her expression giving away nothing.

"You're the one making the house call." I sat down next to her on the couch.

"Mom said you didn't call her back either."

Fidgeting with the magazines on the coffee table, I said, "I'm sorry. Just been really busy."

"Join the club." She frowned at me. "Don't you even care about your nephew?"

"Of course I do." I gently rubbed her belly in a circular motion. "But he's not even born yet."

"I thought you were going to brainstorm names with me," she said, brushing my hand away.

"It's only been a few days, Claire. And I have been thinking about it."

"Really," she said doubtfully.

"Yes, really."

Sounding positive she could call my bluff, she said, "Throw out a name then."

Crap. Think fast. Boy's name. Boy's name. "William!" *Et tu, Brute?*

Claire gave me a funny look. "William?"

"Yes," I said, nodding my head enthusiastically.

"You want me to name my son William Williamson?"

*Shit.* "Why not? It's a family name."

"It's a stupid name."

"Then don't ask for my help."

"What's with you, little sister?"

I reclined against the sofa throw pillow. "I have a lot going on. You wouldn't understand."

Claire removed her purse from the floor, placed it in her lap, and put her hand inside. Holding up a clear plastic bag with my red lace thong inside, she said, "Getting to the bottom of what your panties were doing at my apartment is taking longer than Magellan's expedition around the world."

I snatched the bag out of her hand as my face got hot in recollection of my afternoon with Buddy. "It's a funny story."

Raising an eyebrow, Claire said, "Let me be the judge."

"After the whole Cory mess, followed by Bob and Trish's party, I needed to blow off some steam. I met this guy and we..." I tucked a strand of hair behind my ear and stared at my hardwood floors. "I had a one-night stand with him at your apartment. Actually, a one-*day*-stand is more accurate." I giggled before meeting Claire at eye-level.

Claire stared at me, her mouth slack and her full cheeks flushed with anger. "You brought a strange guy to my apartment?"

I bit my lip. "I didn't want him to know who I was and ruin the mystery. Your place seemed like a good idea at the time. But nothing was stolen and we used protection. All's well that ends well, right?" I smiled hopefully.

Claire blinked at me. "Who are you and what have you done with my sister?"

Sinking deeper into the couch, I said, "I'm here."

"The Jane I know would never do something so stupid and reckless. How am I supposed to trust you with my child?" Her brown eyes flashed with anger.

"I'm sorry. I didn't think it was a big deal. I was just trying to have fun."

"Screwing some random and potentially dangerous guy at your pregnant sister's apartment is fun to you?"

"I'd never do anything to hurt my nephew." I reached out to pat her belly again, but she flinched. "It was a dumb thing to do, but I didn't mean any harm. Like you said, I don't have it in me to be horrible."

"I don't know what you're capable of anymore." She stood up and flung her purse over her shoulder.

I felt tears burning the corners of my eyes and blinked them away. "You don't understand. You have Kevin and a baby on the way—the perfect life. Nothing ever works out for me. I was just trying..." I sniffled. "I was just trying to have some harmless fun for a change."

Claire rolled her eyes. "We clearly have different definitions of 'harmless.' This guy could have raped and murdered you before doing the same to Kevin, me, and your unborn nephew, William." She looked at me in disgust. "And by the way, you've been single for less than two years of your adult life. Get a grip. Yes, it's true I have a husband and a baby on the way, but you of all people know my 'perfect life' didn't fall into my lap. And you of all people should be happy for me. But instead you're being bitter and immature." Claire put her coat on and walked to my front door. Turning around to look at me one more time she said, "And, by the way, no one has the perfect life. No one." She walked out and slammed the door behind her.

# Chapter 40

The following Saturday, I sat in the passenger seat of my father's Audi and rolled down the window, letting the refreshing breeze brush against my face.

Taking a quick sideways glance at me before looking back toward the road, my dad asked, "You hot, Pumpkin?"

"No. Just need a little air." I felt suffocated riding to my parents' house from the train station. I wanted to be anywhere else, but my mom broke down all of my excuses for not coming home for the day. I told her I had a tentative date planned, thinking that would make her happy, but she said "tentative" and "definite" were not the same, and if he really wanted to take me out, he'd nail down plans.

My dad pulled up the driveway and turned off the engine. "Home sweet home."

I tossed my bag over my shoulder and followed him up the multicolored tile pathway to the front door. I smelled cinnamon. "What did Mom make?" I hoped she'd waited for me to make breakfast.

"Mom made French toast," I heard her say, before she walked out of the kitchen. She wiped her hands on the midnight blue polka dot apron she wore over a turtleneck sweater of the same color and winter white pants and pulled me in for a hug. "Hi, sweetheart. How nice of you to grace us with your presence."

I dropped my arms to my sides and mumbled, "Sorry. Been so busy lately."

She motioned for me to take a seat at the kitchen table. Sitting down too, she said, "For instance?"

"Like work. Is there any coffee?"

"Have you had any yet today? You shouldn't drink more than one cup a day or it will—"

"Stain your teeth." I gave her a toothy smile. "My teeth are neither yellow nor brown, Mom. And I haven't had any coffee yet today," I lied.

"Here's your coffee. Just the way you like it. Skim milk and one Sweet 'n Low." My dad placed the cup in front of me. When my mom got up again to check on the food, he whispered, "Don't worry, I used cream and sugar."

I whispered back, "Thanks" and smiled softly at my dad, wondering how such a down-to-earth, laid-back guy fell for my regimented no-nonsense mother. Another case of opposites attracting.

"How do you think you did?"

At least he asked the dreaded question when my mom was not at the table. "Not sure."

Joining us with the plate of French toast, my mom said, "Columbia or Queens College?"

My dad laughed. "She can do better than Queens College. At least Brooklyn Law, right sweetie?"

"Right, Dad." I dug my fork into a piece of toast and dropped it onto my plate. "Can you please pass the syrup?"

"You'll have to figure out where to apply. Narrow it down to a handful of schools. Application fees are not what they used to be," my mom said before taking a small piece of toast into her mouth.

"It's not that expensive," my dad said. "Better to keep her options open than apply to too few."

I pushed my plate away. "Can we change the subject? Is Claire coming?" We hadn't talked since we fought at my apartment. I hoped we could work things out and bond over how annoying our mother could be in one fell swoop.

"Not this time," my mom said. "Do you not like the French toast? I know it's not as good as your gourmet breakfasts."

"It's fine, Mom. Yummy. Just taking a break." I moved the

plate closer to me and took another bite. I wasn't hungry anymore and listened to the sound of metal crashing against ceramic as I dropped my fork onto my plate. "Why didn't Claire come today?" I assumed Claire hadn't told our parents we fought or else my mom would have laid into me already.

"She said she was tired," my mom said.

"That excuse never works for me."

"You're not pregnant, Jane. Meet a nice man, let us spend too much money on your wedding, and get pregnant. Then you can use that excuse," my mom said, smiling as if she didn't mean it.

I exhaled loudly.

My mom studied me. "When you chew your lip like that I can almost picture you dragging your father all over the mall crying because you lost your favorite Ninja Turtle doll."

"You were so cute," my dad said, shaking his head as if remembering me at six years old in pigtails and Osh Kosh B'Gosh overalls.

"And so spoiled, but leave it to your father to romanticize." My mom looked at my dad fondly. "Your father bought you a new doll just to stop you from crying."

He had actually bought me two—Leonardo and Donatello. I could still remember that day and how I kept crying in my dad's arms, even after he gave me the new dolls, until I fell asleep.

"Did that boy nail down a date?" my mom asked, evidently bored with the current topic of conversation.

"Yes. This week," I said. "He's taking me to BLT Prime." If I was going to have an imaginary life, I was going to be well fed.

"What's his name?"

"William," I said without skipping a beat.

Mom looked at me. "Claire said you suggested naming the baby William. At least I know why now. What does he do?"

I was surprised Claire had mentioned any part of our last conversation. "He's in medical school." Maybe he was. Our respective trades never came up in conversation. "But I'm not sure it's going to work out. He has a beauty mark on his lip."

"It's not going to work out because he has a beauty mark on his lip?" my dad asked. "It's a good thing your mother didn't feel that way about my third nipple."

I got up and took my plate to the sink. "No. He's just focused on school. Not sure he has time for a girlfriend." I turned back to my dad. "Third nipple? Really?"

My dad winked. "Just making sure you were listening."

"Then why are you dating him?" my mom interrupted.

"A girl's gotta eat," I joked.

"There must be more to your attraction to this man than free dinners. I only hope he turns out better than the last one."

I assumed she was referring to Cory, who Kevin had finally outed as having ghosted me. "Can we change the subject?" I asked. Like what time I can go home.

"Again?" my mom said.

"I don't want to talk about boys or law school. Any other topic is fine."

"I spoke to Mrs. Krauss. Bob and Trish are having the wedding at the Water's Edge."

"How nice for them." I wanted to tell my mom that Bob-related news fell under the subject of boys, but I didn't want her to think I was jealous or give me a pep talk about how pretty I was and how I'd meet "The One" at the right time and place. She'd make me feel better for about three seconds before telling me where Bob and Trish were planning to go on their honeymoon. "William wants to be a surgeon. Pretty impressive, huh?"

# Chapter 41

As I sat on the M102 Third Avenue bus after a festive Friday night food shopping at Trader Joe's a week later, I reflected upon my week. Work, followed by dinner, followed by television, followed by sleep. All of the above peppered by the occasional session at the gym in an attempt to de-stress and work out my feelings about Marissa, Lainie, and Claire. I hadn't spoken to any of them in weeks.

Marissa refused to return my calls and Lainie spent most of her time out of the apartment. When she was home, she locked herself in her room with Antoine. I'd attempted to make peace by baking a homemade apple pie and leaving a note for her to help herself, but last I checked, the only slice missing was the one I'd eaten. I thought they were both overreacting and refused to beg either for forgiveness. Since Claire was my sister, I knew we'd work things out eventually and wasn't in a hurry to grovel at her feet. When my phone rang, I pushed aside my wallet and hair brush and removed it from the bottom of my bag, excited someone besides a colleague, the cashier at Trader Joe's, or the guy at the front desk of the gym might want to talk to me. Until I saw who it was—Kevin.

He was probably calling to urge me to apologize to Claire since it had now been two weeks since our fight. He'd tell me she was in a vulnerable state right now and I should be the bigger person. And he'd remind me how screwed up it was of me to bring a strange guy to their apartment for sex. I felt my face drain of color and hoped Claire hadn't actually divulged all of the details regarding that day.

I was certain he'd make me feel horrible, and I didn't want to hear it. I stared at the phone, waiting for it to go to voicemail. It didn't. I felt the color return to my face. I couldn't be expected to call him back if he didn't leave a message.

I turned to the woman sitting next to me on the bus and breathed a sigh of relief. "Happy Friday," I said, as I dropped my phone back in my bag.

She opened her mouth to say something just as I heard my phone alert the receipt of a text message. I muttered, "For the love of God, leave me alone." I read Kevin's message: "Call me."

"Bad news?" The woman next to me asked.

Still staring at my phone, I said, "Kind of. My brother-in-law is stalking me."

Looking at me with concern, she said, "Stalking you?"

I exhaled deeply. "Not exactly stalking. But first he called and didn't leave a message, and then he sent me a text to call him."

The woman, who I guessed was around the same age as my mom but looked like she either didn't use as expensive moisturizer, spent too much time in the sun, or smoked, drew her eyebrows together. "Maybe something's wrong. Is this your husband's brother or your sister's husband?"

"I'm not married." Thanks for reminding me. "He's my sister's husband. I'm sure he wants me to apologize to my sister."

"Are you not sorry for whatever he thinks you did?"

"Not exactly," I said, feeling my face get red. "I messed up."

The woman smiled. "Saying the words 'I'm sorry' is easy. Putting aside your pride to actually do it is the hard part."

I debated telling her she had a poppy seed stuck between her two front teeth but didn't want to hurt her feelings, and it was small enough that only someone sitting right next to her, like me, would even notice. "I guess. But she's such a know-it-all. She doesn't understand me."

"Older sister?"

I nodded.

"I had one of those too. I think they're all know-it-alls."

At last, a kindred spirit. "She's always giving me advice and acting like she has so much more life experience than me. We're less than two years apart in age. I'm an adult too, but just because she's married and pregnant and I'm not, she thinks my life is simple and easy."

Lips pursed, the woman nodded. "Your life is complicated and difficult?"

"Compared to hers. She already found a husband."

"And you don't think marriage is difficult?"

"Not as difficult as finding a husband." I pointed out the window of the bus. "Especially in this Godforsaken city."

The woman laughed, flashing the poppy seed again. "May I ask how old you are?"

"Twenty-six." *And counting.*

"I thought so. Why are you in such a hurry to find a husband? Speaking with thirty-plus years of marriage experience, I assure you marriage has ups and downs. Many downs."

"Yet you've been married for thirty-plus years." I hated when married women insisted marriage was overrated. I'd bet if *Glamour* magazine surveyed one hundred married women, ninety-nine would say they wouldn't trade places with a bachelorette, despite the freedom they claimed to miss so much.

"I got lucky, for the most part. But I didn't have the choices you had. There weren't many twenty-six-year-old women living on their own in the big city. This was years before *Sex and the City,* and twenty-somethings weren't encouraged to play the field." Winking at me, she said, "And those who did had bad reputations."

"I had a long-term boyfriend and I've played the field. I gotta say, I much prefer being in a relationship."

"The grass is always greener, I suppose. What else do you do besides date?"

"I'm supposed to go to law school."

The woman repeated, "Supposed to?"

"I messed that up too," I said, looking down at my thighs.

"Do you want my honest opinion?"

*Only if it agrees with mine.* Nodding, I said, "Sure."

Looking straight ahead, the woman paused for a second and then turned back to me. "I think you're way too young to be so focused on getting married."

"I know twenty-six is not old. It's just..." I sought the right words to explain. "I always thought I'd have my first child by thirty at the latest, and at the rate I'm going, I'll still be single at thirty-five. When I was a kid, I thought everyone got married at twenty and died at a hundred. By those standards, I'm way behind schedule."

A light chuckle escaped the woman's lips. "While you're so worried about the future and your 'timeline,' your life is happening. And sweetie, you're missing it." Staring off in the distance, the woman said, "If I was young again and living in the city, I'd see and do everything. I'd go to plays and museums, dance at the hottest clubs, dine in the trendy restaurants, and meet interesting people." Facing me again, she said, "It's too late for me, but it's not too late for you."

"And I'll probably find 'The One' when I stop looking, right?" I asked hopefully.

The woman laughed again. "There are no guarantees in life, hun. But I don't see why not. But a man won't make you happy unless you're already a happy person. Even then, he might make you miserable."

The bus pulled over to the right and the woman stood up. "This is my stop. Good luck to you."

I stood up to let her into the aisle and gave her a closed-mouth smile. "Thanks for your advice, I appreciate it."

With a wave, she said, "My pleasure." She began walking toward the rear door, but then turned back around to face me. "One more thing. Call your sister." Her voice shaky, she said, "I wish I could call mine, but she's not with us anymore." As if acknowledging the finality of her statement, she shrugged and with a turn of her heel, walked down the steps of the bus onto the sidewalk as the doors closed behind her.

The bus continued its trip uptown, but the woman's voice stayed with me. She wasn't the first person to say a man wasn't the recipe for happiness. But I wasn't looking for a man to make all my pain go away. I was just ready to move on to the next stage of my life, and it seemed like so many other people my age in the city were satisfied with the status quo and had no desire to grow up. They wanted to live the post-college experience indefinitely, staying out late, getting drunk, having one-night stands and not being accountable to anyone. I had dabbled in that world over the past few months, and it wasn't for me. I wanted what Claire had. And I hated that I was supposed to feel guilty for wanting to be in a relationship before it just magically came to me. Who were Lainie, Claire, and Andrew to dispense advice as if they were members of some secret love society that wouldn't let me join until I completed some stupid journey?

I looked out the window as the bus passed 79th street. I reached over to press the stop request button, gathered my things, and stepped into the aisle until the bus slowed to a halt. I said, "Thanks" to the bus driver and walked down the steps, debating what to eat for dinner.

I was certain Lainie wouldn't be home, so I'd have the entire kitchen to myself to make a masterpiece. I recalled making my famous rack of lamb for Jim. He was so impressed. Apparently, impressed enough to take me to bed, but not quite dazzled enough to take me out again.

As I made a left onto 82nd Street in the direction of my apartment, my phone rang again. Without looking at it, I took a deep breath and answered, "Hi. Sorry I didn't pick up before. Was on the bus. Too loud."

"Where are you?"

"Mom?"

"Kevin's been trying to reach you. Get to Lenox Hill Hospital right now." My mom's usual take-charge voice contained an unusual quiver.

My heart racing, I said, "Wha...What's going—"

Without waiting for me to finish, my mom said, "It's Claire. She's bleeding. Go to the Emergency Room. Your father and I are on our way."

The Trader Joe's bag hit the ground, splattering a glass container of stewed tomatoes at my feet.

# Chapter 42

*Call your sister. I wish I could call mine. Call your sister. She's not with us anymore. Call your sister.*

"Shut up!" My vision was blurry from tears I couldn't blink away, and I swallowed the bile at the back of my throat, which wanted so badly to form a chunky puddle of regurgitated Caesar salad at the entrance to the Emergency Room at Lenox Hill Hospital.

It was a slow night in the Emergency Room, and I didn't see my sister or Kevin. Just a sweaty teenager gripping his right knee against his chest and an old drunk guy pacing the floor while sniffling his own phlegm.

I waited at the information desk behind a young Asian couple and tapped my foot. The woman behind the desk was telling them, for the third time, where they needed to go to donate blood. For all I knew, my sister was bleeding to death while they needed professional assistance finding the third floor. Wasn't the Emergency Room supposed to be reserved for emergencies?

"Excuse me?"

Silence.

"Er, excuse me?" I stepped forward so I was standing next to the couple. "I hate to interrupt, but my sister's supposed to be here. She's pregnant. And she's, well, she's bleeding. And…" I felt a giant tear hit the top of my lip and wiped it with the side of my hand. To the couple, I said, "I'm sorry. I have to find her."

The lady behind the desk looked at me kindly and turned to the couple. "Just one second, please."

Looking back at me, she said, "What is your sister's name?"

"Claire." I waited for the lady to check her computer, but she just stared at me.

"Her last name?"

"Oh, Claire Frank. I mean Williamson! Claire Williamson."

After being told my sister was admitted to Obstetrics, I rushed to the nearest elevator, realizing as the door closed in front of me that I forgot to apologize again to the couple I cut in front of. They were probably still receiving directions to the third floor. I got off on the seventh floor and immediately turned left, not bothering to check if I was headed in the right direction. As I passed static white walls, the combined smell of sickly get-well flowers, bodily fluids, and antibacterial spray clogged my nostrils until I found myself paralyzed outside of Claire's room, not ready to enter.

Trying to gain my composure, I took a deep breath and ran my hands through my hair. My heart was racing, and I had no idea what to expect when I saw Claire. Or what I was supposed to say. "Are you okay?" or "I love you?" or "I'm sorry I've been a selfish bitch?"

I peeked through the glass panel in the door, hoping to catch a glimpse of her without being seen. She was in bed and Kevin was at her side, holding her hand. She looked normal, if a bit pale, and her hair was lacking its usual fullness and fell flat against her head. I tapped lightly on the door, and they both saw me at the same time. Kevin, looking solemn, signaled with his hand for me to enter.

With my right hand over my heart, willing it to stop beating so fast, I nodded and slowly walked in the room. "Hi," I said, looking mostly at Kevin. "How's it going?"

"Waiting for test results, little sister," Claire said softly.

I forced myself to look at Claire through my damp eyes. "What happened?"

Standing up, Kevin said, "I'll leave you guys to talk before your folks arrive. Going to catch my own parents up."

After he left, Claire motioned to the chair. "Sit."

I sat down, reached for her hand and squeezed it. "I'm so

sorry. For everything. I'm not only saying this because you're in the hospital. What I did was stupid and reckless. I love you." I stopped speaking as Claire acknowledged my apology with a return squeeze of my hand. "What happened? Mom said you were bleeding. From where?"

"Where do you think?"

I looked down at the linoleum floor. "Is the baby okay?"

Claire nodded. "Yes, William Williamson is fine. For now. Dr. Flynn just wants to know what caused the bleeding."

"But the baby is alive?" Embarrassed by the awkwardness of the conversation but needing to know for sure, I said, "I mean, you didn't miscarry?"

"No. The baby has a heartbeat, but bleeding at this stage of the pregnancy could be a sign of something wrong with the placenta or, God forbid, an ectopic pregnancy. But I had no cramping and according to Web MD, abdominal pain is a symptom of that."

"When did you have a chance to check Web MD? Didn't you call the doctor right away?"

"Kevin looked it up on his phone in the cab. Anyway, the bleeding stopped. Another good sign."

"You're so calm."

Claire sat up higher in her bed and placed the longest part of her bangs behind her ears. A habit we shared but I'd never noticed before. "I'm not really calm. I'm just faking it for your sake."

"Please don't do anything for my sake. I don't deserve it."

"You looked like a ghost before. I can't have you fainting and stealing all of the spotlight. I kind of need the medical attention more than you right now."

"I'm sorry for being an awful sister and future aunt."

Claire reached over and took my hand again. "I was really angry, but I'm over it now. If you promise never to do anything so clueless and self-absorbed ever again."

"You have my word." I reached over and kissed her cheek, rubbing the lip mark I left with my thumb. "Just like Nana used to do. I love you, Claire."

"I love you too, little sister. Now do you believe that no one has the perfect life? Still want to switch places with me?"

"If it meant I could take away some of your pain, yes."

Claire put two fingers to her lips and blew me a kiss just as Kevin returned with a middle-aged man in scrubs.

"Test results are in," Kevin said.

I turned to Claire, whose brown eyes were opened to the size of silver dollars. Kevin approached her bed, and she reached out and gave him her hand. When the doctor looked over at me, I said, "I'll wait outside. Mom and Dad should be here soon."

I was tempted to watch the conversation from outside the door and try to read lips, or at least gauge the prognosis by Claire and Kevin's facial expressions, but decided against it. Leaning against the wall with my eyes closed, I prayed softly. "Please, God. Please make Claire and the baby okay. Please." I opened my eyes as my parents were walking toward me. I ran to them with my arms extended, and we had a group hug. After we parted, I said, "The doctor's with them now."

Without saying a word, my mom tapped lightly on the door and entered the room, my father and me behind her.

No one was crying, and Kevin even had a half smile.

"Mom," Claire called out, her face brightening as our mom rushed to her side. "Daddy. Everything is going to be fine."

Turning to the doctor, my mom said, "I'd prefer to hear that from you, if you don't mind."

Holding his clipboard to his chest, Dr. Flynn smiled and shook my father's hand.

"Your daughter is correct. The ultrasound and blood tests showed that Claire and the baby are fine. We were lucky, but I'm still concerned about a preterm delivery. I'm ordering her to stay off of her feet as much as possible for the remainder of her pregnancy. Which means, no standing in front of a classroom of kids five days a week."

"The school will have to make due with a long-term sub," my mother said as Claire nodded.

"I can come by after work and help out," I said. "Anything you need."

My dad kissed the top of my head, "That's my sweet girl."

I flashed back to Claire doing my makeup before Bob and Trish's party and letting me borrow her clothes all through high school. Pointing at her, I said, "Not as sweet as my big sister. Least I can do."

Laughing, Claire said, "I have no idea what's gotten into you, but I like it."

After the doctor said Claire didn't need to stay overnight, my mom suggested we go back to her and Kevin's apartment and order in dinner.

I said, "I could have cooked us up a dinner, but I dropped my bag of groceries on the corner of 82nd and Lex when I got mom's call."

"I appreciate you guys being here. Especially you two," Claire said looking at my parents. "But if you don't mind, I just want to check out as quickly as possible and relax at home alone with Kevin." Frowning, she said, "Are you mad?"

"Not at all, sweetheart," my dad said. "Right, hon?"

"Whatever you want," my mom said sounding less than thrilled.

Claire and I made eye contact, and she gave me a pleading look.

"Why don't the three of us go out? Dad loves the pancakes at EJ's. We can have breakfast for dinner," I said.

"Fine," my mom said. She turned to Claire. "But just relax tonight. You can call the school after the weekend. I can email the doctor's note if you want."

Claire smiled. "Thanks, Mom."

With one hand on her hip, my mom gestured to the rest of us. "Let's leave Claire alone to get changed. We'll walk out with you and then go our separate ways. Kevin can stay."

"Thanks for the permission, Mrs. Frank," Kevin said, laughing.

Giggling like school girl, my mom said, "You're about to give me a grandson. Don't you think it's time you called me Mom?" She kissed him on the cheek.

It always amazed me how easily Kevin could make my mom laugh. She looked instantly relaxed, and I exchanged a knowing glance with Claire who motioned for me to come closer.

She was still in bed, so I leaned toward her and whispered, "What?"

Claire whispered back, "Thanks for rescuing me. And for giving up your Friday night."

"Yes, I had to cancel my other exciting plans of cooking dinner for one. At least now I get EJ's. Even if it *is* with the parental figures."

"What are you guys whispering about?" my mom said. "Let's go."

"Remember to put on your pants. It's too cold out there for butt exposure," I said.

"I'll remember," Claire said with a smile.

I followed my parents out the door and turned back to look at Claire. We shared a smile before I shut the door behind me.

# Chapter 43

I perused the menu at EJ's, contemplating either a Western Omelet or a Waldorf Salad. I had ordered a hot chocolate and dipped my spoon into the dollop of whip cream resting on top of the mug. "Thank God Claire and the baby are okay."

"Amen to that," my dad said, clinking his mug of coffee against my hot chocolate. "How about I get pancakes, you get eggs, and we share? Your mother will probably get a boring California salad of cottage cheese and fruit."

"Or a scoop of tuna salad over lettuce and tomato," I said giggling.

"For your information, Mother's getting a burger."

My dad and I looked at her in shock. "What's the occasion?"

"Your sister and the baby are healthy." She pointed at my dad and me. "I'm sitting in a restaurant with my husband of thirty years and our beautiful, if moody, youngest daughter. Calls for a burger."

"Sorry I've been moody. I'm over it."

"Over what?" My dad asked.

I sighed and placed the menu on my lap. "The angst. I'll meet someone when the time is right. And if I'm not meant to be a lawyer, I'll find something else to do." I skimmed the menu, noting that the word potato in the sides section was spelled with an "e" like it was edited by Dan Quayle. I looked up to find my parents staring at me. "What?"

"What do you mean if you're not meant to be a lawyer?" My mom asked.

Frowning, my dad said, "Did you get your LSAT scores back?"

I removed the elastic band from my wrist, put my hair in a bun on top of my head and contemplated my response. I could tell my parents I did poorly. They'd say something kind, like I was just having a bad day when I took the exam and would do much better the next time around. But they'd discuss it on the car ride home and wonder whether I truly had what it took to be a great lawyer. As much as I feared the repercussions of confessing my lie, it was better than my parents thinking I was incompetent. "Not exactly," I said, my voice a soft whisper.

With an unmistakable trace of annoyance, my mom said, "What do you mean?"

I forced myself to look my mom dead in the eyes. It was actually easier than facing my dad this time. "The LSAT was only two weeks ago and scores take three weeks, but it doesn't matter anyway since I didn't take them."

My mom's eyes opened wide. "You didn't take what?"

My stomach rumbled. I wondered if it was hunger or fear. I felt the same way whenever I was strapped into a rollercoaster and knew the only way off was by completing the ride. "The LSAT. I didn't take the LSAT," I said hesitantly.

My mom raised her voice. "Why the hell not? You had something better to do?"

Placing his hand over hers, my dad said, "Shhh. Keep your voice down."

Then he looked at me and said in a lower voice, "Explain yourself, Jane."

I bit my lip. "I forgot all about it until your email the Thursday before the exam. I knew I hadn't studied nearly enough to get a good score so I skipped it."

My dad furrowed his brow. "You said you were prepared. Each time I asked how the studying was going, you said 'great.'"

"I lied."

"You lied to your father?" My mom's face turned ashen and I held my breath awaiting her next words. The waiter saved the day by coming over to take our orders, but as soon as he walked away, she repeated in a whisper, "You lied to your father?"

I looked at my dad, whose sad face resembled a little boy whose lunch was stolen by bullies at recess. "I'm sorry, Dad. I didn't want to alarm you because I hadn't really studied yet. I had every intention to, but..."

"But what?" he said.

"I was distracted."

"By what?" my mom asked. Her complexion was back to normal, but the tapping of her long, polished nails on the tablecloth still kept me from breathing normally.

"By the dumb jerky boys who keep ruining my life."

My mom scrunched her face, resembling a French bulldog, but I braced myself for an attack by a much scarier breed of dog. "You blew the LSAT exam over a guy? Whose child are you?"

"Not just one boy," I whined. "All of them. Every single guy I've dated since Bob turned out to be a complete assclown. Excuse my language."

My mom closed her eyes and I watched her breathe in and out. When she opened her eyes, she said, "You need to pay us back for the exam fee. We shouldn't be held fiscally responsible for your mistake."

"I will," I said, crumbling my napkin. I glanced between my mom and dad. "I know I screwed up and I'm so sorry." My dad had been awfully stoic and I held my breath for his response.

"Call me daft, but what does any of this have to do with taking the LSAT?" he asked.

I licked my lips. "It's been a more difficult transition into the dating jungle than I expected and I lost my way." Anticipating my mom's next words, I raised my hand. "Please don't say I shouldn't have broken up with Bob. I wasn't in love with him."

Dropping her shoulders, my mom studied me with a more forgiving expression than I'd expected. "I know I gave you hard time about it, but the truth is, when I thought you and Bob might get married, I was actually concerned you would wonder about other men. And what it was like." She paused, her face flushed with embarrassment. "You know what I mean, right?"

"Uh-huh," I said, feeling my face get warm.

"Alright then," my dad said, his complexion almost purple. "Can we get back to the topic at hand?"

"Yes, dear." My mom patted my dad's arm sympathetically, and I could tell she was trying to keep a straight face. When she turned back to me, all humor had left her face. "Well?" she said.

I resumed my explanation. "I found it so hard to focus on my studies because I was too busy trying to figure out what I was doing wrong and how to fix it." I searched my parents' eyes for the magical answer.

"You can't fix it, sweetheart," my dad said.

"And you're probably not doing anything wrong," my mom added.

"Really? You don't think it's my fault?" I asked my mom, shocked.

"Don't get me wrong, neglecting to study is all your fault. You can blame it on as many flakey guys as you want, but it's all on you," my mom said.

My chin trembled in shame. "I know."

She sighed heavily. "But with respect to your love life, no offense to your father, but men can be assholes. No matter how pretty and nice you are, you can't change who they are or what they're looking for."

"None of those men were good enough for you, and you should be happy you didn't waste too much time on them," my dad said sternly. "I'd like to get them alone in a dark alley."

Dismissing him with a wave of her hand, my mom said, "Of course we're sorry you've had such a hard time, but it doesn't excuse your behavior. Life is always going to throw you curve balls and law school won't wait for you to find a husband. You need to compartmentalize better."

I nodded my agreement.

"What now?" my dad asked.

I hadn't given any thought to my next steps, so when the waiter brought out our food, I hoped it would signal the end of the conversation.

My dad placed half of his stack of pancakes on my plate, and I gave him half of my omelet. Then we watched in silence as my mom prepared her burger. First she removed the top half of the roll and covered the burger with lettuce and tomato, leaving the slice of red onion on the plate next to her. Then she reached across the table for the ketchup and spread a thin layer on the roll. Then she swapped the ketchup for the mustard and spread a thin layer of mustard directly over the ketchup. Finally, she cut the burger in half and, with both hands, brought one half to her lips and took a huge bite. It wasn't until after she chewed, swallowed and wiped her chin with a napkin that she noticed us watching her. She put the burger back on her plate. "What is so fascinating about watching me eat a burger?"

My dad and I looked at each other and laughed.

"Getting back to the subject at hand, what is your next move? Have you signed up for the next exam yet?" my dad asked.

"You'll pay for this out of your own pocket," my mom said.

"I haven't signed up yet, but yes I'll pay the fee myself. The next exam is in June. Plenty of time to prepare if I start studying now." I poured a few drops of syrup onto my plate and swirled a piece of pancake in it before taking a bite.

"The question is: will you start studying now?" my mom asked.

"If you need more time, you can always wait until October," my dad said, stealing one of my mom's French fries. "We don't want to pressure her. Do we, Pamela?"

After moving her plate farther away from my dad's reach, my mom looked at me. "Do you need more time, Jane?"

"No. I want to take the exam so I can start applying to schools. I don't want to delay admission any longer, otherwise I'll be thirty-five by the time I graduate. The plan is thirty at the latest."

My dad chuckled. "Reminds me of that saying—'Man makes plans. God laughs.' You've always been a planner, Jane. Remember all of those lists you used to write? What to wear for the week, what games to play at your sleepover party."

"And the pro/con lists," my mom said with a squeal. "You even wrote one before choosing a prom dress."

"No, I didn't. I wrote one to help Bob choose whether to wear a black, white, or silver cummerbund with his tuxedo." The dope wanted to wear red, which would have completely clashed with my pastel pink dress and looked ridiculous in our prom pictures.

Rolling her eyes, my mom said, "Such a life-altering decision. The point is, there are some things you can control. Like remembering to study for the LSAT exam. But most things can't be planned, like meeting the love of your life. I know you like to consider yourself a mature, experienced, woman, and you think you are ready to get married and start your own family, but I'm not sure I agree."

Feeling defensive, I pouted. "But—"

Interrupting, my mom held her hand in my face, which I hated. "Wait a second. I'm not finished."

I didn't bother arguing with my mom and remained silent.

She continued, "You might only be seventeen months younger than Claire, but you've led a completely different existence." Raising her hand again as if anticipating resistance from me, she said, "I don't mean that in a bad way. I just mean Claire has had more life experience than you. She struggled in school. She dated more 'assclowns' than you did. She lost her first teaching job. You've yet to have the world slam the door in your face, although maybe it's happening a bit now. I don't think you're ready to settle down, because I don't think you even know what you want yet. And, really, there is no rush. You're still very young."

I looked at my dad for his reaction. "What do you think, Dad?"

My dad shrugged. "What the hell do I know? I'm a man. Listen to your mother."

My mom winked. "I've trained him well."

I hadn't given much thought to veering from the plans I'd made as far back as I could remember, but maybe my mom was right and I had more living to do. Although I didn't think my mom would encourage more one-night stands under the guise of "life experience." "I promise I'll try to appreciate what I have now and not worry about what will surely happen eventually." I took another bite of my pancake. "Yum. So good."

I looked around the restaurant and took notice of the other diners. I wasn't at all jealous of the people out with their significant others. Well, not that much. I didn't currently have a boyfriend, but so what? I had a loving family and great friends. I turned back to my parents and watched my mother continue to devour her burger. And I watched my dad as he watched my mother devour her burger. Yes, I had a loving family. I stopped chewing the piece of pancake in my mouth and swallowed hard as it dawned on me that whether I still had loving friends was questionable.

# Chapter 44

I placed the box of cupcakes on the stoop and rang the buzzer for Marissa's apartment. My arms hurt from lugging both the cupcakes and my heavy purse, but I needed to apologize to Marissa face-to-face. Voicemails and texts were the lazy way and I knew she deserved better than that.

"Who's there?"

"It's me." In response to silence, I clarified, "Jane." Your ex-best friend.

Sounding less than enthusiastic, Marissa said, "Come on up" and a moment later the buzzer sounded.

I grabbed the box of cupcakes, took a deep breath, and climbed the two stories to her apartment. Usually when I rounded the steps to her floor, she'd already be standing outside the door, propping it open with her body, but when I got to 2D, the worn wooden door was closed shut. I knocked softly and heard her say, "Come in. It's open."

When I walked in, Marissa was in sweats and sitting on her futon bed, staring at the television set with the remote control on her lap.

I planted on a smile. "I come bearing gifts."

Turning to face me, Marissa quickly glanced at the box of cupcakes. "Thanks," she said before returning her attention to the couple figure skating on the television.

"I made them myself. Red velvet, tiramisu, and peanut butter cup, all your favorites. And a cookie dough for me. In the event you're in a generous mood and want to share."

"Help yourself," Marissa said dryly.

I brought the box to her small kitchen and removed two small plates and two glasses from her cabinet. I took out the container of milk from inside her refrigerator and poured us both a glass. Then I placed a red velvet cupcake on one plate and the cookie dough cupcake on the other and returned to find Marissa still riveted to the television screen. I could tell she was trying very hard not to see what I was doing or act like she cared by the way she kept nervously tapping her slipper-clad foot. After I put the plates on her coffee table, I went back to the kitchen for the milk and sat next down next to her. "Are you going to ignore me all night?"

Marissa muted the television and looked at me. "Why are you here, Jane? Is this about another guy?"

I guess I deserved that. "No. I wanted to apologize."

"Really? For what exactly?"

"I haven't been a very good friend lately."

Sounding mildly bored, Marissa said, "Go on," but I could see her hazel eyes dilating and knew I had finally piqued her interest.

I took a bite from the bottom of my cupcake, leaving the frosting for last. "Look, I didn't mean to go all self-absorbed on you. This dating stuff was harder than I thought it would be and, well, it consumed me."

"You think?"

I tucked my hair behind my ear. "If it's any consolation, you weren't my only victim. I fought with Claire too. It wasn't until she wound up in the hospital that I—"

Interrupting, Marissa said, "Claire's in the hospital? Is she all right?"

"She's home and she's fine." When Marissa opened her mouth to speak again, I said, "So is the baby. I'll tell you about it later. Please let me finish. I think you'll want to hear this."

Marissa nodded for me to continue, but still frowned with concern.

"I've been out of control and it's taken its toll on every important relationship in my life. I've lost my parents' trust by forgetting to take the LSAT and then lying about it. We're okay now, but it will be a while before they trust me again. I lost all sense of judgement by inviting Buddy back to Claire's apartment and wonder if she'll ever let me babysit my nephew without fearing I'm going to do something reckless while he's in my care. I was beyond rude to Lainie when she was only trying to be helpful. And then there's you. We've been best friends for eight years now and I behaved like my life was center stage and yours was just a sideshow. I tried to convince myself my attempts to apologize over the phone were enough and that you were also to blame for ignoring me, but you were right. Those attempts were half-assed and not nearly enough to convey how much I appreciate your friendship and miss you."

Marissa wiped a tear from her eye. "You acted like my problems were less important than yours. Like I didn't count. Best friends don't do that."

I nodded as a lump formed in my throat. "I know. I'm done making excuses for my behavior and spewing lame apologies." I put my hand to my chest. "This one comes from the heart. Will you please forgive me?"

Marissa stared me down for a few moments and I felt my chin tremble in certainty she wasn't going to accept my apology. But then she smiled softly. "I forgive you." Raising a finger, she said, "But if you ever treat me like a second-class citizen again, we're done." Her lips curled up again and she finally took a bite from the cupcake she'd been holding the entire time. "And by the way, being single isn't the end of the world. We're only twenty-six."

"No, it's not the end of the world. But it would be if we weren't friends anymore. Best friends. I love you."

"I love you too."

"I'm so happy." I reached over to hug her.

Marissa remained stiff in my embrace before pulling back. "I got the promotion, by the way."

"What promotion?"

Marissa shook her head. "Exactly."

My heart sank. "Did I miss something?"

Marissa frowned. "I told you my project manager had quit and asked for your help making a list of my best qualities to emphasize during the interview. You were too busy lost in Jane's world and comparing yourself to Trish to bother with me. But I got the job. No thanks to you. I know you say I rely on Katherine too much, but she's the one who encouraged me to go for it and helped me prepare. I'm not sure I could have done it without her."

I felt my eyes water and reached for her hand. "I'm so sorry I wasn't there for you, and I'm glad you have Katherine. Sisters are the best." I shook my head in shame. "God, I was awful. I promise to never, *ever* take you for granted again. Please take my word on that."

Marissa nodded and squeezed my hand. "It's a good thing I love you, Frank."

I hugged her firmly. When we separated, I said, "What did you wind up buying Katherine and Martin for their anniversary?"

"The two remaining place settings of their china pattern. They never got a complete set when they originally registered. It was an easier choice than I thought since Katherine conveniently mentioned it to me the day before the dinner."

"Was the dinner awful?"

"Not as bad as I expected." Laughing, Marissa said, "I drank a lot of wine to dull the pain."

I raised my glass of milk in the air. "Well, it's not wine, but I think your promotion and our friendship deserves to be toasted." I motioned to Marissa's glass and, smiling, she raised it in the air with mine. "To your promotion and friendship."

"To friendship," Marissa repeated.

## Chapter 45

Later that night, I went home and signed up for the June LSAT. I even registered for a Kaplan prep class. I didn't make enough money to blow two thousand dollars on a course I wouldn't attend and had a feeling asking my folks to foot the bill wouldn't go over well. An online course would have been more convenient, but I feared it might be *too* convenient, so I chose the live class. And I assured Marissa it wasn't to meet men.

Off to a good, albeit second, start on the road to law school, I returned my focus to mending the relationships I had let go astray due to my unsuccessful quest for a committed relationship. Next up: Lainie.

As happy as I was to have resolved things with Marissa, I hadn't been all that concerned. I was sincerely remorseful for taking her friendship for granted, but I trusted it would take more than a few months living in an "it's all about me" bubble to permanently turn her against me. I was less confident about Lainie. I hadn't known her long enough to know if she was the forgiving type, but she'd mentioned many times that she was a Scorpio and that Scorpios were known to hold grudges.

Lainie was a self-proclaimed expert in everything, so I didn't want to apologize for not blindly drinking the Lainie Kool-Aid, but harsh words were spoken, and I knew I was responsible for our fight. Lainie hadn't changed as a result of her relationship with Antoine; *I* was the one who had changed because I was jealous at the ease with which she found what I was looking for—a relationship—while I tripped over one stumbling block after another. But I knew little about Lainie's background and to assume her path to monogamy had been easy was presumptuous of me. The bottom line was I never should have said some of the things I said and needed to express my remorse.

Lainie hadn't been spending much time in our apartment, but I knew she was home that night because I saw light peeking through her bedroom door and Mary J. Blige softly playing on her stereo. When I heard her go to the bathroom, I quickly left my room and checked the kitchen to see if Antoine was with her. He wasn't. That was a rarity of late, so I took it as my opportunity to have a chat.

I sat on the edge of her bed. While I waited for her to come out of the bathroom, I leafed through one of her gossip magazines. Kim Kardashian was on the cover of almost all of them.

"Can I help you?"

I tossed the magazine to the side and looked up at Lainie. She was wearing a green facial mask and her almond-shaped eyes made her look like an alien. Trying to lighten the mood, I giggled. "Looking hot, Lainie."

"I don't recall inviting you into my bedroom, so if you want to insult me, do it from outside." She stood by the side of her door and motioned toward the hallway.

So much for keeping things light. "I was kidding. I just thought we should talk. I saw Antoine wasn't here and figured it might be a good time."

I nervously tapped my foot against the wooden floor of her bedroom.

"I'm not going to feel guilty about having a boyfriend, Jane," Lainie said, still not moving from the doorway of her room.

I clasped my hands behind my back. "You shouldn't have to. That's actually why I'm here."

Finally moving, Lainie turned her desk chair so it was facing the bed and sat down.

"Say your piece," she said.

Her feet were stretched out next to me on the bed. Normally I'd have joked that they smelled, but it wasn't a good time. "I haven't been myself lately, and I know it's gotten in the way of my friendships, including ours. I'm sorry."

Looking me square in the eyes, she said, "How have you not been yourself? Because you've been immature, spoiled, and controlling? You were all of those things when we met, Jane."

My cheeks burned as if she'd slapped me across the face. I didn't want her to see me cry, so I stood up and walked to her door. With my back to her, I wiped my eyes, said, "I'm sorry I bothered you," and started to walk out.

"Oh crap. Jane. Jane, come back."

I turned around. "Yes?" I didn't know if I could handle further attack on my character and held my breath.

Standing up again, Lainie walked over to me. "I didn't mean...Are you crying?"

"No." When my lips began to quiver and my vision blurred from the tears, I changed my answer. "Yes. Sorry."

"I shouldn't have been so blunt. I'm sorry."

"But you really feel that way?"

Lainie didn't say anything. Our eyes locked and I silently pleaded with her to retract her comments. "Sometimes I feel that way. Not always," she said apologetically.

I wasn't sure that made me feel any better.

"Most of the time, it's endearing. You're a type A, Jane, for sure. And you always think you're right."

Reddening, I said, "I always think I'm right? Pot. Kettle. Black."

Lainie's eyes widened behind the goop on her face. "Me?"

"Uh-huh. 'You should play the field, Jane.' 'The NYC dating world is a zoo, Jane.' 'You should listen to me, Jane.' Sound familiar?"

Lainie smiled for the first time. "Oh."

"Oh," I echoed.

"Can we start over? What did you want to talk about?"

"I wanted to say…" I cleared my throat. "Before you so harshly summarized my most egregious attributes, that I realized you've just been trying to help me. I'm sorry I was a bitch about it."

"Apology heard and accepted. I know how difficult it is for you to admit when you're wrong."

"Yes. And I know how it pains you to rub it in my face."

Nodding in agreement, Lainie said, "Yes, painful. It hurts." She faked a cry. "Hurts so much."

"Oh, shut up, you alien." I grabbed a magazine from her bed and threw it at her.

She looked confused. "Alien?" Then she touched a finger to her face. "My mask!" Running out of the room, she shouted, "How long have we been talking?"

"Not that long. Relax," I said, laughing as I followed her into the bathroom and watched her scrub the mask off her face. "What did you think would happen? Your face would turn green permanently?"

"No, but overexposure could burn my face, right? Or dry it out," she said, patting her face with a towel.

"I wouldn't know. Never used a facial mask."

"You should. We're never too young to start caring for our skin. Down south, girls start getting facials in their teens." Patting the top of my head, she said in her Southern accent, "You might be a few years younger than me, but you're no spring chicken, *Cher*."

"Hmm, don't they say 'Cher' in New Orleans? And isn't your family from Atlanta?"

Lainie threw the towel on the floor and left the bathroom. "Once again, I try to help you and you miss the point." Smiling, she said, "Want to use some of the mask?"

I picked the towel back up, placed it on the towel rack where it belonged, and followed her into the hallway. Glancing back at my room, I said, "I appreciate the offer, but I really should take a practice exam. I signed up for the regular LSAT course, but I think I should take the advanced course instead. It's focused on students who want to get into a top-tier school. I need to get at least a 158 on a practice exam to enroll and, as you might have noticed, I haven't been studying much."

"I hadn't noticed. Been too busy avoiding you."

Chuckling, I said, "But we're good now, right?"

Lainie nodded. "We're good."

"I'm so glad. I'm going to make some coffee and try to get in a few hours of prep." I started walking to the kitchen.

"Jane?"

I turned around. "Yeah?"

"If you meet a cute guy in your class, please don't think it's fate that you signed up for the same course and imagine a life in the law firm of *Jane and Husband LLP*."

"Girl Scout's honor." With my palm facing out and my thumb holding my little finger, I gave her the Scout Sign.

Shaking her head at me, Lainie said, "I should have known you were a Girl Scout."

I shrugged. "I am who I am."

Lainie smiled sheepishly. "I was one too. Troop 442."

At the same time, we sang, "*Make new friends, but keep the old. One is silver and the other's gold.*"

# Chapter 46

I should have realized it wouldn't take forty-five minutes to get across town to West 56th Street. Because I gave myself an extra ten minutes to get a good seat and settle in, I arrived at the class almost thirty minutes early. There was only one other student in the room. He was reading, so all I could see was the dark brown hair that covered the top of his head. He sat in the center of the second row, exactly where I wanted to sit, so I chose the desk next to his and shyly greeted him.

He looked up with a lazy smile. "Hey there. Another early bird," he said before taking a sip of his venti Starbucks.

His eyes were turquoise, like the water in Cozumel, Mexico, where I had gone with Marissa right after I broke up with Bob. They were beautiful, and I was momentarily rendered speechless. Feeling myself blush, I said, "I didn't think the crosstown bus ran so often on Saturday mornings."

Blue Eyes stretched his lean but muscular arms over his head and grinned. "I live in Park Slope. I'm not used to taking the subway into the city this early either and gave myself way too much time. So here I am."

"Do you want to be a lawyer?" Duh, Jane. Why else would he be taking the LSAT?

"Well, I want to go to law school. Not sure I'll actually practice law."

"Why not? I mean, why bother with the law degree if you might not even want to be a lawyer? Lots of time and expense involved, no?"

Maintaining a relaxed position with his head resting against the palm of his hand and his elbow on the desk, Blue Eyes faced me. "I already have an MBA. Having a legal degree too will give me an edge in the biz."

I had no idea to what "biz" he was referring, but he was so cute it didn't matter, and if he already had his MBA, he had to be at least my age, if not older.

"Sounds like a great plan," I said, wondering what else I could do with a law degree besides practice law.

"You like U2?"

"The band?"

Blue Eyes nodded.

"Love them. My best friend's family is practically off-the-boat Irish and loves all things Ireland, including Bono, The Edge, and especially Larry Mullen Jr. I've seen them three times with her and her sister. Why?"

"I love them too. Was just listening to 'Rattle and Hum' on my iPod. They just don't make music like that anymore."

I said, "Agree completely" before turning around to check out the group of people who had joined us in the classroom. We all acknowledged each other's presence with a nod, a smile, and a soft "Hi," but then I turned back to Blue Eyes, hoping to resume our conversation and see what else we had in common. He was on the phone but grinned at me. I smiled back and fidgeted with my notebook while struggling to hear his end of the conversation.

"Me too. Okay, bye," he said. He placed his phone in his messenger bag. "My wife—calling to wish me good luck on my first day of school. She was still sleeping when I left this morning."

My heart skipped a beat. "Your wife?" I hoped I heard him wrong. He wasn't wearing a ring. Gorgeous men should always wear a ring when chatting with single women.

"Yeah, she's a teacher. Kindergarten."

I bit back disappointment I'd heard him correctly. Embarrassed, I said nonchalantly, "I didn't hear what you said before." Boldness and a bit of anger quickly replacing my shame, I gestured toward his left hand and added, "And married men usually wear rings."

Blue Eyes chuckled. "Yeah, my wife took it to be polished. She suggested I wear a cigar ring in the meantime so I wouldn't mislead all the single ladies." He adopted a girl's voice for the last part that I assumed was supposed to sound like his wife. In his normal voice, he said, "But I figured I could manage to stay out of trouble for a few days. Everyone at work knows I'm married, and I doubt anyone in this class would be concerned about my marital status." He laughed again. "There are much cheaper ways to get a date than this."

Feeling my face burn, I said, "Totally." Then I opened my notebook to the first page and wrote my name in script in small letters on the upper left corner. I looked up at the ceiling. *I know, Lainie. I know.* Then I wrote "Focus" in big letters underneath my name.

Drawing to mind the drinking game we sometimes played in college, I silently chanted to myself, "What's the name of the game?" Drum roll. "The LSAT course." "Why do we play?" Drum roll. "To get into a good law school."

# Chapter 47

"See you next week," I said to Roberto (formerly known as Blue Eyes) before walking out of the classroom and onto 56th Street a few weeks later. I had the entire day ahead of me and no desire to spend the afternoon studying. I had received a score of over 160 on my last two practice exams and still had seven weeks to further improve my testing skills. I needed a break. It was a warm, sunny day. I unbuttoned my trench coat, put on my sunglasses, and began walking north, figuring I'd cross town through the park. I heard my phone ring and stepped aside to answer it. "Hey, what's up?"

"Please come over tonight," Claire said, a hint of desperation in her voice. "I can't spend another night playing Candy Crush Saga on Facebook."

And if you update your status one more time about what Kevin is making for dinner, I might have to de-friend you. "Sounds good. We can watch a movie on Netflix."

"Something funny. And no childbirth scenes."

"Will Kevin object to a romantic comedy?"

"I'm letting Kevin go out with the guys."

"Yay. Ladies' night. I won't have time to make any snacks, but I'll stop at Fairway and buy some."

"Pick up Mallomars. Or Double Stuf. Or Chips Ahoy!"

I laughed. "Trust me. You won't go to bed hungry. Seven?"

"Can you make it six thirty? Not sure I can stay up past nine."

I resumed walking at a brisk pace. "Works for me. I want to get up early for the ten-fifteen spin class anyway."

"Ten fifteen is early?"

"For those of us who don't have the luxury of being excused from work all week, yes."

"Luxury? Just wait till you're preggers, little sister."

"Whatev. Bye, Claire." Walking was overrated. I threw the phone in my purse and hailed a cab.

I removed a bag of Tostitos from the shelf and tossed it in the cart with the Milano cookies. After a brief hesitation in front of the jars of salsa, I moved on. It would only take me a few minutes to make something from scratch and it would be so much better. I continued roaming the aisles for the delicious combination of sweet and salty treats when I saw the back of a familiar head examining a box of Bavarian pretzels. I stopped in my tracks.

That Vidal Sassoon haircut was unmistakable. It had to be her, especially since her head was attached to such a freakishly short body. Maybe not freakishly short, but short enough. What was she doing on the Upper East Side? I wondered if Bob was with her. I hadn't seen her since the afternoon Marissa and I ran into her and Bob at Starbucks and she'd been decidedly quiet. She probably thought I was a total freak after my behavior at her party. *I'm just using them for sex.* My body recoiled at the memory. I'd never had a chance to apologize and wanted to do it before Bob appeared by her side. It was a girl thing. I approached her and lightly tapped her on the back. I must have startled her because she jumped and dropped the cereal box she was holding. "I didn't mean to scare you. Sorry." I smiled timidly. "Hi."

"Hi, Jane," she said smoothing down her already perfectly coiffed hair.

I bend down and picked the pretzel box off the floor. Handing it to her, I said, "What brings you to this neck of the woods?"

"Girls' night. Movies and wine. My friend lives on 84th and Third."

"My sister and I had the same idea. We're watching a movie tonight too. She's pregnant and on bed rest. Basically going out of her mind." I looked over her shoulder. "Is Bob here with you?"

Trish shook her head. "No. Just me. I'm heading straight to my friend's apartment from here."

"Too bad. I haven't spoken to him since I saw you guys at Starbucks and don't like too much time to go by." More to myself, I said, "I'll call him soon."

Trish waved me away. "We've been so busy with the wedding planning anyway."

I smiled. "Congratulations again. Bob was an amazing boyfriend. I have no doubt he'll make a terrific husband."

"Thank you—"

"It will probably take me a long time to find someone as special as him."

Trish looked at me with narrowed eyes and crossed her arms. "You're dating though, right?"

"I'm taking a break. Speaking of dating, I wanted to apologize for how I behaved at your party with Todd."

"What do you mean?"

"All those things I said about needing to sow my oats and using guys for sex. I didn't mean them. I was in an odd transitional phase. Bob saw right through it because he knows me so well, but I don't want you think I'm really like that."

Trish studied me for a moment before responding. "Don't worry about it."

"Thanks. I would hate for it to get in the way of us getting to know each other and maybe even double dating sometime. Right now, I'm too focused on the LSAT to date and trying not to take it all so seriously. But someday." I stopped babbling.

"Sounds good." Trish peeked in her purse. "Crap. My friend sent me a text asking how long I'd be. I should get out here."

"Don't let me keep you. Good seeing you." As she walked away, I said, "Tell Bob I said hi."

Happy to have explained myself to Trish, I resumed my shopping trip with focus, stopping only at the cheese guy to sample the goat cheese from Spain.

# Chapter 48

"I think maybe we'll be good friends," I said to Lainie the following day.

"With your ex-boyfriend's fiancé? Doubtful," Lainie said. She was standing on a footstool and handed me the baking sheet we kept in one of the higher cabinets. We were both PMSing and craving chocolate chip cookies. Lainie suggested we run out to buy them, but it was pouring out so I offered to make a fresh batch. The Chips Ahoy! Claire and I had eaten the night before were not nearly as chewy and moist as mine.

I waited for Lainie to safely step off the stool before saying, "Why not? We both care about Bob."

"It's weird."

Furiously stirring the chocolate chips into a mixing bowl with the rest of the ingredients, I blew my hair out of my eyes. "You're weird." I handed Lainie a spoonful of cookie dough and took a spoonful for myself. "Time to shape the cookies and put them in the oven."

Later, we sat at our kitchen table: me with a tall glass of cold milk and Lainie with a tall glass of Baileys Irish Creme.

Lainie took a bite from a freshly baked cookie, closed her eyes, slowly chewed and swallowed. When she opened her eyes to find me staring at her, she said, "These are so good, Jane. Like orgasmic."

I took a bite and agreed completely. Smiling, I said, "Yeah, I'm good, aren't I?"

Lainie took another bite of a cookie. "Fan-freaking-tabulous."

I stood up, flipped my hair, and looked over my shoulder at Lainie red carpet style. "When you've got it, you've got it." Then I walked over to the sink.

"Well, you've got it. And I'm so gonna miss it."

With the water running while I rinsed my plate, I said, "I'll make them again. No worries."

A moment later, Lainie was standing at my side. "Actually, I need to talk to you," she said.

I wiped my hands on the dish towel and sat back down at the table. Gesturing toward the bottle of Baileys, I said, "Uh-oh. Will I be needing this?"

Lainie sat down and frowned while twirling a strand of hair around her finger.

"What is it?"

"Antoine asked me to move in with him, and I said yes." Raising her hand as if to stop me from saying anything, she said, "But don't worry. I'm not moving out until our lease expires in August. You have plenty of time to find a new roommate. Assuming you want to stay here."

I ran to Lainie's side of the table. "Oh my God. You guys are moving in together."

Still sitting down with a stoic expression on her face, Lainie nodded.

"That's amazing! Stand up so I can give you a congratulatory hug."

Lainie stood up and I embraced her fiercely. When we separated, she looked at me with her brow furrowed. "You're not upset about this?"

"Why would I be upset?"

Lainie raised an eyebrow and sat back down. "Something about the cheerleader for the terminally single chick finding cohabitational bliss while the cheerleader for the hopelessly romantic sleeps alone night after night after—"

"I catch your drift. But no, I'm sincerely happy for you. You're my friend. If your time to settle down is before mine, however nonsensical that is, I'm fine with it. My time will come. My finding love is not mutually exclusive with you finding love. I have to focus on law school now anyway."

Wide-eyed, Lainie said, "Wow. I'm so impressed with your maturity, Jane."

"See? I'm not always immature, selfish, and controlling. Was just going through a bad phase."

"Really? I didn't notice any weird phase. Your personality has been totally consistent since we've met."

"I was all jealous and bitter for a while, remember? I'm not like that now."

Lainie stared at me blankly. "I don't see any difference."

"C'mon. Really?"

Lainie burst out laughing. I threw my dirty napkin at her before joining in.

"How do your parents feel about this? Antoine doesn't exactly qualify as a 'polite Southern Boy,'" I said.

Lainie bit her lip. "I still haven't told them. But I will. And they'll have to deal with it. I'll blame it on them for not throwing me a bigger cotillion with more appropriate suitors." She smiled. "It will be fine. Don't worry your pretty little head about me."

As I lay in bed that night, I felt tightness in my chest thinking about how my living situation would change in a couple of months. I'd ask Marissa if she wanted to move in, but if she was happy living on her own, I'd probably have to go through Craigslist again. I slowly breathed in through my nose and out my mouth and tried to free my mind of all thoughts. As my dad liked to say, "It will all work out. It always does."

# Chapter 49

I had a lot of regrets over the last several months, including getting a ticket for drinking in public. Standing in the endless line to get into the court room, I glanced at my watch. Thank God they were calling us in alphabetical order or I'd have to take a week off from work instead of just a day.

I glanced around at the other people in line. Most looked to be around my age, give or take a couple of years. No one seemed particularly seedy, and I wondered out loud if it was always so crowded.

The guy behind me said, "I'd say at least eighty percent of the people here got tickets at the Hoboken St. Patrick's Day Parade."

I turned around in surprise. "Really? That's why I'm here."

He smiled. "Open container?"

"Yeah. You too?"

He nodded and whispered, "We're the cream of the crop. The guy behind me got caught taking a whiz by a car."

"Gross."

Shrugging, he said, "Not that I never took a piss in public, but open container is much classier."

"Agreed." Speaking softly in case anyone was listening, I said, "The cop purposely made my ticket void."

"Wrong spelling of your name?"

"No, wrong birthday."

"Right. Same shit."

I smiled and turned back around as we were ushered into the

court room. As the court officer directed me to one side of the room and my new friend to the other, I waved. "Good luck."

He waved back. "You too."

Two hours later, I walked out onto Washington Street and breathed in the fresh air. The case dismissed as promised by the police officer, I said, "Free at last. Thank God almighty, we are free at last."


"I spent four and a half hours waiting around, and my case was dismissed in about thirty seconds," I told Marissa later that night over dinner. Marissa was craving Pad Thai. I was mostly excited for Thai iced tea.

"Did you have to plead your case or request that the judge go easy on you since it was your first offense?" Marissa paused. "This *is* your first offense, right?"

"Of course. Aside from that little manslaughter charge in '99." I rolled my eyes. "Seriously, Marissa?"

"Hey, you're not the same goody-goody you used to be. All I'm sayin'."

"I've never been a goody-two-shoes."

Marissa raised her eyebrows.

"Fine. So I've been an upstanding member of society for most of my life. Sue me." I took a long sip of my iced tea, stopping only because I didn't want to finish it yet. It was so sweet and creamy, I could have sucked it down in a single sip, but I was determined to pace myself to prolong the pleasure. "Anyway, what were we saying?"

Eyeing my iced tea, Marissa said, "That the case was dismissed in thirty seconds. Can I have a sip?"

I knew she'd regret ordering just a water. I reluctantly pushed the glass to her side of the table. "That's right. They called my name, I walked up to the judge, and when the court-appointed attorney said the police officer put the wrong date of birth on my ticket, the case was dismissed. Just like that. Really boring, actually. Please kill me if the only job I get after law school is a defense attorney for the state trying these ridiculous cases."

Marissa laughed. "Well, you can always make up a more exciting version to tell your dates."

"I have no idea when I'll be going on another date, but feel free to use my story on one of yours."

Marissa leaned forward. "Speaking of which, any cute guys there?"

"Where?" I leaned forward too, mimicking her body language.

"In court."

I visualized myself back on the endless line to get into the courtroom, but was unable to picture any of the other people on line. "I have no idea. I was reading Anthony Bourdain's memoir while I waited. I only spoke to one person the entire day."

"Girl or boy?"

"Boy."

"Was he cute?"

"I don't know." Back in line in my head again, I squinted as if doing so would allow me to see him better. It always worked when I watched television. But all I got was a faceless guy with brown hair. "Maybe. I don't remember."

"Frank, you're slipping."

Laughing, I said, "Next time I get a ticket for open container, I'll do a better job scoping out men in court. What about you? Any dates coming up?"

Marissa nodded excitedly. "Yes. His name is Jason, he's a computer programmer, and he's seriously sweet and cute. We had our first date on Friday night. We met at the City Bakery for hot chocolate and cookies. He has a major sweet tooth but you wouldn't know it from looking at him. He—"

"Slow down. You're talking a mile a minute," I laughed. I hadn't seen Marissa this animated in a long time. "When's your second date?" I held my breath, praying he had already asked her out again.

"Tomorrow!"

I raised my hand to give her a high five.

Marissa clapped her hand against mine. "I'm excited but trying not to get my hopes up too high. It's only a second date."

"You have a right to be excited. Maybe it will get so serious, you'll move in with him instead of me." Marissa agreed to be my roommate when I told her Lainie would be moving in with Antoine at the end of our lease. The timing for us to live together had never worked before because she already had a roommate when I moved into the city and by the time her roommate moved out, I was living with Lainie."

"You sound like the old Jane Frank getting way ahead of yourself, but this time I hope you're right." She frowned. "No offense."

"None taken and even if doesn't work out, at least you'll know there are still guys out there you actually like. But I will cross my fingers and toes it works out. I'll even cross my eyes." I crossed my eyes at Marissa to prove my point.

"Ha. I appreciate it."

"Between Jason and your promotion, looks like things are looking up for you. You deserve it."

"Thanks, Jane. We both deserve it."

"Agreed. But for now, I think we should get the check." I glanced around the restaurant hoping to spot our waiter. "I have some studying to do."

# Chapter 50

I was putting the finishing touches on my tuna casserole, a new recipe I had dreamed up, when my phone rang. Bob. I hadn't spoken to him in a while and wondered if his call had anything to do with my recent encounter with Trish. Cheerily, I answered, "Hey there. How's my favorite ex-boyfriend?"

Bob laughed. "I'm good, Jane. How are you?"

"I'm fabulous."

"Wow, you sound like you're in good spirits."

"I am. I'm more than prepared for the LSAT, about to be an aunt, on good terms with my friends and family, and making a mess in my kitchen, cooking up a storm. Life could be worse." As the words left my mouth, I felt warmth in my heart in the realization that I really *was* happy. "To what do I owe the honor of your call?" There was silence on the other end of the phone. "Bob? You still there?"

"Yeah, I'm still here."

"What's going on? You sound weird."

I heard Bob exhale into the phone. "Jane, I, uh, have to tell you something, and I really don't want to."

I felt my pulse beat faster and the warmth in my heart changed to goosebumps on my arms. "What the hell? Is everything okay?" I remembered when Bob's aunt passed away and her brother had emailed the news to Bob and asked him to tell his mother. He knew the death would hit his mom hard and hated being the messenger. I didn't think I'd heard him so reluctant to talk since then. "Bob? Just tell me. I can take it." I sure hoped I could take it.

Bob sighed loudly again. "Trish doesn't think we should be friends anymore."

Confused, I said, "You and Trish? That makes no sense." Then I realized what he meant. "She doesn't think you and me should be friends anymore? Why?"

"She thinks it's inappropriate since we dated for so long and now I'm going to be married to her. She said it's awkward and too close for comfort."

I sat down at my kitchen table. "I don't understand. She told me at your party she wanted us to be friends. Even thanked me for training you so well."

"Yeah, but that was before you acted weird."

"I apologized to her for that. Didn't she tell you I saw her in Fairway?"

"She did, but..."

"Didn't you tell her I'm completely normal?"

"Yeah, but..."

"But what?" I stood up again and paced the kitchen floor, one hand holding the phone and the other chewing on my cuticles.

"She thinks you acted weird because you're still in love with me."

I felt my eyes bug out. "Please. I broke up with you. Did you tell her that?" He probably didn't. He probably told her it was mutual or something to protect his manly pride. Or that he broke up with me.

"I did, but she's afraid your dating disasters have you regretting the decision to split with me."

Ouch. "Well, that's just ridiculous and you know it."

Speaking almost in a whisper, Bob said, "I know and I told her as much. But she's my fiancée, the future mother of my children. I have to do this for her. It won't be forever. Just let her calm down. After we're married, I'll talk to her again."

"Wait, I'm not invited to the wedding?" I felt my eyes water. Despite my fear I wouldn't have a date, Bob had been the most important man in my life aside from my dad. And now he was shutting me out. Why? Because I told Trish I was using guys for sex? Or was it because I mentioned Bob was a good lover? "I can't believe this," I said. I wasn't sure if I was speaking to Bob or myself.

"I'm sorry, Jane. Give me time. I promise she'll come around. I'm gonna miss you."

"Yeah, I'll miss you too," I said absently as the tears blurred my focus. I wiped them away. "I gotta go, Bob. Take care."

# Chapter 51

The night before the LSAT, my phone rang as I was getting into bed, just as it had the last time. But this time, I happily answered it since I had nothing to hide. "Hi, Daddy."

In his usual good-natured voice, my dad said, "How are you, Pumpkin?"

"I'm good. Just taking it easy tonight." I removed my pink bunny slippers and slid under the covers, ready for the Lifetime movie to begin.

"No big plans this Friday night?"

"The night before the LSAT?"

After a brief hesitation, my dad said, "Will you be taking the exam this time?"

I shook off my first instinct to be insulted he even had to ask. "Yes, I'm really taking the test tomorrow."

"I had no doubt." Whispering, he said, "Your mother was concerned though."

In the background, I heard my mother yell, "I had every right to be concerned."

"Not only am I taking the LSAT tomorrow as planned, but in the battle between Jane Frank and the LSAT, Jane will emerge victorious. I've eaten, slept, and breathed practice exams for the past three months. I'm confident I have the analytical, reading comprehension and writing skills to get at least a 165, and absent an unavoidable act of God during the exam, there's no reason I shouldn't."

"Then hopefully there won't be an earthquake tomorrow. You

know how prominent they are in the New York City Metro area."

"I was more concerned about a tsunami, to be honest."

"Al Roker hasn't predicted one so you should be fine, sweetheart."

"Then I'm really ready. And we probably shouldn't joke about acts of God." It so happened, the Lifetime movie of the week was about a flood that left a single mother (played by Alyssa Milano) and her children stranded in the basement of their home. I switched the channel to repeats of *The Golden Girls*.

"In that case, I'll just wish you good luck, honey. Even though you don't need it."

Feeling superstitious, I said, "Well, good luck never hurt anyone, Dad."

"I'm proud of you no matter what. Do you want to talk to Mom?"

Without thinking, I said, "Not if she's going to make me more nervous."

"Just call us tomorrow when it's all over."

Laughing, I said, "Will do. Love you both."


As it turned out, there was no earthquake the next day. Nor was there a tsunami, flood, tornado, avalanche, or any other act of God. In fact, it didn't even drizzle, and the breeze in the area was welcome as it was an unseasonably warm June day. It felt more like August, thanks to the trademark New York humidity. The test was hard, but when I left the testing center approximately five hours after I'd arrived, I was confident all the studying I'd finally done was not for nothing. I was even pretty sure my scores would be enough to get me into Columbia. I should have been high on life, but instead I was filled with anxiety. Maybe it was leftover nerves from the last few days, but I couldn't shake it. I wanted to treat myself to something special as a reward for getting my life back on track and knock me out of my unexpected funk, but I didn't know what. I could take a tour of the Columbus campus, but I'd done that with Bob years earlier and wasn't in the mood. I stopped in front of a Mister Softee truck, but wanting something more substantial than a soft serve ice cream cone, kept walking. And then I saw it. On the corner of Broadway and Grand, L'Ecole, the restaurant affiliated with the International Culinary Institute. The menu was expensive, but considering I'd paid $2,000 for the Kaplan LSAT prep course, what was another fifty?

Because it was late afternoon—not yet dinner but too late for lunch—I could have dined at one of the many empty tables covered with fine white linen and adorned with cut orchards, but I sat down at the small bar instead. I was immediately greeted with a smile from a twenty-something male bartender with a shag hairstyle and topaz-brown eyes. "Can I get you a drink?" he asked.

"I wasn't planning on drinking, but I'm celebrating, so what the hell? I'll have a glass of Chenin blanc. Can I please see a food menu too?" I placed my bag on one of the hooks under the bar.

"Of course," he said. "We have a three-course price fix if you're interested." He handed me the menu.

"I'm in." I relaxed my posture as the tension slowly left my body.

"Can I ask what you're celebrating?" he asked.

With a proud grin, I said, "I took the LSAT this afternoon and I'm pretty sure I nailed it."

"Nice. A lawyer, huh?"

"Yes, but don't hold it against me."

He winked. "I wouldn't dare."

I glanced over my shoulder in the direction of the kitchen. "Are you a student at ICI?" The restaurant was a working school where students at the culinary institute interned as servers or chefs.

"Sure am," he said, pouring me a glass of wine.

"Do you like it?" I took a sip of my wine.

"It's a dream come true."

A barrage of questions whipped through my brain. "Do you want to be an executive chef somewhere? Or do you have a specialty like rotisseur, saucier, or poissonneir? Or are you more interested in front of house? You think you'll open your own restaurant one day?" I took a breath and looked at him in awe.

The bartender's eyes opened wide. "Wow. You know your stuff."

I felt heat creep across my cheeks. "I love food and everything associated with it," I said with a swirl of my glass.

He smiled. "You've come to the right place. To answer your many questions, I'd like to work my way up to executive chef somewhere high end and eventually co-own a restaurant with my girlfriend. We met in the program."

"To fall in love with someone who shares your passion must be amazing," I said. I took another sip of my wine.

"So far, so good." Topping off my glass, he said, "This is on the house because it's a special occasion."

"Thank you so much." I removed the glass from the bar and brought it to my mouth again.

"Since you love food so much, did you ever consider a career in culinary arts or did you always know you wanted to be a lawyer?"

I immediately responded, "I've always wanted to be a lawyer," but it came out more like a question and the bartender gave me a funny look.

"You sure about that?" he asked.

I'd been answering the question for so long, I never asked myself if I was telling the truth. A chill ran through my body and as my hands trembled, I carefully placed the glass back on the wood bar. My heart racing, I said, "I just remembered I have to be somewhere." I removed a twenty-dollar bill from my wallet and handed it to the bartender, whose name I never got. "Will this cover my wine?"

He shuffled back in surprise. "It's fine, but are you all right?"

I tossed my wallet back in my bag, stood up, and plastered on a smile. "It was so nice talking to you. Best of luck with school, your girlfriend, and the future." With a quick wave, I hurried out of the restaurant and onto the street where I leaned against the building and took a long, deep breath.

*   *   *

I sat up in bed and sucked in my breath. I looked down at the shape of my body under the covers and at the walls of my bedroom and realized it was just a dream. I had been dressed in a navy suit, sitting at a conference table, ironing out the details of an agreement between my client and a third party. I was a fifth-year associate at my father's law firm and well on my way to making partner. It was everything I'd always wanted.

So why was I sweating?

# Chapter 52

"Pack it up, Frank," Andrew said to me the following Wednesday.

I looked up from my computer and over at Andrew. "What are you talking about?"

"Let's get a drink. We're working too hard." Standing up, he said, "C'mon, you can finish whatever you're working on later."

Grabbing my purse from my desk drawer, I said, "Just one."

"You can drink one for my two. Deal?"

"Deal. You think I need a jacket?" It had been warm earlier when I had picked up lunch, but it was after eight p.m. now and the necessity of outerwear at night was unpredictable this time of year.

"Nah. We'll just go to Hillstone."

I grimaced. The last time I'd been to Hillstone was when I thought Andrew liked me and I'd convinced myself the feelings were mutual. I still thought he was a great guy, but my romantic feelings for him had disappeared in a New York minute. Similar to Randall, Jim, and Cory's romantic interest in me. Single New Yorkers sure were fickle, I thought with a chuckle.

"What's so funny?" Andrew looked down at his black shoes, up the length of his gray pants, and back to me. "Did I skip a button on my shirt or something?"

Ignoring his question, I said, "Hillstone it is."

A few minutes later, we were sitting at the bar. Well, I was sitting. Andrew insisted I take the last bar stool.

"So what's going on, Jane?" Andrew said, his back to the guy on the barstool to the right of me.

"Nothing much. What about you? How's Farah?" I was genuinely pleased for him now.

"The honeymoon phase is over and I still haven't cheated."

Rolling my eyes, I said, "Am I supposed to award you a medal or something?"

"Maybe a gold star."

"You're pathetic, Andrew," I said, laughing.

"What about you? You've been quiet this week. Is there a new douche bag in the picture? Need my expert advice?"

The girls next to me on the other side got up to leave. I slid over a barstool and motioned for Andrew to take my seat. "Dating isn't even on my radar right now."

"I can set you up with Brandon or Don. Just pick one this time."

I stuck my tongue out at him, but then chuckled. "Maybe ask me again in a few months."

He narrowed his eyes at me. "That's it? No complaining about being single? No ranting that guys suck?"

"I'm not saying guys don't suck. I'm just saying they're not at the forefront of my mind right now."

"As impressed as I am with the calm, cool, and collected Jane, something is on your mind. Care to share?"

I disguised my frown by bringing my glass to my mouth. Ever since the day I took the LSAT the previous weekend and talked to the bartender at L'ecole, I had trouble focusing. The only reason I was at work late tonight was because it was taking me twice as long to get things done. Once I'd acknowledged the future looming before me wasn't the one I wanted, it was all I could think about.

I faced Andrew, who was studying me with concern. "Does this have anything to do with the LSAT? You took it last weekend, right?" he asked.

"Yes to both questions." Maybe I'd feel better if I told someone.

"Did you blow it? If so, no big deal. You can take it again."

"I actually think I did really well," I said, placing a strand of hair behind my ear.

Andrew pursed his lips. "So what is it?"

My eyes welled up and I took a deep breath. "I don't think I want to be lawyer." There. I said it.

His eyes bugging out, Andrew said, "You don't? Since when?"

As a tear dropped down my cheek, I choked out, "I don't know. I've been talking about working with my dad since I was in fourth grade, but I never thought about the actual work part." I wiped my eyes. "Seems so stupid, I know."

Cocking his head to the side, Andrew said, "Not stupid." He gestured to the bartender for another round before looking back at me. "I think you need another glass."

I smiled timidly. "With enough wine, maybe I'll forget I've been living a lie."

"I think you're being way too hard on yourself. Do you know what you want to do instead?"

"I do. I want to be chef." My lips curling up, I said, "I want to create food." As the words came out, I felt my face light up at the image. "First stop, culinary school."

Andrew's eyes opened. "Wow. Have you told your parents?"

"Not yet," I said, my breath catching in my throat.

"At least you decided before you spent any money on law school, right?"

"For sure, a bright side."

Andrew gave me a friendly tap on the leg. "I know it's hard, but the sooner you tell them, the better you'll feel and the quicker you can start your new life—the one you really want to live."

I swallowed hard. "I know you're right, but I don't want to disappoint them." I pictured their faces when I told them and shuddered. My dad would be crushed and my mom's ears would turn red in anger.

"Better now than after a year or two of law school. Unless you'd rather go along with your parents' plans for you than be happy." He raised an eyebrow.

"Neither option is looking too hot right now."

"Let's drop this topic for now. I'm a good wing man. How's about we get you laid?"

I took another sip of wine. "I've already had my share of meaningless sex this year."

"Ah, yes. You never did tell me about that one time."

Without thinking, I said, "Which one time?"

Eyes wide open, Andrew said, "How many 'one times' were there?"

I stared off into the distance pretending to count. When I looked back at Andrew, he was gazing at me expectantly. I smiled. "Just two."

"Two is better than one. But three would be better." High-fiving me, he said, "It's a start."


After I finished my glass of wine and Andrew chugged one more beer, he walked me back to the office before heading to Farah's apartment. Slightly buzzed, I changed my mind about doing more work and headed home.

When I walked into the apartment, I heard voices coming from the kitchen. I tossed my keys on the rack, hung up my jacket, and greeted Lainie and Antoine. "Hey, guys."

Antoine looked up from his laptop. "What's up, Jane?"

Before I could respond, Lainie said, "You're home late. Do anything fun tonight?"

I kicked off my shoes, leaving them in the middle of the floor, and, ignoring the surprised look on Lainie's face, sat down. "Worked late. Had a drink with Andrew. Went back to the office."

"How'd that work for you?" Lainie asked.

Not sure if she was referring to the drink with Andrew or working late, I asked her to clarify.

"Both, actually. You're a major lightweight, Frank. Drinking and working?" Shaking her head, she said, "Not likely."

"Now be nice, Lainie," Antoine said softly, but I could see the amused look in his eyes even from behind his long eyelashes.

I waved my hand in the air. "She's right. I didn't accomplish much."

"And how was Andrew? Still dating the slut?"

Wincing, I said, "She's not a slut, Lainie. But, yes, they're still an item."

Lainie shrugged. "It's his loss. I'm sure you're prettier and no doubt more ambitious."

"Amen, sister," Antoine said.

"Maybe he's intimidated by you," Lainie said.

I got up and poured a glass of water from the Brita container. "He's not intimidated. He just doesn't think of me that way."

"But he'd nail you anyway," Antoine said with a cackle.

"And now it's my turn to say Amen." Lainie laughed.

"Seriously, guys, Andrew and I are just friends. My guy is out there somewhere. Like Michael Bublé says, 'I just haven't met him yet.'" Tired and anxious to go to sleep, I walked out of the kitchen.

In response to my off-key rendition of the lyrics, Lainie called after me, "Don't quit your day job, Frank," quickly adding, "Unless it's to make me dinner or bake cookies."

As Lainie's statement hit entirely too close to home, my heart skipped a beat and I muttered, "I'll take it under advisement," before closing my bedroom door behind me.

# Chapter 53

After getting the go-ahead from Dr. Flynn, my folks planned one last adults-only family cookout at their house the following Saturday. From the back of Kevin's car as he parked in my parents' driveway, I silently repeated, "I can do this." Next time I sat in this vehicle, it would all be over. I might be an orphan, but I'd be an orphan on her way to culinary school. I chose to make my proclamation today hoping Claire and Kevin would have my back if things got heated. Of course, I hadn't mentioned it to them yet, but I'd practiced my speech in front of both Marissa and Lainie.

Claire knocked on the back window. "What are you waiting for? I'm the waddling pregnant chick who will need a Handybar to get in and out of the car if I don't give birth soon. What's your excuse?"

Willing my heart to slow down, I took a deep breath, opened the door, and stepped out of the car. "I'm coming. Did Kevin open the trunk? I need to grab my dishes." I'd volunteered to bring all of the food aside from what my dad would grill on the barbeque. I did it because it was fun, but also to support my conviction that I was a talented cook, food was my passion, and I wanted it to be my career as well. I spent my Friday night and Saturday morning preparing a feast of carrot and apple slaw with raisins, creamy potato salad with bacon, macaroni and cheese, tangy cucumber-dill salad, and maple corn bread. The menu was over the top even for me, but I needed all the help I could get.

Kevin and I were debating who would carry what into the house, when my dad walked down the porch steps and approached the car. "Let me help you with that," he said, removing two of the aluminum containers from my hand. He kissed me on the head. "You went all out, didn't you, Pumpkin?"

"I did," I said before following him into the house and to the kitchen where my mom was mixing a punch bowl of sangria. "Hi Mom."

My mom licked her finger. "The sangria needs something. What do you think?"

I liked the idea of my mom a bit liquored up before my announcement and the twitchy feeling in my stomach lessened a bit as I brought a spoonful of sangria to my lips. "More white wine."

"Sounds about right," my mom said pulling me in for a quick hug. "Tell us more about the LSAT. You think you nailed it?"

I waved a hand in protest. "First things first. I need to set up my food." As the waves in my stomach crashed in full force once again, I feared it might be my last supper.

I managed to put off the LSAT talk for another half hour. While my dad and Kevin hovered over the grill, I put finishing touches on my dishes, and my mom and Claire gushed over the impending birth of baby boy Williamson. (He still didn't have a name.) But all too soon, the Frank and Williamson family were feasting al fresco on my parents' patio and conversation turned to me.

"Tell us about the LSAT. Did you need all of the allotted time or did you leave early?" my dad asked.

"I made really good time," I said before biting into my cheeseburger.

"A very good sign." My dad beamed.

"Oh my god. I love this mac and cheese," Claire said. She helped herself to another heaping spoonful as the rest of us watched in amusement. Well, my parents and Kevin were amused. I was thrilled for the distraction.

"When will you get the results?" my mom asked.

"In about two weeks," I said. "The thing is—"

"Call us right away," my dad said.

"I will, but—"

"What happens next?" my mom asked.

I closed my eyes and reminded myself to breathe.

"Are you all right, Jane?" Claire asked.

"Not really," I mumbled with my eyes still closed.

"What's wrong? Is it the burger?" my dad asked.

I opened my eyes. "It's not the burger."

"What then?" my mom asked.

My lips trembling, I said, "I have to tell you something and I'm afraid you're not going to like it," I said.

"Don't even tell us you skipped the test again," my mom said as her face turned white.

I shook my head. "I took the test and I'm confident I did well. The thing is..." I felt faint, but it wasn't going to get any easier if I put it off. "I don't want to go to law school."

My dad furrowed his brow. "You need more time?"

"I don't think another year as a paralegal is going to make a difference, Jane," my mom said.

To my mom, my dad said, "Probably not, but if it makes her more comfortable."

"Waste of time," my mom said.

I stood up and tapped my plastic knife against my plastic cup. Unfortunately, plastic on plastic doesn't make much noise so I raised my voice and said, "I don't want to be a lawyer at all."

There was a collective gasp around the table followed by silence, and then all eyes were on me.

Trying to keep my voice steady, I said, "I've been saying I want to be an attorney forever and I just about convinced myself it was true, but it's not." I made eye contact with my dad. "I know we had plans, and the idea of working with you makes me so happy, but I'd prefer to work side by side in a kitchen over a conference table or before a judge."

"A kitchen?" my dad looked confused.

"A chef," Claire said. She smiled at me. "Jane here wants to be a chef. Don't you?"

A lump formed in my throat rendering me speechless, but I nodded my answer. When I found my voice, I said, "I want to go to culinary school at The International Culinary Institute. The basic program is six hundred hours and tuition is about $50,000. It's a lot cheaper than Columbia Law School, but I'll understand completely if you don't want to pay. I'll get a loan."

My parents' response was to gape at me. I pressed my hand against my chin to stop it from quivering. Claire rose from her seat and waddled toward me with her arms outstretched. I stepped into her embrace and she whispered, "I think it's a brilliant idea. I'm so proud of you." She released me and squeezed both of my arms. Coming up behind her, Kevin said, "Congratulations, Jane."

Smiling at them and so grateful for their support, I said, "Thank you." Then I faced my parents again. "Say something. Please."

"I'm concerned you haven't thought this through," my mom said.

I argued, "I've been thinking about it for years. I just didn't know it because law school had been so firmly etched into my brain."

My mom shook her head in dismay. "The food industry is not for the meek. Crazy hours for less than impressive pay. You'll have to start at the bottom. And chefs are known to be cruel to their staff."

Since I was terrified my parents would shut me down immediately, I was thrilled with my mom's questions. I was also prepared with answers. "Everything you said except, perhaps, for the pay, can be said about the legal field as well—crazy hours, starting at the bottom, power-hungry partners." I turned to my father. "Am I right, Dad?"

My dad nodded. "You sure are."

"The difference is that I'm passionate about food preparation and I can't say the same for the law. All of the hard work will be worth it because I'll love what I'm doing."

"Not many people can say that, Mrs. Frank," Kevin said.

My mom froze in place and I could feel the tension in the air as the rest of us braced ourselves for her next words. She slowly turned to Kevin. "Mom. You're supposed to call me Mom. Remember?" When she laughed, Kevin followed suit until eventually everyone except me was chuckling.

I cleared my throat. With a shaky voice, I said, "Does this mean you're okay with my decision?"

My parents glanced at each other and seemed to have a silent conversation. After a moment, they nodded and turned to face me.

My mom spoke first. "We're fine with it. We only wish you'd told us sooner so we didn't expend so much energy worrying about the LSAT."

Taking a step closer to me, my dad said, "It takes but a single bite of one of your culinary creations to know you have a gift for food. If your passion matches your gift and you have the ambition to make it a career, far be it from us to stop you. We'll support you all the way, kiddo."

With those words, all of the tension I'd been holding let loose. I threw myself in my father's arms and burst into tears. I'd never been happier.

When I got home that evening, there was something I wanted to do. I walked to my closet, knelt down, and reached to the back for the DVDs of *Beverly Hills 90210.*

I was going to send them to Bob. It was time for him to start over with Trish, and I didn't want to hold onto anything that technically belonged to her now.

As I put the DVDs in a mustard-colored padded envelope I had bought at CVS, I thought better of it and decided to send them directly to Trish. That way, I wouldn't be blatantly breaking the "no contact with Bob" rule. I removed a sheet of scented stationary I had purchased back in high school and rarely used and lay on my stomach. With the back of a ballpoint pen in my mouth, I contemplated my note.

*Dear Trish,*

*Bob told me you were a big fan of 90210. I did a clean sweep of my apartment this weekend and found these DVDs in the back of my closet. I thought you might like them. I loved the show too. We have that in common. What we also share is affection for Bob. Although my feelings stopped being romantic many, many years ago, I still care about him. He was an important part of my life, and I truly want him to be happy. You clearly make him happy, so I will respect your wishes to stay away, although I must confess it hurts to lose a friend I've had since I was sixteen. I hope someday you will reconsider, but in the meantime, I wish you and Bob a lifetime of happiness.*

*All my best,*

*Jane.*

I folded the note, inserted it in the envelope, and pulled off the label before sealing it closed and dropping it in the mail.

# Chapter 54

Lost in thought, I gazed out the window of my crosstown bus. Seeing Dos Caminos Mexican restaurant on my right, I realized we were only in the 50s and turned back to my book. Marissa was right; it was a pretty fast read. But I still had two more of the series to go and we were supposed to have a movie marathon that weekend. Marissa insisted I choose sides in the teenage love triangle. Not like she was twenty-seven years old or anything...

I finished a chapter and looked back up to see a familiar face in the opposite aisle one row ahead. As I stared at her fifty-something profile, I wondered if she was the mother of one of my friends or a friend of my mom or maybe a former colleague. Then it dawned on me and I sucked in my breath. What were the chances of randomly running into a person twice on the same crosstown bus?

I leaned over and tapped her on the shoulder.

She quickly jumped in her seat and turned around. "Yes?" But then she smiled in recognition. "Oh, hello."

"Hi," I said cheerfully. "Small world, huh?"

Shifting her body so her legs were now facing the aisle, she said, "I'll say. How are you?" I noticed there was no poppy seed stuck in her teeth this time.

"I'm well. Really well, actually."

"Let me guess. You're engaged?"

I raised my ringless left hand. "No. Still single, but I'm at peace with it. For now at least."

"Good for you. Life's too short."

I nodded. "And I'm going to culinary school next semester instead of law school. I'm following my passion."

"How wonderful." Glancing out the window, she said, "Oh, my stop is coming up." Leaning over the man sharing her row, she pulled the lever to request the stop and stood up. "I wish you the best of luck in culinary school and beyond, and maybe I'll see you on the bus again sometime."

When the bus stopped at the light before her stop, she waved and began walking to the front exit. Suddenly, I remembered something. Realizing I never got her name, I grabbed my shopping bags and ran after her. I tapped her shoulder once again and she turned around, startled.

"Hi, again," she said with a crooked grin.

"I forgot to tell you something."

"What's that?"

"My sister and I made up. She'll be giving birth to my precious nephew any day now." The lady smiled, but I could see sadness in her eyes. I figured she was thinking of her own sister. "Thank you for your advice and for telling me about your sister. I'm sorry for your loss. It helped me see the big picture."

Her eyes welled up, and I felt guilty for bringing up bad memories. She took my hand in hers. "I'm glad I could help you. You're a sweet girl." Looking embarrassed, she said, "Woman. You're a sweet woman." The light changed and the bus pulled over to the right. When it came to a complete stop, we exchanged one more goodbye and she stepped off into the street.

I held my book against my chest the rest of the way home and closed my eyes. I was too exhausted to read and would probably enjoy the movie more if I didn't know the ending. This is what I'd tell Marissa when she pouted about my lack of preparation for our movie night. My red velvet cheesecake should be preparation enough. I opened my eyes just in time for my stop, tossed my book in my Trader Joe's bag, and walked to the rear door. As I stepped off the bus, my phone rang. It was my mom.

Her voice catching, she said, "It's your sister."

# Chapter 55

Since Claire's water had just broken and my mom said it would be a while, I stopped at my apartment to put away my groceries and change into leggings and a long t-shirt. I was happy the food made it into my refrigerator this time, rather than in a puddle on the corner of 82nd and Third. I walked briskly to the hospital, my heart beating rapidly with the knowledge I was going to be an aunt by the time I went to sleep. Unless she was in labor all night. I hoped the delivery would be quick, but not so fast that she'd give birth before my parents and I got there. We were lucky we lived close enough to wait in the hospital. Poor Kevin's parents would have to wait by their phones in Philadelphia.

The nurse wouldn't let me see Claire, so I sat in the waiting room and texted Marissa the news. Not a minute after I sent the text, she called me.

Feeling uncomfortable talking on the phone from a hospital waiting room, I whispered, "Hi." I made eye contact with the couple sharing my space and gave them a closed-mouth smile.

"Are you excited, Aunt Jane?"

Still speaking softly, I said, "Totally. Just waiting for my parents to get here. Could be a while."

"Friday night traffic from Long Island? With any luck, Grandma and Grandpa Frank might arrive in time for Baby Boy Williamson's first birthday."

I giggled at the thought of my mom as a grandmother. She still freaked out when her roots came in and the gray in her hair was visible.

"Earth to Jane."

Jolted out of the vision of my mother twenty years from now in a house dress with her teeth in a glass by her bedside, I said, "I might have to postpone movie night. Depends on how Claire is. She might want me to come over."

"Or she might have postpartum depression and want nothing to do with you."

I bit my lip. "I hadn't thought of that."

"Don't worry. She'll probably be fine. But it happens sometimes."

"Thank God my mom will be here. I hope they don't want to sleep over at my place. Lainie and Antoine might be there."

"So? You afraid your parents will catch them humping on the kitchen table or something?"

"Perish the thought. I eat off that table. But get this. I met a woman on the Third Avenue bus a few months ago. I was in my 'all about me' phase and venting to the woman about Claire. She said her sister died and urged me to appreciate Claire while I still could. Claire was admitted to the hospital the very same night."

"Interesting coincidence." Marissa laughed.

Anxious to tell her the rest, I said, "It gets better. I ran into her again tonight on the same crosstown bus. The very same night Claire went into labor."

"I thought things like that only happened in movies. Bizarro world."

"I know." Adopting a creepy voice, I said, "*Do do doo do doo do*, you just crossed into the Twilight Zone."

After we hung up, I glanced at the wall clock in the waiting room. Even in light traffic, it would probably be at least twenty minutes before my parents arrived. Kevin was with Claire, so having no one to talk to, I sent texts to Lainie, Andrew, and even Bethany to occupy my time.

I heard someone call my name and looked up to see Kevin in scrubs grinning like a three-year-old boy. I deleted the text I was drafting and stood up. "Did she have the baby?"

"Not yet. Her contractions are getting closer though. I figured you'd want to know the status." Glancing around, he said, "Your folks here yet?"

"Nope. On their way."

"I'm gonna call mine," he said before walking to a corner of the waiting room.

"Wait," I called out.

Kevin turned around and grinned. "Yeah?"

I bet that wide grin had been on his face all day. I only hoped he had the common sense to remove it during Claire's contractions. "How's she doing?"

"Surprisingly calm. Not yet screaming for an epidural, but that might have changed by now."

"Make sure they don't wait too long and lose the window of opportunity."

Kevin shook his head. "She'd kill someone before giving birth without drugs. Trust me."

"Good. Please tell her I'm here and can't wait to meet little Nathaniel."

Kevin raised an eyebrow. "Nathaniel, is it?"

"Or whatever you two decide to name him," I said, rolling my eyes. He walked away to make his call.

For the next hour, I flipped through the hospital's collection of *New York Magazine*, but looked up every two minutes hoping to see my parents. My mom sent me periodic texts, updating their estimated time of arrival, but I was impatient. I also had to use the bathroom but didn't want to leave the room in case Kevin came back. Or in the event one of the doctors burst out the double doors bearing bad news.

Despite the bed rest, I knew this was a relatively routine delivery and not an episode of *Chicago Med*, but ever since my date with Andrew at Hillstone (the first one), I liked to prepare for the worst-case scenario.

The waiting game would be much more fun if the hospital invested in a movie room. There was a television, but I was too embarrassed to change the news station to something more exciting like *NCIS*. I returned the magazine to the stack, reclined my head, and closed my eyes.

"There she is. Sleeping."

With my eyes still closed, I said, "I'm not sleeping, just resting my eyes." I opened them to see my mom standing over me with a large Barney's bag. "What's the story?" she said.

Eyeing the bag, I said, "Do some shopping on your way?"

My mom sat down next to me. "No. I brought my knitting needles. And a few magazines for your father."

"You're really getting into this grandma thing, aren't you? Since when do you knit?"

"It has nothing to do with becoming a grandmother." Removing what looked like the beginnings of a yellow bootie from the bag, she said, "We're reading all of those knitting novels in book club. Seems to be the newest 'it' activity, so Barbara and I signed up for lessons."

"Cute."

"I'm not cute, Jane. I'm trendy."

Standing up, I said, "And I'm dying to take a piss."

My mom's eyes opened wide in either amused or annoyed surprise. I wasn't sure which, and didn't want to stick around to find out. "Sorry. I really have to go. Claire's still in labor."

Dismissing me with a wave of her hand, my mom said, "Don't let me stop you. Go."

After I went to the bathroom, I decided to be nice and buy coffee for my parents.

On the way, I walked past the vending machine, which, as usual, beckoned to me with its tempting individual bags of Fritos and Cool Ranch Doritos. I turned away just before my stomach grumbled, and I knew if I didn't succumb then, I'd be back within ten minutes. I decided on the healthier bag of Baked Lays, but somehow entered the code for the Cool Ranch Doritos instead. I squatted down to remove the chips from the machine. When I stood back up, I felt a presence behind me.

"I'll be out of your way in a second. I just want to get something for my..." I turned around mid-sentence, looked up at the tall, lanky guy sharing my space, and felt my face turn white as I remembered doing a striptease for him.

# Chapter 56

"Jim." I firmly gripped the bag of chips and swallowed hard, remembering how I never heard from him again after a sexual encounter I barely recalled being party to.

Jim removed his Tigers baseball cap from his head, ran his hands through his black hair, and put the hat back on, this time backward. "Hey Jane. Come here often?" he said cheerily, his facial expression hinting no recollection of how things ended between us.

Embarrassment quickly turning to anger, I removed a hair from behind my left ear, twiddled it around my finger, and coldly said, "Not quite. My sister is in labor."

Jim gave me a wide grin. "Congrats! Wish I had such an exciting excuse to be here."

As unenthusiastically as I could, I said, "Why are you here?"

"Just being a good colleague. A guy on my team had trouble breathing at happy hour and we insisted he have it checked out." Jim shrugged his narrow shoulders. "Not the Friday night festivities I was hoping for."

I couldn't believe I used to think his laugh lines were cute. And that he was actually a decent guy. Now I just thought they were signs of old age and he was a prick. I narrowed my eyes at him. "Yeah, I'm sure you'd rather be picking up chicks." Jim didn't say anything, and I watched his eyes dart around the room, probably to avoid eye contact with me. "It was...interesting seeing you again. But there's no reason to make small talk," I said.

A film of red rising from his neck up to his face, Jim said, "Look, Jane, I'm sorry I never called you."

"First of all, please don't 'look, Jane' me. I've moved on. But for the record, it was very douchey of you. Just because sex isn't mind-blowing the first time doesn't mean it won't get better. It's certainly no reason to blow a girl off."

Grimacing, Jim said, "Oh God, Jane. That's not why I didn't call."

"So you would have blown me off even if I screwed like a porn star?"

Reddening more, Jim said, "No."

"I figured as much. Seriously? You're a dog."

Stammering, Jim said, "No. That's not...That's not what I meant." He leaned his tall frame against the vending machine and removed his baseball cap again. "The truth is, Jane, I really liked you."

Rolling my eyes, I said, "Yeah, you made that abundantly clear."

"No, really. I thought you were adorable. And sweet. And romantic." Jim looked down. "Perfect, really."

I *was* all those things. "You liked me so much you had to ghost me? Is that really the excuse you're going with?"

Jim shook his head in shame, resembling an eight-year-old boy in a man's six-foot-two-inch body.

"Well?" I didn't feel the slightest bit guilty about bullying him.

"The girls I met in the city before you were so insincere and desperate. And cynical. It's like they assumed I was dating a different girl every night, and were basically unwilling to believe I was interested in a committed relationship. They'd tell me all about other guys they went out with, the restaurants they went to, and even how many dates I'd need to take them on before they'd sleep with me." Jim looked hard at me. "You weren't like that."

"Then I'm going to ask again. What happened?"

Jim went to remove his baseball cap again and, infuriated, I quickly grabbed it from him and hid it behind my back. "Speak," I demanded, wondering when I became such a tough bitch and kind of liking it.

"You were so sweet on our first two dates, but, I don't know, you changed."

"Changed how?"

Jim rubbed his forehead and closed his eyes. When he opened them, he said, "Well, you kind of freaked me out the way you threw yourself at me."

This time it was my face that turned beet red as I took in his words. "You're complaining that single girls in this city are insincere? Well, why do you think that is, Jim?"

Jim looked at me blankly.

"It's because of the men in this city. You dump us when we don't sleep with you. You dump us when we *do* sleep with you. And sometimes, you dump us for no reason at all." I raised my arms and dropped them to my sides dramatically. "No wonder we're so cynical. I'll have you know the reason I slept with you so early was because I told the guy I dated before you I wanted to take things slow and he blew me off. I liked you, Jim, but I didn't want to sleep with you so soon. I just thought I had to." Feeling tears in my eyes, I rubbed them away. "I *am* sweet and I *am* sincere. And I'm a freaking romance-aholic. I felt horrible when I never heard from you again."

Biting the nail on his thumb, Jim looked at me sheepishly. "I'm sorry, Jane. I really did like you. I just thought it was weird and unexpected."

"Not weird enough to turn down my advances, apparently."

Jim averted eye contact again. "Yeah. Uncool. But a pretty girl comes onto me, it's hard to resist, you know?"

I sighed. "No. I really don't know. It's impossible to play the game, because the rules keep changing."

"That's just it. I don't want to play games at all." Jim exhaled loudly. "Call me old-fashioned. Crap, the guys call me gay, but honest to God, I just want to meet the right girl and go from there."

I turned my back to Jim, leaned my head on the vending machine, and muttered, "I don't want to play games either. I just want to love someone and be loved." I raised my head and turned back around to face Jim. He was smiling at me. "What are you so happy about?"

His lips still curled up, he said, "It looks like we want the same things, Jane."

After I let his words sink in, I nodded and gave a half grin back. "I guess we do."

"Do you think we can start over?"

Start over? He'd disappeared on me without so much as a Post-it note. He ruined my parents' anniversary party for me. And he put a damper on Claire's pregnancy announcement. He hurt me, and I honestly didn't know if I could handle being disappointed again. I shook my head. "I don't know, Jim. That was then. And I barely know you. All I even remember about you is that you hate when your team loses football. And it's not even football season." Was it football season? I really had no clue.

"I remember things about you."

"Like what?" Besides that I lacked the requisite stripping skills to get a job at the Bada Bing.

Jim smiled softly. "I remember how thoughtful you were to pick a sports bar that had television screens at each booth so we wouldn't have to worry about getting a table near the wrong game. And how you agreed to a second date even after seeing my lack of sportsman-like behavior." Jim paused and gazed into my eyes. "And I remember how much I liked kissing you."

I remembered that too.

Jim took a step closer to me and reached for my hand. "What do you say? Second chance?"

Who was I kidding? I still thought his laugh lines were sexy. "You win. I'll give you a second chance. But the second time better be the charm, because there will be no third." I squeezed his hand.

"I'll take my chances."

"And there will be no striptease this go-around."

Making a sad face, Jim said, "No striptease?"

I shook my head and pursed my lips. "Nope."

"Ever?"

I cocked my head to the side. "Well, I wouldn't say never. But not for a long, long time." I looked at Jim's full lips as he bent his head towards mine. I felt the soft touch of his lips and mumbled, "Well, not until at least the fourth date this time."

Jim pulled away from me and raised an eyebrow. "Final answer?"

I wrapped my arms around his neck, stood on my tippy toes, and drew him in for another kiss. But as my lips met his, I thought better of it and quickly pulled away. "No."

"No, what?" Jim took a step closer to me, closing the distance between us.

I stepped back but maintained eye contact. "No. It's not my final answer."

"What do you mean?"

"I can't make any promises about a fourth date until I know we'll actually have a first, second, and third date."

Jim moved toward me again, running his fingers up and down my arm. "I promise this time will be different."

I didn't move his hand away, but only because it felt nice. "We'll see. You give me a call, ask me for a proper date, and we'll take it from there. In the meantime, I have a nephew who, at this moment, might be taking his first breath. I gotta run." I smiled sweetly at Jim, then turned around and walked out of the cafeteria.

As I made my exit, back straight and head held high, I knew full well Jim was watching me, his mouth probably wide open. I kept smiling, not because of some presumptuous daydream about our honeymoon, but because I knew that no matter what happened, even if Jim never called, I'd be okay.

# Meredith Schorr

A born-and-bred New Yorker, Meredith Schorr discovered her passion for writing when she began to enjoy drafting work-related emails way more than she was probably supposed to. After trying her hand penning children's stories and blogging her personal experiences, Meredith found her calling writing chick lit and humorous women's fiction. She secures much inspiration from her day job as a hardworking trademark paralegal and her still-single (but looking) status. Meredith is a loyal New York Yankees fan, an avid runner, and an unashamed television addict. To learn more, visit her at www.meredithschorr.com.

**Books by Meredith Schorr**

JUST FRIENDS WITH BENEFITS
A STATE OF JANE
HOW DO YOU KNOW?

**The Blogger Girl Series**

BLOGGER GIRL (#1)
NOVELISTA GIRL (#2)

## Henery Press Books

And finally, before you go...
Here are a few other books
you might enjoy:

# BLOGGER GIRL

Meredith Schorr

## The Blogger Girl Series (#1)

(From the Henery Press Chick Lit Collection)

What happens when your high school nemesis becomes the shining star in a universe you pretty much saved? Book blogger Kimberly Long is about to find out.

A chick lit enthusiast since the first time she read *Bridget Jones's Diary*, Kim, with her blog, *Pastel is the New Black*, has worked tirelessly by night to keep the genre alive, and help squash the claim that "chick lit is dead" once and for all. Not bad for a woman who by day ekes out a meager living as a pretty, and pretty-much-nameless, legal secretary in a Manhattan law firm. While Kim's day job holds no passion for her, the handsome (and shaving challenged) associate down the hall is another story. Yet another story is that Hannah Marshak, one of her most hated high school classmates, has now popped onto the chick lit scene with a hot new book that's turning heads—and pages—across the land. It's also popped into Kim's inbox—for review.

With their ten-year reunion drawing near, Kim's coming close to combustion over the hype about Hannah's book. And as everyone around her seems to be moving on and up, she begins to question whether being a "blogger girl" makes the grade in her offline life.

Available at booksellers nationwide and online

Visit www.henerypress.com for details

# GIRL MEETS CLASS

Karin Gillespie

(from the Henery Press Chick Lit Collection)

The unspooling of Toni Lee Wells' Tiffany and Wild Turkey lifestyle begins with a trip to the Luckett County Jail drunk tank. An earlier wrist injury sidelined her pro tennis career, and now she's trading her tennis whites for wild nights roaming the streets of Rose Hill, Georgia.

Her wealthy family finally gets fed up with her shenanigans. They cut off her monthly allowance but also make her a sweetheart deal: Get a job, keep it for a year, and you'll receive an early inheritance. Act the fool or get fired, and you'll lose it for good.

Toni Lee signs up for a fast-track Teacher Corps program. She hopes for an easy teaching gig, but ends up assigned to Harriet Hall, a high school that churns out more thugs than scholars.

What's a spoiled Southern belle to do when confronted with a bunch of street smart students who are determined to make her life as difficult as possible? Luckily, Carl, a handsome colleague, is willing to help her negotiate the rough teaching waters and keep her bed warm at night. But when Toni Lee gets involved with some dark dealings in the school system, she fears she might lose her new beau as well as her inheritance.

Available at booksellers nationwide and online

Visit www.henerypress.com for details

# JUST FRIENDS WITH BENEFITS

Meredith Schorr

(from the Henery Press Chick Lit Collection)

When a friend urges Stephanie Cohen not to put all her eggs in one bastard, the advice falls on deaf ears. Stephanie's college crush on Craig Hille has been awakened thirteen years later as if soaked in a can of Red Bull, and she is determined not to let the guy who got away once, get away twice.

Stephanie, a thirty-two-year-old paralegal from Washington, D.C., is a seventies and eighties television trivia buff who can recite the starting lineup of the New York Yankees and go beer for beer with the guys. And despite her failure to get married and pro-create prior to entering her thirties, she has so far managed to keep her overbearing mother from sticking her head in the oven.

*Just Friends with Benefits* is the humorous story of Stephanie's pursuit of love, her adventures in friendship, and her journey to discover what really matters.

Available at booksellers nationwide and online

Visit www.henerypress.com for details